A BODY
AT
LAVENDER
COTTAGE

DEE MACDONALD

Published by Bookouture in 2022

An imprint of Storyfire Ltd.
Carmelite House
50 Victoria Embankment
London EC4Y 0DZ

www.bookouture.com

ISBN: 978-1-80314-853-3
eBook ISBN: 978-1-80314-852-6

This book is a work of fiction. Names, characters, businesses, organizations, places and events other than those clearly in the public domain, are either the product of the author's imagination or are used fictitiously. Any resemblance to actual persons, living or dead, events or locales is entirely coincidental.

ONE

Kate Palmer, feeling all of her sixty-one years, yawned and rubbed her eyes as she stumbled into the kitchen of her Cornish hillside cottage at six o'clock on a grey Sunday morning. She'd given up on sleep, thanks to Barney's incessant barking for half the night, and the springer spaniel was still at it – and scratching madly at the back door.

'What's *wrong* with you?' Kate asked crossly as she opened the door and peered out at the cloudy, mid-October gloom.

Barney made a beeline for the area behind the garage which was a mass of nettles. There was probably a dead animal of some sort there, left as a gift from one of the neighbour's cats on its nocturnal foray.

Aware that she'd forgotten to bring in the washing from the clothes line before she'd gone to bed, Kate headed out in her blue dressing gown to get the laundry. It was almost dry and, as she unpegged and folded the items into the basket, Kate looked in vain for Woody's dark blue tie, bearing the crest of the Metropolitan Police in London, with whom he'd served for many years before coming down to Cornwall as detective inspector. She'd met him when she and her sister, Angie, had moved from the south-east to this beautiful spot on the North Cornwall coast a few years previously. They had fallen in love with Lavender Cottage with its panoramic sea views, and Kate had fallen in love with Detective Inspector Woody Forrest as well. They'd finally married back in the spring.

Woody was extremely fond of this particular tie but had managed to spill ketchup on it, which had caused him, with much sighing, to say that it would most likely have to be specially dry-cleaned. Kate had said no, it could quite easily be washed, and assured him she'd be very careful with it. In fact, she thought it had washed well and was keen to see it now that it was hopefully dry and pristine. But where *was* the damned tie? There was no wind, so it was unlikely to have blown off the line. It had to be *somewhere*.

Then she wondered why Barney was still barking so manically at the back of the garage. Laying down her basket, Kate went to investigate, expecting to find a dead squirrel, rabbit or even a fox.

Instead, the first things she saw were two upturned, dirty-trainer-clad feet, just visible round the edge of the garage. Her blood ran cold. Why would anyone be lying there unless they'd been very drunk and forgotten how to get home from the pub down the lane?

Her heart in her mouth, Kate approached slowly.

She found the feet attached to two long, equally scruffy jean-clad legs, which led to a checked shirt and, finally, a grey-bearded old head.

This man, in the bed of nettles, was not asleep. This man was waxy-faced, and very, very dead, apparently strangled by a dark blue tie bearing the crest of the Metropolitan Police.

Afterwards, Kate couldn't remember if she'd shouted or not. She wasn't a screamer, so she wouldn't have done that. But she *was* a trained nurse and she could tell immediately that this man was well and truly dead and had been for some time.

As she neared the kitchen door in a daze, she met a half-asleep Woody, dressed only in trunks, asking, 'What the hell is all the noise about?'

Kate pointed dumbly towards the garage, holding the edge of the door for support. 'Put some shoes on; go and take a look.'

Woody rammed his feet into a pair of Kate's flip-flops and hobbled his way up the path towards the garage. Kate deposited the laundry on the kitchen table, braced herself and followed him.

She found her husband almost as white-faced as the corpse, as he stared in horror at the unfortunate man. Woody, having spent most of his life in the police, was not given to being easily horrified, but then again, he'd probably never found a body in his own garden before.

He turned slowly. 'I'm going to phone Charlotte.'

Charlotte Martin was the extremely glamorous detective inspector at the police station that served both Upper and Lower Tinworthy, the position Woody had held before retirement.

'What on earth was that man doing in our garden?' Kate asked as they re-entered the kitchen.

'Getting himself killed,' Woody muttered, 'with my bloody tie!'

'This is a nightmare!' Kate said as, with shaking hands, she struggled to prepare some coffee.

Woody looked directly at Kate. 'Thing is,' he said, 'I know who the guy is.'

'You *know* who that man is?'

'I'm almost sure it's Frank Ford. He was a petty criminal, and a case I handled in the Met a good twenty, twenty-five years ago. He went to jail for killing his wife.'

'So what on earth is he doing *here*?'

'I knew he was coming to Cornwall because he wrote to me. But what he was doing in our garden: your guess is as good as mine!'

The coffee maker had given a little gasp and died too, and Kate was now trying not to cry with shock and frustration as she searched in the cupboard for a cafetière. They were certainly going to need coffee, because, at this hour of the morning, they could hardly hit the brandy bottle, much as she would like to.

Kate studied her husband, noting the worry in his dark brown eyes; these same eyes, and his Mediterranean colouring, had melted her heart when she had first set *her* eyes on him. Even now, at sixty-three, with his dark hair rapidly greying, he was a handsome man.

'Why would he have been coming to visit you in the middle of the night?' Kate asked, finally unearthing the cafetière and spooning coffee into it.

'That, Kate, is the million-dollar question. And why is my Met tie wrapped round his neck? Because, sure as hell, *I* didn't strangle him.'

Kate looked at him in astonishment. 'Well *of course* you didn't!' For a brief moment, she wondered if she could have slept through him getting up, going downstairs, going out into the garden to strangle a passing old acquaintance, and then quietly getting into bed again! Of course not! She always knew if he got out of bed.

'Thing is, he mentioned in his letter that he'd like to meet me, but he didn't say why,' Woody said. 'I can't imagine what he wanted to see me about, given that he's just come out of jail after twenty years.'

Kate poured the coffee. She had a distant recollection of him receiving a letter from 'an old lag', as he put it. 'You really have *no* idea why he'd want to see you?'

Woody shook his head. 'None at all. Have you seen my phone? I must ring Charlotte.'

Kate nodded. 'I think you'll find it down the side of the sofa.' Kate placed the mug of coffee on the table in front of her husband. 'Tell me about this guy,' she said.

'Frank Ford?' Woody took a gulp of his coffee. 'He was a small-time criminal in South London, and he wasn't very good at it. His whole family was dysfunctional. For some reason, he took to me after I'd arrested him for the umpteenth time, and he became an informer; gave me all manner of tips on who'd done what, when and where. Then, out of the blue, he supposedly killed his wife.'

'Supposedly?'

'He was very keen to admit to it, suspiciously so. I mean, he wasn't a very nice character, but I didn't have him down as a killer.'

'But he was sentenced to twenty years?' Kate asked, becoming increasingly confused. 'Surely the jury were convinced? It must have been a nasty murder?'

'Yeah, but I was never convinced he did it, and I told him so. I wonder if that's why he wanted to see me now?'

'Where's this letter?' Kate asked.

'It's upstairs somewhere. I'll go and look for it after I've had my coffee and rung Charlotte.'

While Woody looked through his paperwork upstairs, Kate stood at the front sitting-room window from where there was a panoramic view of the beach and the sea, and the village of Lower Tinworthy with its little shops and galleries on either bank of the River Pol, including her sister Angie's bar and bistro, The Old Locker.

They had both been single again: she, Kate, a long-time divorcee, and Angie a widow. They'd thought Cornwall would be the perfect place to live out their golden years. Then Kate had fallen in love with Woody, and Angie with Irishman Fergal, after which a sort of musical chairs took place in terms of who lived where. Angie and Fergal moved down to take over The Old Locker bistro, and Woody bought out Angie's share of Lavender Cottage and moved in with Kate, letting out his own cottage on the other side of the valley. Everyone was happy with the arrangement, apart from the elderly postman, because he kept getting confused as to who lived where and with whom.

Life, however, had not been quite as tranquil as might be imagined. Kate thought she'd left crime well behind her in the London area, but, as well as renovating the cottage, and working part-time as a nurse at the local medical centre, she'd also gained a reputation as Cornwall's answer to Agatha Christie's Miss Marple, following a series of very unfortunate incidents.

But none of those had been anything like as problematic as finding a dead body in her own garden!

TWO

Charlotte Martin and her team from Launceston Police Station were there within thirty minutes, having instructed Woody not to touch or move the body but to cover it loosely with a tarpaulin or something if the heavens opened, which they looked like doing at any minute.

Charlotte was one of those women who always looked good, even first thing in the morning. Now here she was, slim and svelte, her blonde hair tied up in a tidy chignon, her make-up perfect, clad in a crisp white shirt, grey skirt and black blazer. Kate, standing alongside, still in her dressing gown, and constantly battling with her weight, felt like a sack of potatoes.

Charlotte, like Woody, had come down from London in the hope of finding peace, tranquillity and, at worst, possibly the odd pub brawl or petty crime to deal with in idyllic Cornwall. Also like Woody – and Kate – she'd certainly got *that* wrong.

Woody, now fully clothed, went out with Charlotte and the team to where the body lay. American born and bred, Woody had inherited not only his Italian mother's colouring but also his English father's serenity, which meant he had quickly overcome his initial horror and was approaching the situation with calm professionalism. .

While the team were at work on the body, Woody and Charlotte came into the kitchen. Kate could scarcely believe the event unfolding in her own cottage!

Charlotte refused the offer of coffee. 'We need confirmation of who this man is,' she said, 'but if you're right and he is this Frank Ford, then it doesn't look good for you, Woody.'

Woody groaned. 'I'd already worked that one out.'

'And I need to see this letter you mentioned when we were outside,' Charlotte added as she went out again.

The white-clad forensic team were still checking on the body, while two uniformed police officers were busily taping off the whole area. Charlotte watched them for a few moments and then came heading back towards the house, just as Woody reappeared downstairs, clutching the letter.

'OK, folks,' said Charlotte, 'I'm going to have to hear this from the beginning. I'm sorry, but you're both going to have to come with me to Launceston Police Station.'

'Is it OK if we follow on in our own car?' Woody asked.

'Yes, I think I can allow that,' Charlotte said.

After Charlotte had left and the body was removed, Woody poured himself a large Scotch. 'I need this! Would you mind driving today? You *know* I didn't do it, don't you, Kate?'

'Of course I know. But you've been set up, my love.' Kate sighed. 'Surely, once the body's been properly examined, they'll come up with *something*? What about fingerprints, for example?'

'Unlikely,' Woody said. 'Most probably they'll have worn gloves.' He took a swig of his whisky. 'Poor old Frank, banged up for twenty years, comes down to Cornwall and gets done in.'

'Poor guy,' agreed Kate. 'Never mind, we'll have our Sunday roast dinner tonight, and try to forget the whole thing.'

She thought for a second. 'I'm dreading going to work tomorrow because I'll bet the news has already got around.' Then she rapidly changed the subject, determined to talk about normal things and to remain as calm as possible for Woody's sake.

Kate sat in a state of disbelief as she stared across the table at Charlotte and a young male detective sergeant. She took comfort from the fact that he had a kind face.

Charlotte leaned across the table and switched on the recorder. 'OK, Kate,' she said, 'let's hear it from the beginning.'

Kate told the detective about Barney barking, coming down early, removing the washing from the clothes line, realising the tie was missing and then finding the body.

'And did you recognise this man?' Charlotte asked.

'No, but Woody thought it was a man called Frank Ford, who was a petty criminal and a grass, who'd just finished serving twenty years in jail for killing his wife. Woody told me that this man had written to him to say he and his family were coming down to Cornwall for a couple of weeks and he'd like to meet with him.' Kate realised that the words had tumbled out in a mad rush due to her extreme nervousness.

'Why would he do that?' Charlotte asked calmly.

'I don't know,' Kate said, 'but Woody did tell me he never really believed that Frank Ford had killed his wife.'

'Why didn't he believe it?'

'Honestly, I've no idea. Woody just had a gut feeling that Frank Ford wasn't that type of man.'

'What time would you say you went to bed?'

Kate thought for a moment. 'Well, we had a couple of drinks in The Greedy Gull, and I suppose we got home about half-past ten. Then we watched the end of a James Bond film on TV, and I guess we went to bed around eleven, half-past eleven latest.'

A few minutes later, it was Woody's turn to be questioned, and Kate had to wait, shivering, in a chilly corridor until he emerged. She had no idea how that wretched man had ended up in their garden, but she was absolutely sure that her husband was no killer.

Hours later, as they were driving home, Woody said, 'If it wasn't for you giving me an alibi, Kate, I think they would have kept me in.'

'Thank God, I'm a light sleeper!' Kate thought for a moment. 'Charlotte asked me why you didn't think Frank Ford could have killed his wife, and I just said you had a gut feeling, but you never told me the details.'

'Frank's testimony was that he'd accused his wife of having an affair with another man, and she'd taunted him for a bit, followed by an almighty row. That's what he said anyway. He fled the scene, and it was her father – Frank's father-in-law, Sid Kinsella – who found Pauline Ford's body. Her skull had been caved in. I just don't think Frank was capable of doing that.'

'What a horrible end!' Kate remarked.

'From what I saw of the body this morning,' Woody said, 'I think it's possible that he might have been killed before the tie was placed around his neck. That will obviously have to be verified, but hopefully they'll find out in the post-mortem.'

'You really think so?' Kate asked.

'Well I didn't put the damned tie round his neck,' Woody snapped.

Kate reached across and caressed his knee. 'I know you didn't, but whoever *did* kill him meant it to look as if it *was* you,' she said. 'I'm going to use all my contacts to find out if anyone by the name of Ford has booked accommodation round here. He must have been staying *somewhere*! Do you really have no idea why he might have wanted to see you after all this time?'

'*You've* seen the letter,' Woody retorted. 'If you read it, you'll see that he's given no details whatsoever.'

'You're right, there were no clues in the letter, but I'm going to find out.'

It was unusual, to say the least, to see Woody so stressed, and it made Kate more determined than ever to clear his name.

When they got back to Lavender Cottage, Kate was relieved to be in her cosy home and not locked up in a police cell. The dog needed a walk, and Kate was keen to escape for an hour or so after being cooped up at the police station.

'Do you mind if I take Barney down to the beach?' she asked Woody.

He shook his head. 'Of course not. As Charlotte instructed me not to leave the village, I'm virtually housebound, so I'm going to sort out my paperwork – something I've been planning to do for months.'

Kate's heart was heavy as she led Barney, on his lead, down the lane to the beach, where she let him run free, throwing sticks for him to retrieve. The sky still looked ominous, but it wasn't raining yet, and Kate walked the length of the beach, sat down on her favourite rock and gazed out to sea. Normally, the sound of the Atlantic rollers soothed her soul and put everything into perspective, but, for some reason, today it wasn't working.

Since she'd met Woody she'd become used to being involved in helping to solve crimes of one sort or another, but this was different in that Woody was the only suspect. Furthermore, she couldn't shake the image of that grey old man in the bed of nettles. When Woody had told her about the letter from

Frank Ford, she'd had no idea that matters could become so serious. She remembered Woody saying, 'He probably wants
money or a favour or something.'

If only, Kate thought.

'Come on, Barney,' she called. 'I think it's time we went to
visit Angie.'

THREE

As most of the tourists had now departed, Kate knew that it would be unlikely if many, or any, customers had yet arrived at The Old Locker for their afternoon refreshments. She badly needed to talk to someone.

However, as she pushed open the big, old oak door, all thoughts of bodies and suspects vanished for a brief moment because, sitting on the bar, as if it owned the place, was the most gigantic ginger cat Kate had ever seen. Barney began to bark excitedly, leaping up and down in an effort to reach it. The cat gave him a cold, green-eyed stare but remained aloof and completely unperturbed.

Just then, Angie appeared. Her sister was a little shorter and considerably plumper than Kate. 'I wondered what the noise was all about, but I see you've met Maximus.' She patted her immaculate – as always – blonde hairdo.

'*Maximus*?'

'Our adopted cat. He moved in a couple of days ago, had a good wander round the whole place and decided to stay.'

Kate stroked the cat's head, and he immediately began

purring very loudly. 'I wonder where he came from? I assume it's a tom?'

'Oh yes, Maximus is all male. He likes it here. You know what cats are like.'

Kate did indeed know what cats were like, having been adopted by several over the years. She wondered briefly about health and safety regulations regarding animals in catering establishments and was about to mention it when Angie asked, 'What the hell were all the police cars doing screaming up and down your lane at the crack of dawn this morning?'

'You aren't going to believe this,' Kate stated, immediately transported back to grim reality, 'I found a body in our garden.'

'*A body?*' Angie stopped in her tracks at the coffee machine.

'A *dead* body,' Kate clarified.

'In the garden of *Lavender Cottage?*'

'In the garden of Lavender Cottage.' Kate shuddered. 'I found him. He was at the top of the garden, behind the garage.'

'Well I've heard of fairies at the *bottom* of the garden, but this is ridiculous!' said Angie.

'And Woody is the main suspect.'

'Woody? Wonderboy? *Never!*'

'I agree, Angie. But this Frank Ford was apparently coming to visit and, in the process, managed to get himself strangled with Woody's Metropolitan Police tie.'

'Why would anyone be coming to visit in the middle of the night?' Angie asked, placing a large cappuccino in front of Kate.

Barney, in the meantime, had quietened down but remained standing and staring up at the cat, emitting low growls at regular intervals.

'He was obviously put there by whoever *did* kill him.'

'And what about the tie?'

'Well, the tie was dangling on the clothes line and must have been a real temptation to point the finger at Woody,' Kate replied.

'And you're absolutely sure it wasn't him?' Angie asked with a mischievous look in her eye.

'Of course I'm sure. I heard Barney barking during the night, so I guess that's when it all took place.'

'Well it must have been somebody who knew Woody, and knew where he lived.'

'Yes, I'd thought of that,' Kate said, 'but the only people we can think of are the victim's family. Woody said they were a dysfunctional lot.'

At this point, Fergal appeared. 'Hello, Kate, what brings you here this afternoon , and how do you like our cat?'

'Your cat's magnificent,' Kate replied, 'but I haven't had the best start to my Sunday.'

'Oh, why's that then?' Fergal asked. He'd grown a beard of late, black like his hair, which seemed to make his blue eyes even more intense.

She went on to tell him the whole story.

'Jaysus!' he exclaimed. 'Shall I put a drop of brandy in your coffee?'

'Do you know what, Fergal? That's a brilliant idea!' Kate pushed her cup along, and Fergal poured a generous measure into it.

'Get that down you!' he instructed, stroking his black beard thoughtfully. 'Well, Woody's ex-police and you're the local Miss Marple, so if anyone's going to solve this thing, it'll be you two!'

Kate gulped her coffee. 'We're going to have to do just that, Fergal, to clear Woody's name.' She glanced at the cat. 'Who decided to call him Maximus?'

'I did,' said Fergal. 'What the hell else would you call a big lad like that? He's a very nice cat, I'll have you know.'

'Yes, I'm sure he is, but I'm not sure Barney agrees.'

Kate glanced at her watch then drained her coffee. 'I'd better go home and get us something to eat.' She felt a tiny bit more relaxed after her fortified coffee.

FOUR

Kate worked as a practice nurse at Tinworthy Medical Centre two days a week. These days varied from week to week, but on this occasion, Kate was on duty the following day.

Tinworthy Medical Centre was in Middle Tinworthy. Middle Tinworthy was situated above Lower Tinworthy, and beneath Higher Tinworthy. The higher part of the village lay on the edge of the moors and was home to some large, luxury houses, the Atlantic Hotel and stunning panoramic views of the coastline.

Middle Tinworthy consisted of the school, the church, the village hall, the hairdressers, assorted shops and a large housing complex.

Lower Tinworthy had the River Pol flowing into the sea. There was a white, sandy beach, several shops along the riverside, and houses, including Kate's, dotted up towards the clifftops on both sides of the valley.

Kate was working, this particular week, on Monday and Tuesday, and she knew that word would have got around about an 'incident' – as Charlotte called it – and about which she could say nothing. She'd already rung Angie again to stress that she wasn't to tell anyone anything, whilst hoping fervently that Angie hadn't already told some of her regulars.

Saying nothing was going to be made difficult by the insatiable appetite for gossip of Denise, the receptionist at the medical centre. Denise, Kate knew, would do her utmost to wheedle out as much information as she could regarding the body in the garden.

'What on earth was going on at your place yesterday morning then?' she greeted Kate as soon as she walked through the practice door on Monday morning. 'My friend, Patsy, lives down the bottom of your lane and she said there were police *everywhere*.'

'There was an incident,' Kate replied, 'about which I can say nothing for the moment. Now, who have you got on your list for me this morning?'

Denise was determined not to be fobbed off so easily. 'Patsy told me there was an ambulance too,' she continued, 'so did someone need to go to hospital?' She studied Kate hopefully. 'Or was there a *body*?'

Kate smiled. 'Full marks for effort, Denise, but I can say nothing for now.'

As she glanced at her list of patients, Kate was well aware that more questions would be forthcoming. If there was one thing she'd learned after three years in a Cornish village, it was that word got around *fast*. And with each telling, so the story became further embellished.

Ida Tilley, housekeeper to Seymour Barker-Jones up at Pendorian Manor, in Higher Tinworthy, was the first patient on Kate's list.

'It's me knees,' she informed Kate, 'cos I'm needin' new ones.' Ida sat down and tapped both her podgy knees to illustrate the point.

Kate knew Ida suffered from arthritis, but the knees were

nowhere near ready for replacement, although it was becoming more and more difficult to convince Ida of this.

'It's scrubbin' all them floors what's done it,' Ida continued.

Since Seymour rarely appeared at Pendorian Manor these days, Kate couldn't work out why Ida needed to do so much floor scrubbing.

Ida leaned forward, bright-eyed, knees forgotten for the moment. 'I hear there was a mass murder up at your place on Saturday night?'

'I'm afraid you've got that wrong, Ida,' Kate said calmly as she wrote out a prescription for Ida's painkillers.

'Oh no, I don't think so, dear,' Ida persisted. 'See, I got it from Postman Pat, who got it from Polly Lock, who, I'm thinking, got it from your own *sister*!'

Kate groaned inwardly. Why couldn't Angie keep her mouth shut? She'd have to call in at The Old Locker on her way home to reinforce the instruction, although by now she imagined it could already be too late, with the locals having it down as a mass murder.

The woman who came into Kate's treatment room next was short, tubby, sixty-two years old and had a strong Northumberland accent. What made her particularly interesting was her address: Sunshine Caravan Park. This was the place where Kate's *almost*-daughter-in-law had worked the previous summer – until her son's romance had come to a most unexpected end. This woman had lived there for years apparently, but must have been relatively healthy, apart from her arthritis, because Kate had never seen her before. Her name was Mavis Owen, and she, along with her husband, were the wardens of the park, she told Kate.

'Me and Ricky have been runnin' that place for years now,' she said, 'but we're gettin' on, and I don't know how much longer we can carry on.'

'Are you busy at the moment?' Kate asked casually.

'Well, it's quietened down a bit now, but we've got this lot from London who've taken *three* vans. *Three*! I mean, them's big vans, three bedrooms an' all. And they're all one family, so they could easily have managed with one van, but no, they had to have three. Thing is, you see, we're short of cleaners now. We had some lovely lasses here in the summer, but they've all gone now.'

'Yes, I remember one of them very well,' Kate said drily. 'Would these people with the three caravans be called Ford, by any chance?'

'Yes, that's their name: Ford. Do you know them then?'

'No, I can't say I do, but I've heard of them,' Kate replied, rapidly changing the subject. 'OK now, I've renewed your prescription, but we're right out of these tablets at the moment, Mrs Owen. So if you can manage for a few days, I can bring them up to you as soon as they come in.'

Mavis Owen sniffed. 'Well, that's right kind of you, but it's a bit out of your way, isn't it?'

'Oh no, not at all,' Kate lied. 'I quite often come up your way.'

'Well, thank you very much, dear. But I better warn you that the police are visitin' that lot I was tellin' you about every five minutes, and they've been askin' us all sorts of stuff too. But they won't tell us what's goin' on!'

Kate gave her a sympathetic smile. 'That's the police for you!'

It would appear that not only had Frank Ford been ensconced at the Sunshine Caravan Park, but so was his entire family.

That morning, Woody had been summoned again to the police station at Launceston and he had lots to tell Kate when she got in from work that afternoon. 'Apparently, on Sunday morning, a hysterical man, by the name of Wayne Ford, came rushing in to report that his elderly father was missing. He insinuated that the old boy wasn't quite the full shilling and had been known to wander off. Seemingly, the family have rented three caravans up at Sunshine Park, with the intention of visiting the daughter, Wayne's sister, Sharon, who's married down here and lives near Crackington Haven.'

'Yes, I'd heard that they were up there. How many of them are there?' Kate asked, remembering Mavis Owen's remarks.

'Well, Wayne was sharing one caravan with his dad and, when he woke up yesterday morning, discovered he'd done a runner. Then Damian Ford, and his wife Jackie, who normally live in Spain, had another one and, finally, the youngest son, Jason Ford shared the third caravan with his wife and his grandfather, Sid Kinsella.'

'That's a lot of Fords,' Kate said, trying to keep count.

'And none of them on the straight and narrow,' Woody put in, 'apart from the daughter, who had the good sense to get out.'

'Tell me what you know about them,' Kate asked.

Woody scratched his head. 'Well, Wayne is the eldest, if I remember rightly. He was dealing in drugs in the nineties, and was convicted and imprisoned several times. But as far as I recall, he wasn't particularly violent. I don't know much about Damian, the middle son, other than I think he was done for armed robbery and absconded to the Costa del Sol. I know even less about the youngest son, Jason, other than he shouted abuse at his father at the arraignment and vowed to get vengeance one day.'

'Which he just might have done?' Kate suggested.

'Indeed he might,' Woody replied. 'Now, Sid Kinsella was Pauline Ford's father, and it was him that found her body on the kitchen floor. He was a scrap merchant and dodgy second-hand car dealer, but as far as I know, he had no convictions. What I *do* know is that he never wanted his daughter to marry Frank Ford in the first place.'

'It seems strange then that they're all holidaying together, doesn't it?' Kate asked.

'Yes, it does,' Woody agreed. 'They'd obviously come to visit Sharon – that's the daughter – to celebrate the old boy getting out of prison.' He hesitated for a moment. 'Or to get rid of him.'

'And lay the blame on you,' Kate added.

'Charlotte's hoping to get more details from Forensics, but, in the meantime, I'm still not to leave Tinworthy. I suppose I should be glad that I'm not in custody,' Woody said, 'and neither of us is to discuss this with anyone, OK?'

'OK,' Kate said, making a mental note again to tell Angie to keep quiet.

Already, her mind was whirring with a list of suspects.

FIVE

'I'm sure I didn't tell *anyone!*' Angie wailed when Kate popped in a short while later.

Kate was aware of a cold stare emanating from Maximus, who was sitting on the bar in exactly the same place as he had previously.

'Does that cat *ever* move from there?' Kate asked, momentarily distracted.

'Yes, of course he does!' Angie retorted. 'He goes outside to do his business, and he sleeps upstairs with us at night. But he really likes sitting there, and the customers *love* him!'

'Hmm,' said Kate, giving the animal a cautious stroke. 'Anyway, as I was saying, are you absolutely *sure* that you didn't tell anyone about the body in our garden?'

Angie thought for a moment. 'Well, I *suppose* I might have mentioned it in passing to Polly last night, but she promised not to tell.'

'So did *you* promise not to tell, if I remember correctly,' Kate said, irritated. She sighed. 'I don't suppose it'll be a secret for long anyway. Now I'd best be heading home.'

As Kate walked up to her cottage, she found three men, of

varying shapes and sizes, pointing cameras in her direction. Reporters! The bane of her life! Yet she knew they had a job to do and so she always tried to be polite.

'Ah, Mrs Forrest!' called out the shortest one of the three, clad in a black leather jacket with a tartan wool scarf tied artfully round his neck. 'Why's your husband been arrested? Is it true he's a suspect for this killing? Who found the body?'

Kate emerged warily from her car and shook her head. 'I'm not at liberty to say anything. Sorry!' She walked quickly towards the back door, shutting the garden gate firmly behind her. Woody arrested? Of course not!

'Can you show us where the body was found?' one of the others shouted out.

For a second, Kate had visions of dozens of reporters swarming around their garden. She shook her head and entered the house.

She hoped Woody was busy oiling the hinges of the spare bedroom door, which had been creaking for months. She decided that her husband being confined to barracks was no bad thing, as this was just one of an endless list of small jobs around the house that needed doing.

'Have you seen all those reporters out there?' she called out as she mounted the stairs.

There was no reply. No sound. No bedroom door hinges being oiled.

'Woody! *Woody*?' Kate shouted, going from room to room.

She rushed down the stairs and checked all the downstairs rooms. It was when she got to the kitchen that she saw the note, which he'd placed underneath the wine bottle on the work surface.

They're taking me into custody. Please don't worry. I'm sure I'll be home soon.

Kate read the note several times in disbelief. The reporters out there were right! Woody *had* been arrested! How *could* Charlotte arrest him? Surely she knew he was a decent man, a man who'd done her job and who'd helped her to settle in down here? What possible proof could they come up with?

Kate went to the cupboard, found a glass, picked up the bottle which had been guarding the note and poured herself a glass of wine. Then she dug her phone out of her bag and rang the police station.

'I need to talk to Detective Inspector Charlotte Martin,' she said firmly to the constable who answered the phone.

'Is it important?' he asked. 'She's very busy at the moment.'

'It's *bloody* important!' Kate yelled. 'She's got my husband, Woody Forrest, there, and I want to know what's *going on!*'

'Ah,' he said. 'I'd better put you through.'

'Yes, you'd damn well better!' Kate snapped.

She waited for several minutes before Charlotte came on. 'Kate,' she said.

'Why have you arrested Woody? This is *incredible!*'

Charlotte gave a long sigh. 'Because, Kate, he's the obvious suspect. The *only* suspect.'

'The whole Ford family is down here, and surely any one of them could be a suspect?' Kate said.

'We will be interviewing all of them,' Charlotte replied crisply, 'but, at the moment, Woody is helping us with our inquiries.'

'But I can verify that he was with me all the time on Saturday night and Sunday morning,' Kate said, hoping she didn't sound too desperate.

'Yes, but you're his wife and you would be loyal, wouldn't you?' Charlotte paused. 'Kate, let me spell it out for you. This Frank Ford wrote to Woody to say he was coming down here and wanted to see him. The family arrive and, within hours,

Frank Ford is found dead, in *your* garden, having been strangled, with *your* husband's tie around his neck. You don't need to be Sherlock Holmes to work out that this appears suspicious, do you?'

'But—'

'We're keeping him in until we get the forensic report, which may throw some light on the situation. I'm sorry, Kate, but there it is. He'll be able to call you later.'

With tears streaming down her face, Kate cut off the call. She took a large gulp of wine as she glared out of the window at the cluster of reporters standing at the gate and decided she'd stay in the house. Woody was going to phone, so she'd wait for that.

He rang at seven o'clock that evening. 'Don't worry, Kate! Charlotte really *is* only following police procedure and everyone's being so nice to me. They're hoping to get the forensic reports tomorrow, so that may help. Just don't say anything to anyone for the moment, will you?'

'Of course I won't, Woody. I'll keep everything crossed that you get home tomorrow,' Kate said.

She shuddered at the very thought of going to work the next day.

Kate slept little, her thoughts with Woody. Was he spending the night in a little cell, on a hard bed with just a not-very-hygienic blanket with which to keep warm? Who had killed that wretched Frank Ford? It certainly wasn't Woody, and she was not going to rest for one minute until she'd proved his innocence and found out who the killer was.

When, next morning, Kate arrived at the medical centre, Denise, as ever keen for gossip, asked, 'What were all the reporters doing outside your house?'

'They just wanted more information on the body in our garden,' Kate said.

Thankfully, it seemed that nobody at work knew that Woody was even a suspect, and Kate certainly wasn't about to tell them that, or about his arrest.

For the first time in her life, as far as she could remember, Kate had difficulty in concentrating on her job. A vision of Woody, peering sadly through prison bars, haunted her all day. She had to force herself to dismiss this reverie and give all her attention to what she was doing. Making a medical mistake was not an option.

She'd told no one of Woody's arrest. She even hesitated to tell Angie, although she desperately needed to share it with somebody, but Angie wasn't the best at keeping secrets. Before they knew it, Polly Lock would have wheedled the information out of her, and then it would become public knowledge within minutes. Kate certainly couldn't say anything at work either because Denise would have a field day gossip-wise.

Somehow or other, Kate got through her shift and set off for home. Surely they couldn't keep Woody in custody for more than twenty-four hours without good reason, or some sort of proof? Her spirits plunged at the prospect of another solitary meal, and an evening on her own.

As she trudged through the kitchen door, she thought she heard noises from upstairs. Half hopeful and half afraid, Kate mounted the stairs and, on the landing, found Woody oiling the hinges of the spare bedroom door.

'*Woody!*'

'Well, you did say these hinges needed oiling,' he said with a grin as he laid down the oilcan.

'Oh, *Woody!*' Kate fell into his arms and hung on tightly. 'When did you get home?'

'Around midday, I guess,' Woody replied. 'Shortly after they got the forensic results. I've got lots to tell you. Is it too early for a drink?'

Kate laughed. 'No, it most definitely isn't! And, boy, do I need one!'

SIX

Woody refused to say anything until they were both seated and clasping large glasses of Malbec.

'I worried about you all day,' Kate said, taking a large gulp. 'I could see you looking out through bars... Oh, it was horrible! But it must have been so much worse for you.'

'To be fair, I don't think any of them – except perhaps Charlotte herself – thought I should be there, so they were very good to me. I got endless cups of tea, and *dreadful* coffee! They put clean sheets on my bed and even got me bacon and eggs for breakfast. It wasn't bad at all! Not exactly five stars, but...'

'Tell me about the forensic results,' Kate said.

'They've made one interesting discovery,' Woody stated. 'Frank Ford was *not* strangled with my tie. As I suspected, he was strangled, but they reckon it was with a leather belt. They think he'd been dead around ten to twelve hours before they picked up the body.'

'We were in The Gull until about ten thirty,' Kate said.

'Yeah, and Des has vouched for us, so I have an alibi of sorts, thank God! But I'm not altogether convinced that Charlotte doesn't think I was involved somehow. Whoever dumped him in our garden plainly saw the tie dangling on the line and must have thought that was a real nice little touch,' Woody said with the semblance of a smile.

'So does that let you off the hook?'

Woody shrugged. 'Not sure about that. I'd guess Charlotte suspects me less than she did, but she's working on the theory that whoever dumped him here was sending some kind of message that I was involved by placing the tie round his neck. He was obviously killed before he was transported to the garden, with the express purpose of pinning the blame on me.'

'But why would anyone want to do that?'

'That,' Woody replied thoughtfully, 'as I already mentioned, is this week's million-dollar question.'

The following day, at lunchtime, Kate and Woody decided it was time to visit The Greedy Gull, and thank Des Pardoe, the lugubrious landlord, for his statement to the police.

Des leaned across the bar and said, 'I was hopin' you two would come in, cos I been hearin' all sorts of stories about what's been happenin' at your place.' He sighed. 'I nearly came up and knocked on your door! Everyone's wantin' to know, see?'

'Yes, I daresay they do,' Kate said.

'And so here we are,' said Woody. 'I'll have a pint, and Kate'll have a large glass of Pinot Grigio.'

Des frowned, his long face looking sadder than usual as he grabbed two glasses off the shelves. 'So I've been waitin' to *hear*,' he said as he positioned Woody's beer glass under the Tribute tap.

'Well there's not much to tell you,' Woody remarked. 'But thanks for giving a statement to the police.'

'Surely they never suspected *you*?' Des looked horrified. He placed Woody's glass on the counter and took a bottle of wine from the fridge.

Woody shrugged. 'The police will be issuing a general statement soon,' he replied, picking up his glass. 'Suffice to say that
Kate here found the body of a man in the back garden when she
went out early to bring in the washing.'

'As you do,' Kate added drily.

'But who *was* he?' Des stared at them both as he positioned
the wine on the counter.

'We'll know in due course,' Woody said.

Des's new barman, Steve, who had been holding court with
a group of thirsty, exhausted tourists – who'd walked the
coastal path from Bude – came over to add, 'Yeah, people keep
asking me too. And the press have been in here every five
minutes. Do we know this? Do we know that? Bloody
nuisance!'

Steve had arrived at The Greedy Gull in July, when the
place was inundated with tourists, and Des, who was struggling
to cope, had been persuaded to take him on for a few months.
Steve was in his forties, stocky, with a shaven head and a nose
which appeared to have been flattened more than once. Des
admitted that he'd caught Steve snorting cocaine on more than
one occasion, but nobody was perfect. And there were a lot
more women coming in on a regular basis since Steve had
arrived, so he wasn't complaining.

'Blimey,' said Steve, 'that policewoman don't half go on,
don't she? I mean, I didn't see nothing and I've told her that a
thousand times. Just cos I walk up there late at night! I'm too
bleeding knackered to go killing anyone!'

Steve, a surfer, lived in his camper van, which he'd parked
on a scruffy farm on Potter's Hill, leading up to the cliffs on the
south side of the valley. As a result, he walked down the cliff-
path, behind Lavender Cottage, to work each day and walked
back up again at night, by torchlight. He was a Londoner, but
he was here to surf and he needed to earn money. He was, in
fact, a very good barman, and Des was glad to be able to step

back a little, informing everyone that he wasn't as young as he used to be.

'Yes, well, she has her job to do,' Woody said as he picked up Kate's glass and headed towards their usual table near the inglenook fireplace.

Kate followed him.

'You know I can't tell him anything until Charlotte makes it public,' Woody said, taking a large gulp of his beer.

'They're both still staring hopefully at us,' Kate replied, sipping her wine.

'Excuse me.' A male voice.

Kate looked up to see a tall, suntanned, balding man standing beside their table.

'I'm sorry to bother you,' the man said, 'but I overheard the landlord talking to you just now so I reckoned you must be the couple who own the garden where my dad's body was found?'

There was a stunned silence for a moment before Woody asked, 'And you are...?'

'Damian Ford, Frank Ford's son.'

'I heard you and your family were staying down here,' Woody said.

'We're all up at the Sunshine Caravan Park.' He stared at Woody. 'I remember you from Dad's hearing; it *is* you, isn't it?'

'Yeah, it's me,' Woody said, taking another large slug of his drink. 'What can I do for you?'

'I gather Dad's body was found in your garden?' He looked from one to the other but didn't wait for a reply. 'Don't know how the hell he got there, but I gather we're all suspects.'

'I'm sorry for your loss,' Kate said, 'but I wish we weren't involved.'

Damian Ford nodded. 'Can I buy you both a drink?'

Kate was sure Woody would flatly refuse, but, to her surprise, he said, 'I'll just have half a pint of Tribute please. Kate?'

Kate shook her head. 'No, I'm OK, thanks.'

As Damian crossed to the bar, Woody said under his breath, 'I don't suppose we should be associating with him, and he's probably going to be lying through his teeth, but I'm curious to know what's going on with that family.'

'Which son is he again?' Kate asked, studying him as he stood at the bar.

'The middle one,' Woody replied. 'He's the one who absconded to the Costa del Sol.'

When Damian returned with Woody's drink, and a pint for himself, Woody said, 'Pull up a chair then.'

After he was seated, there was an uncomfortable silence for a few minutes before Damian said, 'I'm living in Spain now, you know.'

Woody nodded. 'So I heard.'

'Me and the wife came up to celebrate Dad getting out of the clink. That's what Dad wanted, you see: a big family get-together. I tried to get them all to come to us for some Spanish sunshine cos – no offence – it's bleeding cold here in October, ain't it? Thing is, Dad don't have a passport, see? And he wanted it to be Cornwall, so here we all are.'

'What will you do now?' Kate asked.

He sighed. 'God only knows. We've all gotta stay here, so that bleeding *policewoman* says anyway.' He leaned forward. 'Bit of all right, that one, but don't suppose she could catch a cold, far less a killer.'

Woody exchanged glances with Kate. 'She's proved to be quite efficient,' he said, 'albeit with some help occasionally.'

'Yeah, well, she's gonna have her work cut out for her, cos it could be *anybody*! I mean, Dad's always done a bit of sleepwalking, even when he was young, but since he's come home, he's been wandering off at all times of the day and night. Wayne's in a helluva state; thinks it's all his fault. They were sharing a van, see, and Wayne woke up to find Dad gone. Couldn't find him anywhere; no idea where he was.'

'He was in our garden,' said Woody.

'But that means he must've walked for *miles*! How could he have walked all that way?'

'Perhaps he got a lift?' Kate suggested.

'In the middle of the night?' Damian shook his head. 'Don't make sense.'

He turned to Kate. 'You must wonder why we're all so concerned about him when he was jailed for killing our mother?'

Kate, who'd been thinking precisely that, shook her head.

'It was a crime of passion, see?' Damian was in for the full confessional now. 'Our mum had been messing him about and threatening to leave, like. Dad's got a hot temper, and he got a bit carried away. Awful it was. After he realised what he'd done, he ran off in panic to phone for an ambulance, and it was Grandpa who found her, dead as a dodo.'

'How awful,' Kate agreed.

'He admitted he'd done it,' Damian went on, 'and he's spent twenty years in the clink, so we've all calmed down in the meantime.' He looked up at the ceiling. 'I reckon she'd be pleased to see us all together now. Well, maybe not *too* pleased about what's happened to Dad though.'

'So who else is there at Sunshine Park?' Woody asked.

'Well, Wayne of course. Jackie, my wife, and me. And Jason, the baby of the family. Mind you, Jason's thirty-five now, so he ain't no baby no more. He's with his missus, and they're sharing a caravan with Grandpa. That's Sid Kinsella – remember him?'

Woody nodded. 'Second-hand cars, wasn't it?'

'Yeah, Sid's Super Autos it was called, and he had a scrap-metal business as well. Well, he's ninety now and nutty as a fruit cake, bless him, but we couldn't very well leave him behind. Mind you, he always hated Dad for killing his daughter. But he doesn't remember much about it now cos he's in a world of his own. Jason's taken over the car business.'

'Didn't you have a sister?' Woody asked.

'Yeah, that's Sharon. She married Len Mason, who's got a big building business round here. Mason Enterprises. Know it? Lives near Crackington and don't have much to do with the rest of us. But Dad wanted to see her, so that's why we chose to come to Cornwall.'

'Did he manage to see her?' Kate asked casually.

Damian shook his head. 'Nope, he didn't and for sure he ain't gonna see her now. We only arrived on Saturday, and by Sunday morning Dad's a goner. She's real upset; used to go up to see Dad in jail every month, even though she didn't want to know the rest of the family. Strange girl. Well, she ain't a girl any more either, cos she's forty-three and got three kids. Time passes, don't it?'

'It certainly does,' Woody agreed. He hesitated for a moment. 'So, on Sunday morning, everyone was in Sunshine Park, waking up in their beds, where they were supposed to be – apart from your father?'

'You got it,' Damian confirmed. 'Anyway, I gotta love you and leave you now cos Jackie'll be wondering where the hell I've got to. But I just wanted to come down here and get the lie of the land.'

'And are you any the wiser?' Kate asked.

He shook his head. 'No, I ain't. But *we* didn't kill Dad, that's for sure. Funny that he was found in your garden though, ain't it?'

'I think that was an afterthought to incriminate me,' Woody said.

Damian sniffed. 'Well, *somebody* killed Dad, and the sooner they nab him, the better so we can get back to Spain. I'm pleased to have met you two and been able to explain about the family, like. But I'm damn sure it wasn't one of us.'

With that, he laid down his empty glass and, with a wave of his hand, headed towards the door.

Woody took a deep breath and turned to Kate. 'What did you make of *that*?'

'No idea,' Kate admitted. 'He seemed pleasant enough to begin with, although he didn't seem to be all that upset about his dad's death, did he? And I didn't like the way he insinuated that you could be guilty.'

'No, but don't forget I am a suspect. And he probably isn't that upset if he hadn't seen his father for twenty years. I reckon Damian was the best of a bad bunch,' Woody said. 'He was a villain in his time though. The only one who really broke free from the Ford clan was the girl, the one who's married down here. Interesting that she visited her father in jail; I wonder if any of the others did?'

Kate drained her glass. 'I think it's time we went home.'

SEVEN

On Thursday afternoon, Kate reckoned that just because Woody was more or less confined to Tinworthy for the moment didn't mean that *she* had to be as well. Surely even Charlotte couldn't possibly consider her to be a suspect!

Barney needed a walk and would probably welcome a change of scenery, but if he didn't, Kate certainly did. What need might they have of a builder though? None whatsoever. So what excuse could there possibly be to visit Mason Enterprises? She was none too sure how enterprising Len Mason was likely to be, but she *really* wanted to visit his wife. She had no idea where the Masons lived but hoped it might be close to their business.

The venue was little more than a scattering of buildings on the edge of Crackington, most of which appeared to be colonised by Mason, if the signs were anything to go by. With some relief, Kate found a footpath, which gave her a valid reason for being there – to walk the dog. She and Barney set off alongside a hedge, then over a stream and through a little wood, before deciding to turn round and go back the way they came. This way she could see the buildings from a different angle and spotted a large, sprawling, ranch-type bungalow at the end of a private lane, right alongside the Mason buildings. That could be it.

'You're going to stay in the car for a bit, Barney,' she informed the spaniel, making sure that the window was open a little before locking him in the Fiat. He looked at her with sad, doleful eyes, before settling down with resignation in the back seat.

As she made her way up the lane towards the bungalow, Kate began to wonder if she was crazy. What was she going to say to Sharon Mason, assuming this was where she lived? Honesty was most likely the best policy, and it was worth a try. After all, she hadn't got the title of local super-sleuth for nothing.

The woman who opened the white-painted wooden door was around the same height as Kate – five foot, eight inches – but blonde-haired and immaculately made-up.

Kate cleared her throat. 'I'm sorry to bother you but I'm looking for a Mrs Sharon Mason.'

The woman stared back at Kate for a moment then asked, 'Why?'

'I wanted to talk to her because she recently lost her father.'

Kate could see from the woman's face that she'd hit home.

'How do *you* know Sharon Mason recently lost her father?'

'I'm not prepared to go into detail until I know if you *are* Sharon Mason or not.'

'What if I am?' The woman continued to stare at Kate. 'And what's it got to do with you anyway?'

'My husband and I are personally involved. I'm Kate, and my husband's Woody Forrest.'

'I know *that* name.' She took a deep breath. 'Yeah, I am Sharon Mason, so what do you want?'

'I'd like a chat with you, if possible. You see, your father's body was found in our garden.'

'*What?*' She was glaring now. 'What the hell was his body doing in your garden? Which makes you a suspect, don't it? So what're you doing here?'

'My husband is a suspect,' Kate admitted, 'but I can assure you that he didn't kill your father. His body was placed in our garden at some time during the night, with the sole purpose of pinning the blame on us.'

Sharon opened the door wide. 'You better come in then.'

Kate followed her across a stark, white-painted, wooden-floored hallway into an enormous, equally stark kitchen, complete with the requisite island and bifold doors leading onto a patio. Everything was minimalist. There wasn't a saucepan or even a kettle on show, no dishes in the sink, no pictures on the walls apart from one enormous canvas which featured squiggles in red, blue and yellow.

Sharon pulled out a couple of red-leather-topped stools from under one side of the island. 'Sit down,' she ordered. 'Coffee?'

'Yes please, just with a little milk.' Kate looked round in vain for anything resembling a kettle or a coffee maker.

Sharon opened up one of a line of shiny white floor-to-ceiling doors, exposing a huge Italian coffee machine, similar to what Angie and Fergal had at The Old Locker. Above it was a shelf on which was arranged, with military precision, a row of white mugs.

Kate wondered where the milk might appear from before Sharon opened up the neighbouring shiny white door and withdrew a bottle. There didn't seem to be much else in its cavernous depths. The mugs were filled, the milk frothed and added, after which the doors silently closed themselves.

Sharon perched herself on the stool next to Kate. 'I didn't kill the old villain if that's what you're thinking,' she said. 'I don't know who did, but I reckon you'd be spoiled for choice.'

'We met your brother, Damian, in the pub yesterday and he said much the same thing,' Kate said.

Sharon sniffed. 'Just for a start, Damian owes Dad a ton of money for the naff house he bought down on the Costa del Criminals. He's never paid it back, and they spend money like water, particularly that wife of his. Maybe Dad wanted his money back? Why wouldn't he? He might have been planning a new life for himself – who knows?'

'You don't honestly suspect your own brother?' Kate asked.

'I'd bloody well suspect *any* of my brothers,' Sharon snapped. 'Wayne's weird. He's in bits about Dad, reckons it was his fault being as he should've wakened up when Dad went walkabout. He damned well *should* have done, particularly as Dad must have got dressed and everything before he headed out. Or maybe he never got undressed – who knows? Wayne's snivelling away now, but he never bothered much with Dad when he was in jail. Never visited him or nothing. Too busy chasing women.'

Kate didn't think that gave Wayne much of a motive but didn't comment.

'He got religion, you know, did Dad, probably cos the only visitors, other than me, were the Catholic priest and them women from the church who visit criminals. But I went up there every month to see the old bugger, which is more than my brothers did,' Sharon added. She screwed her eyes up. 'Then you've got my little brother, Jason. Jason hated Dad, hated him for what he did to Mum. Well, we all hated him for that, but Jason was particularly mouthy. Then there's his wife, Meghan, who's a real cow. She looks after Granddad, who's completely doolally now.' She grinned at Kate. 'They're a real bloody shower, they are. The best thing I ever did was get away and meet Len.' She looked proudly round her vast, sterile kitchen. 'All this is paid for, *legit*! My Len works his socks off to put our kids into good schools, give us decent holidays. We just done a cruise – lovely it was. You been on a cruise?'

Kate, who'd never fancied cruising, shook her head.

'Oh well, never mind. Perhaps that husband of yours will take you round the Med or somewhere – that's if he ain't found *guilty* of course!' She snorted. 'We're going to do the Caribbean next – can't wait!'

Kate drained her coffee and set her mug down on the work surface. 'I intend to prove my husband's innocence, Sharon, and I won't rest until I find the murderer.'

'Like I said, you'd be spoiled for choice. And you ask your husband why he bloody well *shouldn't* be a suspect. I mean, what was Dad doing in your garden anyway? Still, if the silly old sod was wandering around in the middle of the night, I suppose he could easily have met some nutcase or other, couldn't he?'

Kate stood up and prepared to leave. She didn't feel she'd made a great deal of progress, but at least she knew a little more about the family. She also felt a little anxious about Sharon's comment about Woody.

'I'd best be on my way,' she said. 'I've left my dog in the car. I hope you didn't mind me calling on you.'

Sharon shrugged. 'I expect you wanted to know what the Ford-that-got-away was like. Well, now you know!'

As she made her way back to her car, Kate fervently wished she'd never had to set eyes on any of this Ford family.

EIGHT

'That Sharon Mason certainly doesn't think much of her three brothers,' Kate remarked as she and Woody sat by the wood burner after dinner.

Woody gave a sigh. 'I can't believe you actually went to find her,' he said. 'Then again, I should know what you're like by now: a dog with a bone!'

'And I'm not letting go,' Kate added. 'Anyway, I got some more details about the family.' She hesitated for a moment. 'All I'm trying to do is prove your innocence.'

'Well,' Woody said, 'I've no doubt you have my best interests at heart, but, let's face it, you're addicted to crime solving. For which I probably have only myself to blame. If I'd been a builder or something, you wouldn't have got involved in all this detective nonsense in the first place.'

Kate grinned. 'But you must admit I'm quite good at it!'

'Yeah, but how many times have you nearly come to grief, Kate? This isn't a game, you know, and you could – and can – easily get yourself killed in the process.'

Kate knew he was right. Since she'd met Woody, she'd experienced some very scary and heart-stopping moments. At least the other killings hadn't been right on their own doorstep. This incident was frighteningly close to home and involved Woody in some way. Otherwise why had Frank Ford wanted to meet up with him after all those years, and why had his body been dumped in their garden?

'Frank Ford must have had a good reason to want to see you after all this time,' Kate said, studying him over the rim of her coffee cup. 'He must have gone to some trouble to find out your address, mustn't he?'

'I don't have any idea how he found my address,' Woody said, stroking his chin. 'I'm wondering if he arranged this family trip to Cornwall purely to see his daughter, or was it to tell me something? I guess I'll never know.'

'If he *did* want to see you, perhaps to tell you something important, then *someone* might not have wanted him to do it, might they?'

'That would be my guess,' Woody agreed, staring at the flames.

'Sharon also suggested that, as Frank was wandering around in the middle of the night, he might have met some weirdo.'

'I wouldn't think we've got many killer-weirdos in Tinworthy,' Woody said, 'although we sure have plenty of eccentrics. Anyway, why would a passing maniac then transport the body here and place it in our garden?'

Kate drained her glass. 'If the killer lived round here, he'd *know* that this is where the detective inspector lived.'

'The *ex*-detective inspector,' Woody reminded her. 'So why didn't he dump the body in Charlotte Martin's garden then? No, Kate, they wanted to lay the blame on me. Let's face it, I was *meant* to be a suspect.'

'*We* are going to find out who did this,' Kate said, patting his knee. *Well,* I'm *going to have a damn good try,* she thought.

. . .

When Kate called into The Old Locker the following morning, after walking Barney, she found Angie humming happily behind the bar.

'You're very chirpy this morning,' Kate remarked as she perched herself on a bar stool.

Maximus gave her a green-eyed stare from his usual spot on the counter as Angie popped a coffee in front of her. 'Fancy a teacake? They're absolutely delicious, if I say so myself.'

Kate hesitated. 'Well, I shouldn't...'

'Oh, go on, life's for living!'

'All right then, thanks.'

'It's not as if you're *fat*, Kate, just comfortably covered, shall we say?'

'Thanks a bunch.' Kate took a large bite. 'You really know how to wind me up.' She'd hoped that walking the dog might counteract these temptations. *But I'm never going to have a figure like Charlotte Martin*, she thought, *because we're* built *differently. That's all. And this is only one little teacake, for goodness' sake. With butter, of course.* What was the point of a teacake without butter? She took another bite. 'Why are you so cheerful today?'

'Well,' said Angie, leaning across the counter conspiringly, 'I can tell you this because Fergal's out and can't be eavesdropping.' She paused for a moment. 'A *gorgeous* man came in here last night.'

Kate sipped her coffee. 'A rare species.'

'Indeed. He was so good-looking, and so *nice*. And do you know what?'

Kate shook her head and wiped some crumbs from her mouth.

'I think he fancied me,' Angie said, beaming.

'What gave you that idea?' Kate asked.

'I surely don't have to tell you, at our age, but you just *know*, don't you?'

'I'm not sure that I do. Anyway, where did he come from?'

'I didn't ask him,' Angie replied. 'He said he was just visiting the area and he thought Lower Tinworthy was delightful, and he *loved* The Old Locker.'

'So you didn't get his name or anything?'

'Kate,' Angie said with mock patience, 'I am *not* nosy like you. I don't give everyone the third degree. But never fear, I shall find out, because I've a feeling he'll be back.'

'What about Fergal?'

Angie sniffed. 'What about him? He's been flirting all summer with everything in a skirt, turning on the blarney. You *know* what he's like. But what's sauce for the goose and all that – high time he had some competition! Anyway, how's that husband of yours? Still under suspicion?'

'I'm afraid so,' Kate said, sighing. She still hadn't told Angie about his twenty-four-hour arrest. 'Problem is, he *knew* this Frank Ford was coming down here, and he knew him from twenty-odd years ago. Then, of course, there's the little detail of the body being found in our garden.'

'You're quite sure Woody *didn't* sneak out of bed in the middle of the night?'

'Angie, how can you even ask such a thing? Of course he didn't!'

'Only kidding. Still, he's going to have to prove it.'

'Yes, and I'm going to do everything in my power to help him do just that. This isn't just like a normal investigation; this is very personal.'

Kate was still trying to work out what her next move should be when she got to the gate at Lavender Cottage. The three reporters were there again, including the short one with the same leather jacket but a different scarf – a bright red one this time – draped several times round his neck. He was plainly the spokesman of the group.

'Mrs Forrest...' he begged as she closed the gate, 'could we have just a *word*?'

Kate felt a little sorry for him. 'What's your name?' she asked.

'I'm Eddie, and I wondered—'

'Eddie, I'd like to help you, I really would. But I have nothing to say and you *know* where to go to get the latest information, and that's the police station.'

'But, Mrs Forrest, we—'

'Sorry, Eddie, that's it.' Kate went inside and closed the door.

The sooner she could solve, or help to solve, this mystery, the sooner these reporters would disappear and life would, hopefully, return to normal.

NINE

Kate had just removed her coat when Woody appeared in the hallway.

'You can put that back on again, Kate,' he said with a rueful smile, 'as I've been summoned to Launceston Police Station.'

Kate stared at him in astonishment. 'Why, for goodness' sake?'

'I'm not too sure, but let's go and get it over with.'

'So why am *I* coming?'

'Because I want you there as a witness and for some moral support. I'd rather not involve a solicitor at this point because it would just make me look guilty.'

'Should I bring my toothbrush? Just in case she's going to arrest *both* of us this time?' Kate asked angrily as she put her coat on again.

'She assured me it was just routine questioning,' Woody said.

Kate sighed and prepared to ward off the reporters yet again.

. . .

Charlotte looked cool, calm and collected as usual. In spite of the fact that the woman had no doubt had a stressful week, she didn't have a hair out of place or a single wrinkle in her smart, navy-blue suit.

'I'm going to need your help, Woody,' she admitted as she sat down behind her desk, opposite the two of them. She laid some folders on the table. Nail varnish immaculate, Kate noted. 'I think the stuff we've had from forensics should help to get you off the hook.'

'I thought I was *already* off the hook,' Woody said sharply.

'Surely you *know* he's innocent?' Kate put in.

Charlotte didn't reply but opened a folder and shuffled some papers around. 'As I told you, your friend, Frank Ford, was strangled some ten to twelve hours before we found him at seven o'clock in the morning. But I want you to tell me more about this family of his, from when you knew them all those years ago.'

'Well, like I told you, they were all villains of one sort of another.'

Charlotte nodded. 'Can you tell me why you doubted Frank Ford had killed his wife?'

'He wasn't a violent man,' Woody said, 'although he had a police record as long as your arm for petty crime. I only got to know him because he grassed to me. I thought he was weak-natured, bit of a wimp in fact, very unlikely to be a killer.'

'He obviously was though. Now, what about this Wayne, the one that came to the station in a frantic state because his father was missing?'

'Drug dealer and not a very nice character, but very popular with the ladies,' Woody said. 'So far as I know, he's never married, unless he's tied the knot in the six years or so I've been down here. I heard he was the one closest to his father.'

'He shared a caravan with his father. Unless he's a very

good actor, he appears to be very shaken by Frank's death. What about the Spanish one?' Charlotte asked.

'Damian. Done several times for armed robbery. Rumour has it he has a very luxurious lifestyle out there, fancy house and all that.'

'Sometimes it's hard to put across the message that crime doesn't pay,' Charlotte said drily. 'What do you know about the wife?'

'Nothing at all,' Woody replied. 'I gather she's here with him?'

'She is.'

'We met him in the pub a couple of days ago,' Kate said, 'and he seemed pleasant enough.'

'He should not, of course, have been there,' Charlotte retorted. 'The whole family are supposed to be confined to Sunshine Park until today, when they're allowed more freedom, although they're still not allowed to leave the area.'

'Once a lawbreaker, always a lawbreaker, I guess,' Woody said.

'We can't watch every suspect day and night,' Charlotte said with a sigh. 'What do you know about the youngest son, Jason?'

'Not a great deal. He was closest to his mother I was told. He's very close to his maternal grandfather, Sid Kinsella, and he's now in charge of Sid's scrap metal and second-hand car business.' Woody sighed. 'Sid, we believe, may have some form of dementia.'

'Anything else?'

'Jason appeared to have been the worst affected by his mother's killing; couldn't believe his father could do such a thing and shouted abuse at him at the court hearing.'

'So he probably had the most motive?'

Woody shrugged. 'Possible.'

'What about Kinsella?'

'Pauline's father,' Woody confirmed. 'He was the one who found her body in the kitchen.'

Kate shuddered. 'How dreadful for him! To find his own child...'

'Not very nice,' Charlotte agreed. 'You were right about the dementia, so I'm not able to get a great deal of sense out of him. He's sharing with Jason and his wife – Meghan, I think she's called.' Charlotte studied her screen. 'She's Kinsella's carer.' She then turned back to Kate. 'Tell me again what time you woke up on Sunday morning?'

'The first time was probably about three o'clock,' Kate replied. 'I lay awake for a bit before I looked at the clock, which was then about quarter past.'

'And that was because you heard the dog barking?'

Kate nodded. 'Yes, and I could hear him running around.'

'Was that unusual?' Charlotte asked.

'Sometimes, if he hears a fox or a badger or something outside in the garden, he gets excited, barks, wants to go out. So I just thought that's what it was, so I tried to ignore it and go back to sleep.'

'Did you get back to sleep?'

'I managed to doze off and on for a while, but around five o'clock I gave up because I was afraid my tossing and turning would waken Woody. It didn't of course.'

'Why "of course"?' Charlotte asked.

'Because he's a deep sleeper,' Kate replied.

'That's my pure conscience,' Woody put in.

Charlotte gave a faint smile. 'If you say so.' She turned back to Kate. 'So you came downstairs?'

'Well, I went to the loo and had a look out of the window and then I came downstairs just before six.'

'And what was the dog doing?'

'He was whining and scratching at the back door, which was unusual, so I let him out, and you know the rest.'

'So, in the middle of the night, he *could* just have been barking at another animal in the garden?'

'He could,' Kate confirmed, 'but what was unusual in this case was his desperation to go out.'

'I guess he's not about to tell us,' Charlotte said as she closed her laptop and gathered her folders. 'I now have the unenviable task of interviewing everyone who lives on your lane because, presumably, Frank was transported – dead or alive – up to your garden. Do either of you recall hearing a car or anything late at night before you went to bed?'

Kate and Woody looked at each other and both shrugged.

'We're at the top of the lane there,' Woody said, 'so we don't get cars passing. If we do hear something, it's because it's coming to us.'

'And you heard nothing?'

'No, because we were watching an old James Bond movie until around eleven o'clock,' Woody said, looking at Kate.

'Yes, it finished around eleven,' Kate confirmed, 'and then we went straight to bed.' She'd already told Charlotte this but knew it was part of the process.

'And you weren't aware of any activity taking place in the back garden?'

'Our bedroom faces the front,' Woody said, 'so, unless there was a loud noise, we wouldn't hear it anyway.'

'So there was complete silence?'

'It's never *completely* silent at that time,' Kate put in, 'because we can hear the sound, in the distance, of cars leaving The Greedy Gull down the lane. They've got some late drinkers.'

'I'm going to interview Des Pardoe and Steve again,' Charlotte said, 'just in case they recall something. That Steve is a bit of a dodgy character, and Des suspects he has a cocaine habit as well. He'd have been making his way up the lane behind your cottage to get home, possibly around the time Frank was being deposited, dead or alive, in your garden.' She looked at Woody. 'All suspects are free to move around Tinworthy, including Kate and yourself. But no further, Woody.'

'*Me*?' Kate bleated. 'Surely I'm not a suspect?'

For the first time, Charlotte gave a glimmer of a smile. 'I doubt you were out there strangling anyone, Kate, but there is such a thing as being an accessory to a crime, aiding and abetting...' Her voice tailed off.

'Meaning that you still suspect Woody?'

'You should know by now that I have to suspect anyone with obvious links to a crime, Kate. And, right now, that includes Woody. That is my job, and it means I'm never going to be winning any popularity contests.'

She paused for a moment. 'I'm sorry I had to ask you to come up here,' she added, 'but I needed some more detail and I've got further questioning to do this evening. In the meantime, if you hear or think of anything at all, no matter how irrelevant it may seem, will you please let me know.'

'Of course,' Woody said as he and Kate got up from their seats. 'So can I at least go up to my allotment again now?'

'Yes, Woody, you can,' Charlotte replied.

Kate breathed a sigh of relief. Woody had been pacing round the house like a caged tiger. The allotment, or the 'community garden' as he liked to call it, was his pride and joy. He'd begun renting it back in the summer and had spent weeks getting it into shape, and chatting to the other enthusiasts who frequently offered conflicting advice. The sitting room was now littered with catalogues, 'Grow your own Vegetables' books, gardening magazines and seed packets. As yet, Kate hadn't seen the fruit of his labours, but, more than anything, she was delighted that he'd found a hobby for his retirement – and one which got him out of the house.

TEN

After an uneventful weekend, Kate was back on duty on Monday morning, but working at the surgery had now become something of a trial. She strongly suspected that the influx of patients requesting to see her, and her alone, had very little to do with their lumbago, arthritis or anything else.

First up was Ida, back with a sore throat this time.

'It doesn't seem to be inflamed,' Kate remarked, peering down at Ida's tonsils with a light.

'Well, it *was* this mornin', m'dear,' Ida replied, 'and very sore it was too.' She gave a little cough. 'Any more news about the corpses up at your place?'

Kate sighed. 'Ida, there was *one* corpse, and one only. I told you that before.'

'Just the one?' Ida looked disappointed.

'Just the one.'

'And where did he come from?'

'Good question, Ida. Now, is there anything else?'

Ida shook her head and shuffled out the door.

Next was Tom Barker, local carpenter and coffin-maker. 'Got a bit of a headache, Nurse.'

'Have you tried paracetamol?'

'Well, yes I did, but there's still a bit of an ache there.' He rubbed his forehead then cleared his throat. 'I heard rumour you got a dead body up there at Lavender?'

'We did, Tom, but it's gone now.'

'Will he be needin' a coffin, do you think? I got some lovely ones in the workshop: oak, pine, and all very reasonable.'

'I don't—' Kate began.

'Or I can get him a lovely wicker one,' Tom interrupted, 'cos I know some folks like everythin' simple these days.'

'Tom,' Kate said patiently, 'this has got nothing whatsoever to do with me. The body is with the police, and I've no doubt his family will be making funeral arrangements in due course. Now, about this headache...?'

He looked puzzled for a brief moment. 'Headache? Oh yes, but it's practically gone now. I'll stock up on paracetamol.'

Shortly afterwards, in swanned Penelope Bowen, fresh from chairing the Conservative Ladies' Club Meeting, or some such. She was one of those women who got involved, and took over, every cause she considered worthy of her administrative talents.

'The Conservative ladies,' she announced without preamble, 'are seriously worried about this killing at your place – *such* an unsavoury incident! We all wonder if it's safe to venture out in the evenings, particularly now that the nights are drawing in.' She sighed. 'We would be extremely relieved to know that the killer is under lock and key, so we can all sleep soundly in our beds at night. Do you happen to know what's going on?'

'No, I don't,' Kate replied with a sigh. 'You must ask the police. Now, what seems to be the trouble?'

'*Trouble?*' Penelope looked askance. 'What trouble?'

'I wondered why you were here?'

'I'm here to find out the identity of the man who was found in *your garden*!'

'Then I suggest you visit the police station, Penelope, not the medical centre. Now, is there a medical problem?'

Penelope shook her head.

'You do realise that making inappropriate appointments is wasting precious NHS resources, which is something I'm sure you wouldn't approve of if other people did it.'

Penelope pursed her lips and waltzed out of the door.

At the end of her shift, Kate approached the reception desk.

'Denise,' she said wearily, 'when people ring up for appointments and ask specifically for me, can you make it crystal clear that I am not – *not* – going to discuss the recent incident at Lavender Cottage. If they want information, they must go to the police station. OK?'

'Thing is,' said Denise, scratching her head, 'the police won't tell them a bloody thing.' She had such a guilty look about her that Kate reckoned she'd already tried that tactic herself.

'Well, *I* can't tell them a bloody thing either,' Kate retorted.

'Point taken,' said Denise meekly.

By the time she'd finished her second shift on Tuesday, Kate was exhausted with trying to ward off the endless barrage of questions. On Wednesday, she decided she just wanted a couple of days without seeing hardly anyone and to soothe her furrowed brow by walking by the sea, either on the beach or along the cliff-path above.

The nearest access to the cliffs was the path which went up behind Lavender Cottage, on the south side of Lower Tinworthy, but this cliff-path was hazardous in places, with rough terrain and steep, stony gradients. As a result, she normally walked down to the village, crossed the ancient stone bridge over the River Pol, before climbing up the other side, passing

Woody's cottage – aptly named 'On the Up' – en route. The coastal path on this side was pleasantly undulating and afforded some spectacular views of the Cornish coastline.

To the north, she could see the rocky headland of Hartland Point, with Lundy Island on the horizon, and to the south, she could see as far as Trevose Head. In between, the majestic cliffs, rocks and little coves were battered, all winter, by the Atlantic gales and high tides. This coast was littered with the wrecks of old sailing ships, which was difficult to believe today as the sun sparkled on the gentle waves of the azure sea. Appearances could be deceptive though, as Kate had found out in more ways than one.

After about ten minutes, she'd got to the seat at the highest point, and was glad to sit down for a few minutes to enjoy the view and rest her legs. On the horizon, she could see the distant shape of a container ship, almost certainly heading up the coast to the Bristol Channel to offload its cargo; probably cars from the Far East.

The Far East! Kate's thoughts wandered back to Singapore and to the early days of her ill-fated marriage to Alex Palmer, the father of her two sons. Tom, the elder, was now a civil engineer, husband and father, happily settled up in Edinburgh with his Scottish wife. And Jack, who'd spent years as a building project manager out in Australia, had come home earlier in the year, gone up to visit his brother and had decided to stay north of the border for the time being. There was never a day when Kate didn't offer up a silent prayer of thanks that her two sons were healthy, thriving and firmly rooted, at least for the time being, on British soil.

Barney wakened her from her reverie. He'd plainly become bored with examining everything worthy of his attention in the surrounding area and was now ready to move on. Kate stood up and prepared to retrace her steps.

She'd been trying very hard *not* to think about the body in the garden – or the Ford family. She was sure that Woody had nothing to do with the killing, but, nevertheless, he was involved because of the letter. Kate also knew that she should leave it to the police. However, as long as Woody was a suspect, Kate felt she should be doing something positive to clear his name. There were so many potential suspects that she needed to make a list.

ELEVEN

In the past, when Kate had been trying to solve the crimes that had taken place in the villages since her arrival, she had found it invaluable to make a list of the likely suspects and then, hopefully, be able to cross them off, one by one, as the alibis appeared. This method didn't always guarantee success, but undoubtedly it helped. Woody was highly amused at her lists but had to admit that it was, of course, a normal police procedure to list likely suspects.

When she got back from her walk, Kate made herself a mug of tea and sat down at the kitchen table with a large piece of paper, a pen and a worried frown.

After a minute, she decided she might as well start with Woody because he was, after all, regarded as a suspect and at least she'd have the pleasure of eliminating him from the list straight away.

Kate sipped her tea and wondered if all three Ford brothers might have motives to kill their father. She knew nothing about Wayne, other than he'd been a bit of a ladies' man, he'd been sharing the caravan with his father, and he'd gone to the police station to report him missing. She entered his name beneath Woody's.

Then there was Damian, who they'd met at the pub. He'd seemed personable enough, but, according to Sharon Mason, he owed his father a load of money. That could be a sufficient motive but not as compelling as the fact that he believed his father had killed his mother. Kate added his name.

The youngest son, Jason, had hated his father for what he'd done and made no secret of the fact. Why then had he agreed to come down here *en famille*? To accompany his wife, who was Sid's carer?

Why had Sid come for that matter?

The killer had obviously chosen to incriminate Woody, but what had Woody ever done to any of them except to speak up in Frank's defence at the hearing all those years ago? Surely that was hardly worth such retribution after so long a time?

Kate wrote Jason's name down under Damian's, and then her thoughts turned to Sharon. Since Sharon had escaped the family to become respectable, what possible motive could she have to kill her father apart from the obvious? In any case, the family had arrived from London on Saturday, and Frank was killed some time that night before she'd even set eyes on him. Or was she in league with one of her brothers? Sharon went on The List.

Kate knew even less about any of the spouses. Wayne didn't have one, but Damian did. What was her name? Jackie? Yes, that was it, Jackie. Why would she have wanted to kill her father-in-law? For the same reason as her husband, because Frank wanted the loan repaid? Sharon had been somewhat scathing about the two of them and their ability to spend money. It was a possibility. She went on The List too.

What about Sharon's husband, whatever-his-name was? Kate couldn't remember, so she wrote down 'Husband – Mason'. She could think of no reason whatsoever why he would want to kill Frank. Still, she couldn't be sure, so she'd leave him on the list.

That left Meghan, Jason's wife and the carer of Sid Kinsella. Perhaps she was exhausted with looking after Sid and worried that Frank was heading in the same direction and that eventually she might have to look after him too? After all, Frank was known to go walking in the middle of the night ever since he'd come out of prison, or so they said. Kate wrote 'Meghan Ford' on The List. Less likely, it would seem, but she knew from experience that the more unlikely, the greater the possibility.

Family-wise that only left Sid, who was suffering from dementia and could almost certainly be omitted from The List. Frank had, of course, bludgeoned Sid's daughter to death, so Sid indeed had a motive for murder. But how could he have escaped from Meghan's confines to do such a deed and then transport the body to the garden of Lavender Cottage?

Then there was the possibility that it was someone else altogether. Kate couldn't rule Steve out, after what Charlotte had said. After all, they knew nothing about him, and he did walk up that path every night. Des admitted that he left Steve in charge of the late drinkers, to clear everything away, to do the bottling up and all the tasks that were required to be done each night. Since the police never checked, The Gull was often still going strong at midnight, so there was every chance that Steve would be making his torchlight walk back to his van in the early hours of the morning. She added him to her list, making a note to find out his surname. But if Frank had been killed between seven and nine that evening, Steve would, of course, have been working. They'd been there themselves, and they'd seen him behind the bar. So, highly unlikely, but she left his name on The List anyway.

Looking at The List, Kate surmised it was much more likely that the Fords had reason to kill Frank. There was no two ways about it – Kate needed to get to know this family. Before she got up from the table, she drew a line through 'Woody Forrest' and drained her mug of tea.

The following day, Kate walked Barney along the beach and, feeling refreshed and in need of company again, decided to call on Angie on the way home. As she wandered into The Old Locker, she found Maximus preening himself on the bar stool where she normally sat. He gave her a disinterested glance, yawned and resumed grooming.

'He's not keen on being disturbed,' Angie said, gazing at him fondly. 'I'd sit on another stool if I were you.'

'Who's the boss around here?' Kate asked, doing as she was told.

'But he's *so* sweet, Kate, you must admit.'

Kate glared at the cat, who glared back. 'Sweet' was not the adjective that sprang to mind. 'So, how's things?' she asked.

'Absolutely tickety-boo,' Angie replied happily. 'I'm feeling very womanly today!'

'*Womanly*? You don't normally feel masculine, do you?'

'Of course not!' Angie retorted. 'I just feel more attractive and *appreciated* than usual.'

Kate stared at her sister for a moment. 'Has that man been in again?'

Angie looked coy. 'Funny you should ask that! Yes, he has; he came back last night and sat just where you're sitting now!'

'Did he indeed? And what did he say or do that's made you feel so *womanly* all of a sudden?'

'He's just so sexy!' Angie gave a little shiver of delight.

Kate shook her head. 'And what does Fergal have to say about this?'

'Fergal? I don't think he notices because he's so busy jawing to anyone and everyone who'll listen to him. I have to say that recently I've been feeling that he takes me for granted much of the time.'

Kate snorted. 'Poor Fergal! And where does this Adonis hail from?'

'Oh, the south-east somewhere.' Angie leaned across the counter. 'He's in a *film*!'

'A film?'

'Yes, he's got a part in some costume drama being filmed somewhere down the coast, near Port Isaac, I think. He and the crew are renting in Higher Tinworthy because they're going to be working here for a few weeks.' She positioned a cappuccino in front of Kate.

'Really?'

'Yes, really. Do you fancy a Chelsea bun?'

'I fancy one, but I'm not going to have it,' Kate replied. *Some people*, she thought, *lose their appetite when they're stressed about something like I am, but, unfortunately, I don't.*

'Oh, go *on*.' Angie placed the bun on a plate in front of her.

'I *mustn't*.' Kate again had a vision of the super-slim Charlotte in her perfectly tailored navy-blue suit. She'd *so* like not to have to be squeezed into Lycra every time she wore anything even semi-fitted. The bun did look delicious though. She decided she'd skip lunch. She picked up the bun and took a hefty bite. 'So, does he have film-star looks? And what's he called?'

'He's very dishy, and his name is Clint. And do you know what? He bears more than a passing resemblance to Clint Eastwood!'

'Oh?' Kate muttered through the crumbs.

'He's probably a bit younger than me though,' Angie admitted.

'How much younger?'

'I didn't ask him, but he's probably in his mid-forties.' Angie was avoiding Kate's eye.

'*Mid-forties*! That's *twenty years* younger than you! I know Fergal's a bit younger than you, but I really didn't think you went in for *cradle*-snatching!'

'I am *not* cradle-snatching!' Angie snapped as she poured herself a generous measure of gin. She added tonic water and took a large swig. 'First today! I do *not* go in for cradle-snatching, Kate. I just happen to like younger men!'

'So I've noticed.'

'I don't want some old geezer who's only looking for someone to cook, clean and look after him in his dotage!'

Kate decided against mentioning the fact that Angie had done something similar with Fergal, who might not be in his dotage but who'd been a penniless drifter before Angie took him over.

'So where *is* Fergal this morning?' Kate asked.

'He's doing his yoga, and then having a cold shower,' Angie replied. 'Did you know that cold showers are very good for you? He should be down in a minute.'

As if on cue, the newly yoga-ed and cold-showered Fergal appeared, beaming. 'Oh my God,' he told them, 'that was terrific! I feel like a new man!'

'That makes two of us,' Angie muttered to Kate under her breath.

TWELVE

Friday was, of course, one of Kate's days off, but, at eight in the morning, a frantic Denise rang to ask if she could come in for a couple of hours to cover for the temporary nurse whose car had broken down on the way from Plymouth. Kate felt obliged to help out and, in retrospect, it turned out to be a very good move.

She'd been waiting for Mavis's painkillers to come in so that she would have an excuse to visit the Sunshine Caravan Park, but they hadn't arrived when she'd finished work on Tuesday. Now, as Kate was leaving at lunchtime, Denise came into the staffroom waving a package, asking, 'Anyone going anywhere near Sunshine in the next day or two?'

It was the sign she'd been waiting for. As Sue, the other practice nurse, and the young doctor both shook their heads, Kate said, 'I am!' She had to think quickly. 'I'm going to Boscastle this afternoon, so I can drop it in on my way.'

'Great,' said Denise, handing her the package. 'It's for Mrs Mavis Owen, the wife of the warden up there. Apparently, their car is off the road at the moment.'

Kate had only ever seen the caravan park in the distance when she'd been driving to Boscastle – a journey she *didn't* plan to do this afternoon, but she felt a little white lie had been warranted.

Kate knew the park was a vast, sprawling place, and not a thing of beauty even in high summer, but there was something particularly forlorn about it on this grey October day. The banner above the gate proclaimed: 'Sunshine Park – The Sign of Happy Holidays!' in lurid red and blue lettering on a bright yellow background. As she drove into the near-empty car park, Kate reckoned that most of the happy holidaymakers had headed home, with the obvious exception of the Ford family of course.

The warden's caravan was a large twin unit, just inside the entrance. It had a tiny, neat garden, bordered by a picket fence and a sign planted alongside the roses informing everyone that this was the warden's residence and that they should proceed to the office, the direction of which was illustrated with an arrow.

The office was a shed at the back of the garden and displayed a further sign which said 'Office', underneath which was printed 'If closed, go to caravan door'. It was closed, so Kate retraced her steps and knocked on the caravan door.

It was opened by Mavis herself.

'Hello again, Mrs Owen! I was just passing and thought I'd drop in your prescription,' Kate said.

Mavis beamed. 'That's so kind of you,' she said as Kate handed over the package. 'I'd just about run out of me tablets, so you come at the right time. Would you like a cup of tea?'

Kate didn't particularly want a cup of tea, but she did want to know a thing or two about this park and the visitors. 'Thank you,' she said, following Mavis into a small, very chintzy lounge, where an elderly bald man with a very large nose was sitting with his feet up reading *The Sun*.

'This lady's very kindly brought me my prescription,' said

Mavis. She turned to Kate. 'Call me Mavis, dear, and that there's Ricky.'

Kate introduced herself.

Ricky laid down his newspaper and regarded her with watery blue eyes. 'Bloody car's off the road again,' he said by way of a greeting. 'Clutch gone, and goin' to cost a bloody fortune to put it right. Just had the bloody gearbox done. If it ain't one thing, it's another, and it all costs a bloody fortune.' He picked up his paper again and resumed reading.

In the meantime, Mavis was filling the kettle in the open-plan kitchen. It was all very cosy, although not quite in the same league as Sharon Mason's featureless expanse.

'You live locally?' Mavis asked.

'Yes, in Lower Tinworthy,' Kate replied.

'Aw, nice down there by the sea, innit? I'd like to be down there cos we're a bit out of the way up here. You need a car to go anywhere. I wasn't about to order a taxi just to go for the prescription, I can tell you. The *price* they charge these days! You need a mortgage to go from A to B. Sit yourself down, dear.'

Kate lowered herself into an armchair adorned with very pink roses and very blue wisteria.

Mavis finished pouring boiling water over the teabags and came to where Kate was sitting. She showed her the swollen fingers on her left hand. 'Terrible arthritis,' she told Kate, 'and them painkillers you buy over the counter don't even begin to *touch* it. So I'm bloomin' glad to get these anti-inflammatories, cos, like I said, I'd only got a couple of days left.' She went back into the kitchen. 'Milk and sugar?'

'Just a dash of milk please,' Kate replied.

Mavis carried the mug across to the table alongside Kate's chair, which was covered in framed photographs and china ornaments. She cleared a space and set the mug down.

'It's time we retired,' Mavis said, sitting down opposite.

'Ricky and me been looking after this place for ten years now, and we're worn out, ain't we, Ricky?'

'Bloody worn out,' confirmed Ricky without looking up from his newspaper.

'It's manic here all summer,' Mavis went on, taking a noisy slurp of tea. 'And we can't get no cleaners for love or money. Awful, ain't it, Ricky?'

There was a grunt from behind the newspaper.

'We have to take all sorts on, but we don't know who we're gettin'. We had to sack a couple this year for stealin' stuff from the vans.' She gulped some more tea. 'And the customers ain't a lot better, are they, Ricky?'

Another grunt.

'Most of them are gone now, thank God. There'll be a few for half-term of course. We've just got a few stragglers at the moment.' She shook her head in despair. 'And that bleedin' family in Bluebell Road of course.'

'Oh?' Kate asked, hoping she'd elaborate.

'They've taken *three* vans, ain't they, Ricky?'

'Yeah,' Ricky agreed, finally folding up the newspaper. 'Them bloody vans sleep four to six people each,' he informed Kate, 'and they could all bloody well have got into one quite easy. But, oh no, they wanted *three*! And us so short of cleaners! Bloody nuisance! And then one old geezer goes and gets himself killed!'

Kate had heard all this before, but it was plainly a sore point.

'*Murdered*,' Mavis corrected, 'and they'd only been here five minutes.' She looked sadly at Kate. 'You couldn't make it up.'

'My goodness!' said Kate, hoping she looked suitably shocked.

'Well, you'll know all about it if you live down in Lower T.'

'Oh yes,' Kate confirmed, 'we certainly did know about it.'

'We got police cars up here every five minutes, ain't we, Ricky?'

'Every five bloody minutes,' Ricky said wearily. 'And what do *we* know? They paid their money, and we don't go askin' them if any of them's likely to be bloody murdered. And now we can't even get rid of them cos the bloody police won't let them leave. How long are they goin' to be here for? You tell me that!'

'And cos we ain't got enough cleaners, they're goin' to have to clean up after themselves,' Mavis added.

'Well, let's hope it all gets resolved soon,' Kate said, draining her tea. She stood up. 'I must be on my way.'

'It was really nice of you to bring me the pills,' Mavis said, accompanying Kate to the door. 'Makes such a difference.'

'Good, and thanks for the tea,' Kate said as she stepped out through the little gate, heading for the car park and her red Fiat. At first glance, she imagined she could see someone in the front passenger seat. At second glance, she was aware that there *was* indeed someone sitting in the front passenger seat.

Full of apprehension, Kate opened the driver's door and looked across at an old man with a white beard, sitting upright as a board, staring through the windscreen.

Kate cleared her throat. 'Who are you? This is my car, and you shouldn't be in here!'

He didn't move. 'Are you going to take me home?' he asked.

'I don't know who you are,' Kate said, trying to work out what on earth to do with this old boy who was plainly sixpence short of a shilling.

'I *know* who I am,' he said, reasonably enough. 'Where's Frank? Frank didn't kill my little girl, you know. I've been waiting here for ages and I want to go home now.'

Kate stared at him in disbelief. *Frank?* He could surely only mean Frank Ford! She tried to think of something to say that would draw him out. 'What do you mean?'

'I need to see Frank. I *told* you. He knows who killed my little girl. Can we go home now, so I can see Frank?'

'Do you mean Frank Ford?' Kate asked, her heart in her mouth.

But the old man's eyes had glazed over and he shook his head. 'I want to go *home*!'

At that moment, a frantic-looking young woman with red hair came rushing into the car park. 'S*id*!' she was yelling. 'Sid, where *are* you?' As she noticed Kate, she asked, 'Have you seen…' and then stopped short when her eyes fell on Kate's uninvited passenger.

'Sid! What the hell are you doing in there?' She turned to Kate. 'I'm so sorry! I only turned my back for a moment and the old bugger was off! Like a flash of lightning! He can certainly move when he wants to!' She opened the passenger door and pulled the protesting Sid out by the arm.

'I want to go *home*,' he said.

This then, Kate reckoned, was without doubt Sid Kinsella, and so this woman had to be Meghan Ford, his carer, and Jason's wife.

'Please don't worry about it,' Kate said soothingly. She thought for a moment. 'Would you like me to help you get him back to wherever he's come from?'

The woman grinned. 'Probably a good idea, not that I think he'll make a run for it, but you never know. At least he doesn't run fast! I must get in touch with my husband cos he's gone off in the opposite direction looking for his grandfather. I'm Meghan by the way.'

'I'm Kate.' She took Sid's right arm, holding him firmly by the elbow, and Meghan took the other arm. They marched him up one of the lanes, the inaptly named Bluebell Road, passing rows of caravans of all shapes and sizes laid out in military precision in small, unadorned plots, with nary a bluebell in sight.

They stopped in front of a long, white single unit, just as a man came running from the opposite direction.

'I've found him, Jay!' Meghan shouted. 'He's sat himself down in this nurse's car!'

Kate had forgotten she was still in uniform.

The man, medium height and of stocky build, with dark hair, came to a halt and wiped his brow. 'God, that's a relief!' He turned to Sid. 'You can't keep going off like this, Grandpa!'

'I was going home,' Sid said.

'You weren't going anywhere,' Meghan informed him. 'And you shouldn't have been sitting in this lady's car!'

Sid sighed but allowed Meghan to steer him inside.

'Apologies!' said Jason Ford. 'He wants to go home. We *all* want to go home!' He held out his hand. 'I'm Jason Ford.'

Kate shook it. 'Kate Palmer.' For a moment, she wondered if the name might ring a bell, but it obviously didn't. She still used her maiden name for work, although officially she was now Kate Forrest, a name he might well have recognised. She noted his regular features and dark eyes; a good-looking man but not as tall as the brother they'd met in The Greedy Gull.

'I'm glad to have been of help,' Kate said. Then, as an afterthought, she added, 'I hope you enjoy the rest of your stay.'

'Are you kidding?' he asked as he walked towards the caravan door. 'But thanks again for your help.'

'You're welcome,' Kate said as she turned back along the row of caravans towards the car park. She hadn't learned too much more from her visit, but at least she was putting faces to the names on her list.

THIRTEEN

'Anyone else,' Woody said with a sigh that evening, 'would have delivered the prescription, gone straight back to their car and driven away.'

'But Mavis asked me in for a cup of tea!'

'You didn't have to accept, did you?'

'No, I didn't have to accept,' Kate agreed, 'but during the time I was in there, Sid obviously found his way to my car and decided he needed a driver to take him home. Just as well I had the cup of tea.'

'Don't you bother to lock your car when you park it?' Woody asked.

'Sometimes. But I only planned to be away for five minutes. Come on, admit it, I found out some interesting stuff I wouldn't have done if I'd gone straight back to the car.'

'Tell me again what the old boy said.'

'He said he needed to see Frank, and that it wasn't Frank who killed his little girl, by which he must have meant Frank's wife, Pauline.'

Woody was silent for a moment then said, 'Don't forget he has dementia. You can't take his rantings as gospel truth, Kate.'

'Nevertheless, I don't think you can ignore them either,' Kate replied. 'And you yourself said that you never believed that it was Frank who killed Pauline. Have you honestly no idea who the killer might have been?'

Woody shook his head. 'No idea at all. I was probably wrong anyway – it was just a *feeling*. And let's face it, Frank paid the price, so it's all water under the bridge now.'

'Except that it's *not*, is it? Because the way I see it, someone killed Frank for a good reason. And why would anyone want to throw suspicion on you?'

'We've been through this before, my love. Someone must have known that Frank wanted to see me and, for some reason, they did *not* want him to do that.'

'Because he probably wanted to bare his soul to you, tell you everything – whatever that was,' Kate suggested.

'Sure, that's what I've been thinking. If he'd become religious, he might have wanted to come clean. Who knows?'

'So perhaps Sid's ramblings weren't so crazy after all?'

'Maybe not.' Woody took Kate's hand. 'You could be in danger if any of that family find out who you are. I've told you innumerable times not to get involved, so I know I'm wasting my breath telling you again. All I ask is that you do *not* go up there alone. The likelihood is that one of these three brothers killed their father, so do not get in a one-to-one with any of them.'

Kate nodded. Woody looked tired and drawn; this thing was taking its toll on him. She felt he was more concerned about this case than he was admitting, which was totally understandable, and she had to do *something* to help. Of course, she didn't want to endanger herself, but surely, in a public place in broad daylight, she would be relatively safe.

. . .

There was no one in the bar of The Greedy Gull when Kate made her way in there at eleven o'clock on Saturday morning, just as they opened.

The bar was still empty, there was no sign of Steve, but Des was busy lining up glasses on a shelf. 'You all on your own?' he asked.

'Yes, Woody's across at his cottage tidying up the garden. I'm not stopping for a drink, Des, but I wanted to ask you something. Do you remember the man who was talking to us when we came in the other evening?'

Des thought for a moment. 'Yeah, was it that tall bloke, goin' bald, in his forties maybe?'

'That could be him,' Kate said. 'I just wondered if he'd been in again?'

'Funnily enough, he has. He came in with a woman last night. Great big knockers she'd got, could be his wife. Must be down on holiday cos I've not seen him around before. I did ask him, but he wasn't sayin' much. Said he might pop in again tonight.' Des was now in full flow. 'You two still bein' quizzed by that woman detective? She's been in here three or four times askin' them damn questions about who was here on the Saturday night that bloke was done in. She had a real go at Steve too.' He shook his head sadly. 'As if I can recall everyone! From what I remember, it was just the regulars anyway cos most of the tourists have gone home now. It's time for Steve to move on too, but he's gotta stay here for the time bein', she says. She's been askin' everyone questions, but she don't seem to be any nearer findin' out who done it though, does she?'

'Can you remember if that man I was asking about was in here the Saturday night of the murder?' Kate asked casually.

Des shook his head. 'Don't recall ever settin' eyes on him until that night with yourselves.' He sniffed. 'Did we see anyone around *outside*, that policewoman asked. *Outside*! When do I have time to go outside when we're busy on a Saturday night, eh? Steve takes in the dirty glasses. Did I hear a car late at night, she's askin'. Course I hear a car late at night, I'm tellin' her, I'm hearin' lotsa cars late at night when the last customers leave. Do you know she was even quizzin' old Cal Cobbledick and Ted Colwill and Parsley Perrin! That's them what plays dominoes all night over in the corner.' Des pointed to the table. 'They're mostly deaf and they don't hear nothin' but the rattle of the dominoes. She got their attention though, cos she's a good-lookin' bit of stuff, that's for certain. Sure you don't fancy a drink?'

Kate shook her head, tempted to ask why anyone would be called Parsley. But this was Cornwall, and most people had a nickname of one sort or another. 'No thanks, Des, but I'll most likely be in with Woody later.'

'So,' asked Des, 'are you lookin' to meet this feller again, or are you tryin' to dodge him?'

'Just at the moment, Des, we'd quite like to meet him again.' Kate gave him a wave as she headed out of the door.

'Shall we have a drink at The Gull this evening?' Kate asked casually as she popped some Cornish pasties into the oven to heat up for lunch.

Woody looked up from his seed catalogue. 'I guess so.' He studied her for a moment. 'I'm usually the one who suggests going to the pub. Are you up to something?'

'Of course not!' Kate retorted. 'I just thought it might be nice to go out for an hour or so.'

'OK.' Woody had returned to his seeds. 'How about some winter cabbage? And leeks for the spring?'

'Yes, that would be lovely,' Kate replied absently.

. . .

Later, as they sat with their drinks at their usual table by the inglenook, Kate was relieved to see Damian Ford and a chubby, busty blonde, presumably his wife, coming in.

Damian glanced across, spotted them and immediately walked over, asking, 'Mind if we join you?'

'No, not at all,' Kate and Woody chorused.

Kate studied the blonde, who was wearing a very low-cut blue dress, revealing an alarming amount of cleavage. Apart from anything else, the woman must be cold, because the evenings were chilly now and she didn't appear to have a coat.

'This is my wife, Jackie,' said Damian. The blonde gave a brief nod. 'Can I get you good folks a drink?'

'No thanks – we've already got one,' Woody replied.

As Damian and Jackie went to the bar, Woody said quietly to Kate, 'You *knew*, didn't you, that he was going to be in the bar this evening?'

'I swear I didn't know!' *Well I certainly didn't know for sure*, Kate thought.

'It just seems strange that you suggested coming here, and then, five minutes later, Damian Ford comes in the door.'

'It's not my fault you've got such a suspicious mind,' Kate murmured.

'It's the result of all those years in the Met, my love!'

'Sshh! They're coming back.' Kate noticed that Cal, Ted and Parsley had looked up from their dominoes and were directing their respective gazes at Jackie's frontage.

Damian pulled out a couple of chairs for himself and Jackie and sat down opposite.

'I've been hearing about you,' said Jackie, settling her ample bottom on the chair and placing her schooner of sherry carefully on the table.

'Well I hope what you heard was good,' Woody said.

Jackie sniffed.

'Of course it was!' Damian put in quickly.

Kate, fascinated, watched as Jackie reached for her drink and her two enormous boobs nearly escaped onto the table. 'You must be finding it a bit cool here after Spain,' she said by way of conversation.

'Yeah, right, and the sooner we get back there, the better,' Jackie said with feeling. 'We're almost locals now, ain't we, love?'

Damian nodded obediently.

'Cos we been down there more than fifteen years,' she added, 'and we ain't comin' back here. No, sirree!' She took a generous slurp of her sherry.

'You must be almost fluent in Spanish now then,' Kate said. 'I've always wanted to be fluent in a European language.'

'Spanish?' Jackie looked askance. 'We don't speak *Spanish*!' She made it sound like some dire disease.

'Everyone down there speaks English, see?' Damian explained.

'Oh,' Kate said, 'I just thought that if you lived in a foreign country, it was only polite to learn their language.'

'No need,' remarked Jackie, 'when everyone we know speaks English.'

Probably all villains, Kate thought. She directed her gaze at Damian. 'I met your brother yesterday.'

'Which one?' he asked.

'Jason.'

'Oh, where did you come across *him*?'

'Up at your caravan park. I was delivering a prescription to the warden, during which time your grandfather decided to plonk himself in my car.'

'Kate's a nurse,' Woody explained. 'She goes out of her way to look after her patients.' He nudged Kate's leg.

'So what was Grandpa doing in your car?' Damian asked.

'Good question. He told me he wanted to go home.' She had

no intention of telling Damian what else his grandfather had said.

'We *all* want to go bloody home,' Damian said.

'That's how I met Jason and Meghan,' Kate explained, 'because they were running around looking for him.'

'Yeah, I bet they were.' Damian picked up his glass. 'That's all they damn well got to *do*!'

'Well, it can't be easy,' Woody said diplomatically. 'Must be like having a small child around, and you probably need eyes in the back of your head.'

Damian took a swig of beer, wiped his mouth and laid the glass down. 'My young brother,' he said, with a sigh, 'ain't used to lookin' after anyone except himself. Ain't that right, Jax?'

Jackie nodded emphatically.

'He was always Grandpa's favourite and, boy, hasn't he made the most of it!' Damian added.

'Got himself a nice little business out of it,' Jackie put in.

Damian nodded. 'So it shouldn't be hard work to look after the old sod for a few days on holiday, eh? I mean, Meghan does it *all* the time. And it's a *caravan*, not a stately bleedin' home! They're all livin' cheek by jowl, so you think you'd damn well *notice* if someone had gone out, wouldn't you?'

Jackie had made short work of the schooner of sherry, which was now almost empty. She leaned forward. 'I reckon he was most likely hopin' poor old Sid would wander off and get himself killed on the main road or somethin'. I mean, he's got Sid's business now, so he don't need the old man around no more.'

'Poor Sid,' Kate said with feeling.

'At least he's still with us, which is more than Dad is,' Damian said with a little sigh.

'And Jason always hated his dad of course,' Jackie remarked, picking up her glass and thrusting it at Damian. 'I could do with another of them, love.'

'Yeah, all right,' said Damian, pushing back his chair. 'Anyone else?'

Both Kate and Woody, who'd been sipping their drinks slowly, shook their heads.

Then, as Damian made his way to the bar, Jackie lowered her voice. 'Like I said, Jason always hated his dad for what he done. Understandable, I suppose, being as he was always Pauline's favourite. I've told the police that, so God only knows why they keep questioning us.'

'I guess they have to keep an open mind,' Woody said.

'Then there's Wayne,' Jackie went on, keeping an eye on Damian, who was still standing at the bar. 'He's no bloody saint either! Supposed to be lookin' after his dad, he was, and he ain't half done a lot of weepin' and wailin' since the old man was killed. But' – she looked furtively at the bar again – 'you tell me, how could he sleep through his father gettin' himself up, dressed and out of the door?'

She sat back for a moment then leaned forward again. Kate noticed that every male in the bar, including Woody, was staring at her boobs in fascination, hoping to see The Great Escape.

Jackie wasn't done yet. 'I'll tell you somethin' else. Did you know that Frank became a Catholic while he was in jail? My God, since we all got here, didn't we all have to listen to him spoutin' on about saints and stuff the whole bloody time, tellin' us we should be confessin' our sins and goin' to church. You've never heard the like!' She lowered her voice again as Damian approached. 'But don't you go sayin' to him that I told you that.'

Damian put Jackie's sherry and another pint for himself on the table.

'Well I'm sure you'll be hoping this all gets sorted out before long so you can get back to Spain,' Woody said as Damian seated himself again.

'Obviously I'm upset about Dad,' Damian said, 'but we

didn't have nothin' to do with it, so I don't know why they won't let us fly back to Malaga.' He glanced at Jackie. 'At least the sherry's cheaper there.'

Jackie hiccupped. 'It's my only indulgence, sweetie.'

'That and a wardrobe full of dresses,' said Damian drily. 'Not to mention the bloody boat.'

'It's a little *yacht*,' Jackie corrected him, turning to Kate. 'All our friends got yachts, for goodness' sake!'

'Theirs are probably *paid* for, Jax,' Damian snapped.

'We won't go into that,' Jackie replied, draining half the glass.

Kate and Woody exchanged glances.

'Well,' Woody said, 'it's been most interesting getting to know you, but I think we should be heading home.'

Damian studied his Rolex. 'It's only half-past nine!'

'I have to be up early,' Kate lied hurriedly, 'so we must love you and leave you!'

'Probably run into you again in here sometime,' Damian said, 'if they haven't arrested you.'

As Kate and Woody made their way towards the door, Kate said, 'I didn't like that last remark.'

'Hmm,' said Woody, taking her arm as they left The Greedy Gull.

FOURTEEN

'On the face of it,' Woody said as, half an hour later, they sat drinking hot chocolate, 'it all seems very plausible that Damian's come back, under sufferance, for a family holiday at his dad's request. Even if he doesn't think a great deal of his family and can't wait to get back to Spain.'

'Where there's a boat that apparently hasn't been paid for,' Kate said.

'Which we must call a *yacht*,' Woody said with a grin. 'They certainly enjoy spending money by the sound of it. But whose money is it? Did he owe it to his father, like Sharon said?'

Kate thought for a moment. 'Would Frank have had the resources to lend Damian a large amount of money in the first place?'

Woody shrugged. 'I honestly don't know, but I guess that he probably managed to stash away a fair bit over the years. And it wouldn't surprise me in the least if he did want it back, because, unless he went to live with one of his sons, he'd probably need somewhere to stay, a car maybe and money to live on. Frank was coming up to seventy, so he was hardly likely to get a job or rob a bank.'

'Poor old Frank,' Kate said with a sigh.

'There's a lot of this that doesn't add up,' Woody said. 'According to the police report, Frank was strangled around ten hours before they found him at seven in the morning, which would make his death somewhere around seven to nine o'clock on Saturday night. According to Wayne, his father wandered out while he, Wayne, was fast asleep. Would he have been fast asleep at that time? That's assuming Frank set off around then to meet his doom.'

'If Frank did leave while Wayne was perhaps dozing in the evening, he would still be fully dressed anyway,' Kate added.

'So you're suggesting that Wayne dozes off in front of the telly?'

'Possible, I suppose,' Kate replied. 'If the programme was boring enough, they might both have dropped off, but Frank woke first.'

Woody was staring at the dying embers in the log burner. 'Assuming that was true, where would an elderly man go, in the evening, to get himself strangled?'

'Perhaps he was visiting one of the other sons who was still up and awake? Perhaps Damian saw it as an opportunity to get rid of some of his debts?'

'Perhaps Jackie enveloped him in a hug and smothered him with her boobs?' Woody suggested with a grin.

'Very funny. Or he went to Jason's – we know that Jason hated him.'

'Are you saying Jason attacked him with a rope or something?'

'Well, someone must have done if he was strangled. Either that or he started walking down here to Lower Tinworthy,' Kate said. 'And why would he do that? To see *you*?'

'It's several miles, Kate. So you're suggesting he got hijacked en route? That's very unlikely.' Woody paused. 'I've got no gut feelings at all on this one.'

'Then he must have got himself killed up at Sunshine Park and was transported down here to our garden?' Kate mused.

'I guess it's still the most likely explanation.'

'Yet nobody heard a car coming up here late at night? I doubt very much they physically carried him.'

'Well, Miss Marple, you're going to need all your skills to figure this one out! In the meantime, shall we go to bed?'

Next day, Woody asked, 'Would you mind if I watch the Chelsea match tonight?'

'Of course not,' Kate replied. Then a thought occurred to her. 'I might just pop down to see Angie. I haven't seen her for a day or two and she's been swooning over some actor who's been visiting The Old Locker in the evenings.'

'Are you planning to swoon too?'

'I might just do that! Time you had some competition!'

'Well try not to swoon while the match is on because I don't want to be disturbed and have to carry you home. Unless you do it at half-time of course.'

'I'll bear that in mind,' said Kate.

Kate left Barney asleep and Woody sprawled on the sofa in front of the TV, a few cans of beer by his side, and made her way down the lane, past the pub and the couple of cottages lower down. Whoever had transported Frank Ford's body up to their garden must have had *some* mode of transport, she reckoned, even if it was only a wheelbarrow. She smiled to herself at the vision of someone pushing a body in a wheelbarrow up the lane, passing the pub, where people were going in and coming out all evening, until late. Unless they carried him down from the cliffs above? Even more unlikely considering the rough path.

The Old Locker was fairly busy with more than half the tables occupied and half a dozen people at the bar, one of them stroking Maximus, whilst waiting to be served. Fortunately, her usual bar stool in the corner wasn't occupied, so Kate climbed quickly onto it.

Fergal saw her first and gave her a brief wave as he served some frothy cocktails to a young couple.

Angie was at the till, and as she turned round to give change to a customer, she caught sight of her sister. 'On your own, Kate?'

'Yes, Chelsea are playing. Need I say more?' Kate noticed Angie was wearing more make-up than usual, her hair was lacquered into position and the aroma of Chanel No. 5 was nearly knocking her off the bar stool. 'Expecting someone?'

'You have a suspicious mind,' Angie said. 'So, what do you want to drink?'

'I'll have one of Fergal's Irish coffees please.'

Angie relayed this information to Fergal, who was at the far end of the bar. He winked and called out, 'I'll make it a good one, Kate!'

Kate had no doubt he would, because he was known to be heavy-handed with the whisky bottle, but always managed to soothe the taste with the mountain of cream on the top. She paid for it and took a few delicious sips of the hot liquid through the cream. She'd had a few Irish coffees in her time, but Fergal's were undoubtedly the best.

'Solved your murder yet?' Angie asked cheerfully as she came back opposite Kate.

'I'm trying to forget it for the moment.' As Kate spoke, she noticed Angie's eyes light up and she patted her hairdo, moistened her lips and turned her attention to the man who'd just approached the bar.

'My goodness!' he said. 'You're looking very delectable tonight, Angie!'

'Oh, Clint! Such flattery! Now, what can I get you?'

'A shandy's fine because I'm driving.'

While Angie was pouring his drink, Kate took the opportunity to study him. Tall, dark and undoubtedly handsome, with an almost Romanesque profile. Yes, he was good-looking. He was casually dressed in a black sweater, white jeans and trainers, and Kate noticed he had a gold stud in his left ear. She couldn't see the other ear from where she was sitting.

As Angie positioned the drink in front of him, she said, pointing at Kate, 'Oh, by the way, this is my *married* sister.'

He turned to face her and, for a moment, Kate was transfixed by his dark, fathomless eyes. And yes, he had a stud in his right ear too.

'Hi,' he said, 'I'm Clint, and I'm wondering how many beautiful sisters there are in this family?'

'Oh, just the two,' said Angie coquettishly.

What a smoothie, Kate thought. A professional flirt. She couldn't quite make out his accent, which varied from London to mid-Atlantic. But there was something familiar about him. Had she seen him on TV or at the cinema?

He grabbed a vacant bar stool and brought it along next to Kate. 'Mind if I join you?'

'No, not at all,' Kate replied, wishing she'd washed her hair this morning, or at least put on some mascara. She decided not to know about his acting. 'Are you here on holiday?'

'Um, no, it's kinda business. They're shooting a movie just down the coast and so we're all holed up in Higher Tinworthy for now. We generally finish shooting around five o'clock, when the light begins to fade.'

Kate couldn't help being mesmerised by his eyes and was beginning to wonder if she was being hypnotised. 'What's the film about?'

'Oh, it's a costume drama about the shipwrecks on this coast, along the lines of *Poldark*. Tell me about yourself; do you live near here?'

'Oh, just up the lane.' Kate waved an arm in what she hoped was the right direction.

'And your husband…?'

'Is watching football.'

'Ah,' said Clint. 'Chelsea's playing tonight, right?'

'Right,' Kate agreed. 'I gather you're not a Chelsea fan then?'

'Arsenal's my team,' he said.

In the meantime, Angie was serving some customers and sending worried glances in Kate's direction every few seconds. *Does she think I'm flirting with him?* Kate wondered. *And why wouldn't I? He's damned attractive.*

'So, are you an actor?' she asked.

'Yes,' he said, 'and I play the baddie in this movie. I try to steal the main character's *wife*.'

'And do you succeed?' Kate asked.

'I'm not about to tell you that,' he said with a wicked grin. 'You'll just have to see the film for yourself when it's released next year.'

Kate shivered. She'd never met anyone with such intense eyes.

Angie arrived back on the scene. 'Kate and Woody,' she informed Clint, 'solve all the murder mysteries round here.'

'Do you indeed?' said Clint, suddenly looking at her with interest.

'Oh, we help the police sometimes,' Kate said modestly. 'My husband was a detective, you see.'

'But not now?'

'No, he retired recently. We have a lady in charge now, and she's very efficient,' Kate replied.

'So do you get many murders around here?' He looked from one to the other, visibly shocked.

'Oh, *lots*!' said Angie cheerfully. 'And Kate will tell you that they found a body in *their* garden two weeks ago!'

'*What*?' Clint sounded horrified. 'Who was it? Someone you knew?'

Kate sighed. 'Well, my husband knew him from years ago when he was with the Met in London.'

'But,' Angie put in, 'Woody – that's Kate's husband – *didn't* do it, but it was made to look as if he *did*.'

'This is unbelievable,' said Clint, 'in a little village like Tinworthy! Here was I thinking that a few weeks in the wilds of Cornwall would provide a blessed relief from London crime!'

'Yes, we all thought that,' said Kate drily, draining her coffee. 'That was delicious, Angie, but I'd better be getting back now.'

'*Must* you go?' Clint asked, leaning slightly towards her.

Kate hesitated. He was gorgeous, no doubt about it. No wonder Angie had gone overboard with the make-up! She reprimanded herself for acting like a gullible teenager.

'One of Fergal's Irish coffees is generally enough for anyone,' Angie said firmly, looking pointedly at Kate and then at the door.

Kate glanced at her watch. 'Well, maybe I'll have a little glass of red, because there's still half an hour to go.'

'My treat then!' said Clint, producing a note from his pocket.

Angie didn't look too pleased, particularly as she had to go and serve some new customers. She plonked a glass of Merlot in front of Kate.

Clint wanted to know if she had a career. A nurse! How wonderful! He adored the medical profession, and nurses in particular. Did she have children? Two sons – fantastic! In Edinburgh: lovely city! He told her about some filming experiences, including on a French farm, where a bull had made a run for him and he'd had to vault over a six-foot fence to escape. 'Of course, I was younger and fitter then,' he said.

'You still look very fit,' Kate said admiringly, and then wished she hadn't. Would he take that the wrong way? He must know that she was flirting with him, but, what the hell, he was very, very attractive!

She had, of course, a very, very attractive spouse at home, and the Chelsea game must be nearly finished by now. Perhaps they'd go into extra time? She'd quite like some extra time to have a little flirt. She couldn't remember the last time she'd had any size of flirt, and she'd forgotten just how enjoyable it was! This man had a way of looking at you as if you were the only woman on earth! And a naked one at that.

Kate looked up to meet Angie's hostile stare, bringing her back down to earth. She drained her glass quickly. 'It's been lovely meeting you, Clint, and thanks so much for the wine. Perhaps we'll run into each other again.'

'I sincerely hope so,' he said, standing up in a gentlemanly manner and giving a little bow. Then he gave her a dazzling smile, and Kate noted his beautiful teeth. Surely he should be playing the hero and not the baddie? Ah well.

With a smile on her face, Kate made her way up the lane, thoughts of dead bodies and killers far from her mind.

FIFTEEN

In spite of Woody's warnings about not meeting any of the Ford family on her own, Kate badly wanted to see Sid Kinsella again, in the hope that he might have some more interesting comments to make. The man may be senile, but Kate couldn't get 'Frank didn't kill my little girl' out of her mind. That had come from somewhere deep inside the old man's subconscious, and it also tied up with Woody's hunch that Frank hadn't killed his wife.

She was also keen to meet the third Ford brother, Wayne, who she hadn't yet set eyes on. But what possible excuse did she have to go back up to Sunshine Park again? Perhaps Barney might like a walk on the nearby moors? *I was just walking the dog and wondered how your grandfather was?* That sounded plausible, didn't it? It was certainly worth a try.

On Wednesday morning, Woody decided to spend a few hours at his allotment. 'Why don't you come with me?' he asked Kate.

'I would, but Barney needs a long walk, so I think we'll set off shortly,' Kate replied. 'Perhaps we'll call in at the allotment later, on our way back.'

'On your way back from *where?*' Woody asked, looking at her suspiciously.

'Oh, we'll probably wander on the moors, above The Edge,' Kate said casually. She knew that would pacify Woody because they were extremely fond of both the restaurant and the surrounding moorland. The Edge of the Moor was their favourite eating place and where Woody had taken her on their very first date. It was an ancient stone building, converted into a renowned restaurant and, as the name indicated, situated on the edge of Bodmin Moor.

Woody was placing spades and hoes into the back of his car. 'I'm going to make that shed secure today,' he said, 'so I don't have to bring my stuff home each time.' He gave Kate a kiss, got into the driving seat and, with a wave, he was off.

Kate looked for the dog, who was sniffing around the garage and the shed. 'You won't find any bodies there today, Barney,' she said, 'but perhaps we can find out more about the one we *did* find. Let's go walkies!'

There was a cold wind blowing on the moor above Sunshine Park, and the sun kept dipping in and out of the clouds. Kate pulled her hood up and surveyed the scene below where the moorland gave way to fields of sheep and cattle, the cliffs and the sea. The only blot on the otherwise idyllic landscape was the sprawl of caravans which constituted Sunshine Park. Sited in military rows, there was an awful lot of them; hundreds, Kate reckoned, as she tried to count them but soon gave up. She tried to imagine having a holiday in the place, just a very few feet away from your – unknown – neighbours on each side. The 'sunshine' could certainly not be guaranteed, it was some miles from the beach and the bus service was erratic, to put it mildly.

She turned round to look for the dog. 'Come on, Barney,' she called, 'we're about to go visiting!'

. . .

The first person Kate saw as she walked up Bluebell Road was Jason Ford standing outside the door of his caravan. He looked agitated and was pulling on his walking boots.

Kate had rehearsed what she was going to say, but before she had even opened her mouth, Jason Ford said, 'The old bugger's gone *again!*'

'Gone?' Kate asked.

'Yeah, gone. God knows where. Gone walkabout.' He looked at Barney. '*You* know what he looks like, and you got a springer there, so he should be able to trace someone. We're going to check the surroundin' area, but perhaps you could be checkin' round the park?'

'Well, I—'

'I'll get an item of his clothin',' Jason said, 'and let your dog have a sniff.'

With that, he disappeared inside and then emerged with a grubby grey sock which he stuck under Barney's nose. 'Go find him, boy!'

Barney looked confused but wagged his tail.

Next door, Damian and Jackie were outside pulling on anoraks and shoes.

Kate unfurled her collar and turned her head away quickly. She didn't want Damian to recognise her, because Jason had no idea yet who she was and, for the moment, she wanted to keep it that way.

'Where's your other brother?' Only after she'd spoken did Kate realise that he'd never said anything about having another brother. Fortunately, he didn't twig.

'Damian's right there, next door.'

'No, er, your oldest brother?'

'Wayne?' said Jason. 'God only knows. Probably gone bird-watching.' He pointed at the next caravan along from Damian's.

'He ain't in there.'

'Surely you should phone the police about your grandfather?' Kate suggested.

'Not bloody likely,' snapped Jason. 'They'll ask a lot of questions about how he managed to escape and then probably contact social services to say we ain't lookin' after him properly. We'll find him ourselves.' He hesitated. 'You'd better make a note of my number,' he added, 'so you can give us a call if you find him on-site.'

Kate frantically listed Jason's number and gave him hers before they all raced off, Meghan included. She'd pulled her hood up, and fortunately Damian didn't look in her direction as he was busy getting into his anorak and shouting at Jackie to get a move on because they all had to start looking.

Kate looked at Barney hopefully. 'You're supposed to be a sniffer dog,' she informed him, 'so let's see what you're made of!' She looked briefly at Wayne's caravan, where the curtains were drawn and there was no sign of life. At least now she knew that they had their three vans in a row.

She looked back and saw the two couples racing towards the gates.

Kate and Barney set off along Bluebell Road, where no bluebell was ever likely to sprout between the seas of concrete. Most of the caravans were empty except one, near the end, where a pot-bellied man was sitting on his doorstep, staring into space.

'Have you seen an elderly man passing by here?' Kate asked.

'No, I 'aven't, and you ain't supposed to have dogs in this park,' he yelled at her.

Kate ignored him and carried on walking quickly, turning into Daffodil Way. Barney treated Daffodil Way in the same manner as Bluebell Road, sniffing an occasional lamp post and, finding no interesting smells in this canine-free place, looking thoroughly bored.

There was no sign of Sid or anyone else on Daffodil Way, Magnolia Avenue or Primrose Parkway either, and Barney's encounter with the sock was showing no results whatsoever. Where had the poor old man gone? Where could she look next?

Kate checked on Bluebell Road again on her way out, but all three caravans appeared to be empty. Where had the poor old boy gone this time? And why was he so keen to escape? She decided not to call on the Owens because it would be difficult to explain what exactly she was doing there.

Kate stood outside the park and looked in all directions. She could see three figures heading towards Higher Tinworthy and presumed it was the Fords looking for their grandfather. Where had the old man gone?

SIXTEEN

Woody got back mid-afternoon, mud-splattered and happy. He was making good progress, he told Kate, but he'd had quite enough for today. He wasn't as young or as fit as he once was, his back was playing up and he wanted a nice hot bath. *After* he'd had a mug of tea.

As he sat in the kitchen drinking the tea, Kate told him about her expedition up to Sunshine Park.

Woody slammed down his mug. 'What the hell were you doing up there?'

'Oh, Woody, don't go blowing a fuse! Honestly, I just wanted to give Barney a walk and I wondered how poor old Sid was.'

'I *told* you not to go—'

'I know, I know!' Kate interrupted. 'Thing is, he'd *gone*! They were all going mad getting ready to go and look for him, and I was instructed by Jason to check round the site with Barney, who's a springer spaniel of course and supposed to be able to find people. Needless to say, Barney didn't find a damned thing.'

'Kate,' Woody said wearily, 'it's really none of our business.'

'But it *is*! Their *father* was found in our garden. Their *grandfather* was found in my car, and mumbling on about how Frank didn't kill his little girl. And *you* are a suspect. *Of course* it's our business!'

Woody drained his mug of tea. 'So where are they all looking?' he asked in a resigned tone of voice.

'Well they seemed to be heading towards the Higher Tinworthy area last time I saw them. Now I come to think of it, I should probably have gone down towards the cliffs, but I could see no sign of him in the distance and, to be honest, I was becoming tired at that point.'

'I expect they've found him by now,' Woody said hopefully.

'I'm not too sure about that,' Kate replied. 'We exchanged phone numbers, so I think I would have heard if they'd found him.'

'They were probably heading in the wrong direction. Why weren't they looking on the slopes up towards the cliffs?'

'Do you think that may have been where he was heading?'

Woody grinned. 'I'm having one of your famous "feelings"! Next thing you know, I'll be making lists!'

'Don't be sarcastic!'

'I'm not being sarcastic. If your Ford friends haven't found him yet, then what's the betting he *did* head for the cliffs?'

'You don't suppose he planned to throw himself off, do you?' Kate asked in alarm.

'I have no idea. But if it makes you happy, even before I have my bath, I'll have a look up on the cliffs.'

'Oh, Woody, that's so kind of you! And I'm coming with you,' said Kate.

Kate stumbled several times as she scaled the steep path behind
Lavender Cottage and was out of breath by the time she got to
the top.

Woody was breathing heavily too. 'I must be crazy,' he said,
'after tilling the soil all day!'

The craggy coastal path ahead disappeared down into stony
dips, reappearing again further along. This pattern repeated
itself continually on this part of the coast, which was why Kate
always preferred to walk on the north side of the Lower
Tinworthy valley. Barney, at least, was happy. Two walks in
one day!

'Sid's ninety years old,' Kate reminded Woody as they
scrambled down one dip and up the other side again, 'so I don't
think he'd be able to manage this kind of terrain.'

'Yes, I was going to suggest we head inland.' He pointed at
the rough ground dotted with gorse bushes. 'Surely they'd think
to look round here though?'

Kate shrugged. 'They're city boys – probably haven't much
clue.'

'Then they'll surely have called the police?'

'I don't think so. Jason was adamant that he didn't want the
police involved in case they contacted social services about their
suitability to be looking after Sid in the first place.'

'Bloody right,' muttered Woody. 'I can't see how he can
possibly escape twice from right under their noses. But I don't
suppose they want to draw attention to themselves, being the
villains they are.'

They trudged on for a further ten minutes before Kate said,
'I think we're wasting our time. I'm going to phone Jason's
number to see if they've found him.'

As she dug her phone out of her pocket, Woody held up a
restraining hand. 'Hold off a minute,' he said quietly as he
headed towards a large gorse bush where Barney was running
round in circles and barking excitedly. Behind the bush, Kate

spotted what looked like a strip of grey material. She followed Woody cautiously for a few steps, and then they both stopped in their tracks.

Before them lay the body of an old man, with half of the left side of his head smashed up against the rock. Kate gasped with shock.

SEVENTEEN

'I think he'd been dead a little while,' Kate told Charlotte later, after they'd got back to Lavender Cottage. They'd waited up there for the police to arrive, along with a helicopter from Plymouth.

'What was he doing there on his own?' Charlotte asked.

'I don't know. But I did know he was missing.'

'How did you know that?'

Kate swallowed. 'Because I'd seen the family earlier and I knew they were looking for him.'

Charlotte rubbed her brow. 'You'd better tell me why you were in contact with the family and how many times you've been in touch with them.'

Kate told her about delivering the prescription, finding Sid Kinsella in her car and, as a result, meeting Jason and Meghan.

'We'd already met Damian and his wife at The Greedy Gull, purely accidentally,' Woody added. 'But neither of us have met Wayne.'

'So you're not stalking them, are you, Kate?' Charlotte asked.

'Absolutely not,' Kate said, annoyed. 'I was concerned. Poor

Sid, he was a confused old man, and he certainly didn't deserve this.'

Charlotte gave a sigh. 'No, I don't suppose he did. At first, we thought he'd fallen and bashed his head against a sharp rock, but, on closer inspection, we've established it most certainly was *not* an accident, due to the extent of his injuries. It would appear that whoever killed him wanted to make sure he was well and truly dead.' She then made careful notes about the time that Kate found the family preparing to go looking for him. 'And you saw all of them heading towards the Higher Tinworthy area, did you?'

Kate thought for a moment. 'Four of them left the caravan site, but I'm not altogether sure all four of them were going towards Higher Tinworthy, but I could certainly make out three. It was difficult to see from some distance away, and they were all wearing anoraks with the hoods up because it was windy and it had started to drizzle.'

'So, assuming there were three of them and not four, then the fourth one could presumably have gone in a different direction, and could even have killed him?'

'I suppose so.' Kate wished she'd counted them more carefully, but she'd had no idea at the time how important the information was to become.

'Tell me again what Kinsella said to you when you found him in your car?'

'Just that he wanted to go home, and that Frank hadn't killed his little girl.'

'So, possibly whoever *did* kill his little girl wanted him out of the way before he started spilling the beans?'

'Which narrows it down to Damian, Jason and their respective wives,' Woody said. 'And Wayne of course.'

'Well it seems extremely unlikely that a passing stranger would take such a dislike to a doddery old man heading towards the cliffs that they'd batter him to death,' Charlotte said. 'I'm going to get the whole family into the police station as soon as I finish here, and I intend to be interrogating them individually this evening.'

'I wish I'd never set eyes on that damned family,' Woody said with feeling. 'If only I could wind the clock back...'

Charlotte gave a long sigh and looked at them both as she packed away her recorder. 'I have no idea how you two manage to get yourselves involved in every murder going. Come to think of it, I've never known such a succession of killings, bearing in mind this is a comparatively small village. You know what? I'm about ready to go back to the Met for a rest.'

The following day, Woody was summoned to the police station to repeat, more or less, what he'd already told Charlotte. The atmosphere there, he told Kate, was very tense. Two murders in the one family! It would not encourage tourists to visit Tinworthy, Charlotte had said; the tourist board and the hoteliers were all up in arms and badgering her to get a move on to solve this thing.

After a quiet, uneventful weekend, Kate was relieved to go to work the following Monday morning, if only to forget the Ford family for a few hours. As she came out of her door, she saw half a dozen reporters again, including Eddie, waiting at the gate.

'We understand your husband's a suspect for the murder of both Frank Ford and Sid Kinsella, from London, who were staying at the Sunshine Caravan Park. Can you confirm that?' The spokesman this time was a tall, thin, gaunt-looking man in a donkey jacket.

'I have nothing to say,' Kate replied primly as she got into her Fiat.

'Were you friends with the Ford family in London?' Eddie

shouted, to which Kate replied with a loud and forceful 'No!' before driving off down the lane.

As she and Sue approached the reception desk to get their lists of patients, they found Denise beaming from ear to ear. When she saw Kate, the smile disappeared.

'Is it true you found *another* body?' she asked, her eyes widening.

'News travels fast round here,' Kate said through gritted teeth.

'Really?' muttered Sue.

'Well,' said Denise, 'my nephew was walking up on the cliffs Wednesday afternoon and he couldn't believe his eyes when he saw the helicopter landing and picking up someone, and then he saw you and Woody talking to the DI. I put two and two together, Kate, knowing how you tend to come across bodies and that. Anyway, you *know* how it is, and he hid behind one of those bushes up there and listened in.'

'My lips are sealed, Denise,' Kate replied. 'Now, can we change the subject please?'

'Don't go badgering Kate,' Sue said, 'but I must say I did hear the helicopter going over and wondered what was going on. Anyway, *you're* looking mighty pleased with yourself today, Denise.'

'I am,' Denise confirmed, beaming some more. 'I think I may be in love!'

Kate and Sue exchanged amused glances. Denise was famed for falling in and out of love.

'So who's the lucky man this time?' Kate asked, glancing at her appointment list.

'Oh, just someone I met in The Tinners on Saturday night,' Denise replied airily.

'Don't keep us in suspense,' said Sue. 'Tell us all!'

'He's gorgeous: tall, dark and handsome with a smile that would light up the room!' Denise said dreamily.

'Well The Tinners could certainly do with some extra illumination,' Sue remarked.

'I'm seeing him again tonight,' Denise said coyly.

Kate laughed. 'I hope he's taking you somewhere nice?'

'Just The Tinners. Nothing wrong with the Tinners,' Denise snapped.

The Tinners' Arms was an ancient pub situated in Middle Tinworthy, near the medical centre, the church and the school. It had low, beamed ceilings, wonky slate floors and nicotine-stained walls from years back. The Tinners was greatly favoured by the more elderly locals, for whom The Greedy Gull was far too modern, being only a couple of hundred years old, and far too touristy, being so close to the beach. The Tinners was also the village centre for pub quizzes, darts matches and the like. Kate and Woody did visit the place occasionally, but they couldn't walk home from The Tinners like they could from The Greedy Gull. Kate always found the sloping walls and uneven slate floor disorientating, and that was *before* she had her first drink. She couldn't quite see the place as the ideal setting for a fledgling romance.

'So tell us about him,' encouraged Sue.

Denise glanced at the door to ensure no patients had begun to arrive. 'Like I said, tall, dark and handsome, and he's here to write a *book*!' She gave them a look to ensure they were as impressed as she was.

'He's never writing it in The Tinners surely?' Kate said, laughing.

'Of course not!' retorted Denise. 'He's renting a tiny room at the Wayfarers Guest House, so he can have peace and tranquillity.' She leaned across the desk. 'Creative people *need* peace and tranquillity, you know.'

'Doesn't he have peace and tranquillity at home, wherever that is?' Kate asked.

'No, because he lives in a very noisy block of flats in Peckham. That's in *London*, you know. So he needed to get away.'

'What's his book about then?' Sue asked.

'Oh, mystery, crime, that sort of thing.' Denise sounded vague.

'And what's the name of this Adonis?' Kate asked.

'Lloyd. Lloyd Bannerman. Isn't that classy? I mean, you can just *see* it on a book cover, can't you?'

Sue gave a snort. 'Well I hope he's going to take you somewhere more salubrious than The Tinners while he's here, Denise.'

'As a matter of fact, he's going to book a table for the Atlantic restaurant on Friday night,' Denise said triumphantly. She then cleared her throat as an elderly man approached. 'Good morning, Mr Potter! Take a seat! The nurse will call you in shortly!' She looked pointedly at Kate, who decided it was time to start work.

Charlie Potter wanted to see Kate because he'd been getting heart palpitations, and was it any wonder what with everything that was going on?

'What do you mean?' Kate asked, taking his pulse.

'Well, you know my sister, Mattie? Her what lives out at the bottom of the hill?'

Kate nodded.

'She's hangin' out her washin' and her hears this helluva noise from above, so up her looks and there's this bloody great helicopter screamin' over her head and lookin' to land. Well, Mattie's a bit shaken like, but her's figurin' that maybe someone's in trouble, so off her goes at the double, up the hill, to have a look at where it's landin', see? And there, on the ground, is someone bein' put in a black bag, and we all know what *that* means, don't we?'

Kate said nothing but recalled Mattie having two bandaged knees and moaning about being unable to walk any distance, far less sprinting up hills.

'Anyway,' Charlie continued, 'her keeps herself hidden behind one of them bushes, and her sees the police havin' a chat with you, like, and then the 'copter takin' off again. Don't think Mattie's had that much excitement in years, cos not a lot happens in her bit of the village, if you know what I mean.'

'Quite,' Kate said, visualising half of Tinworthy crouching behind the gorse bushes getting their excitement fix. 'Now, I've given you a further prescription, so see how you get on, Charlie.'

'So who was in the bag, Nurse?'

Kate shrugged. 'No doubt the police will issue a statement soon.'

'But you must've seen whoever it was, didn't you? Was it somebody you knew?'

'No,' Kate replied, 'no one I knew.' *Just wish I'd known him better.*

An hour later, Ida Tilley waddled into the treatment room. Kate sighed. *Here we go again.*

Before the old woman could sit down, Kate said, 'Hello, Ida! And no, I *don't* know who the man was, and the police *will* be issuing a statement in due course.'

Ida looked somewhat perplexed. 'What man was that then?'

'The man the helicopter took away on Wednesday afternoon.'

'Wednesday afternoon?' Ida sat down heavily on the chair. 'Didn't hear no helicopter Wednesday afternoon. Must've been havin' me forty winks. Have I missed somethin' then?'

EIGHTEEN

Kate and Woody had just finished lunch on Wednesday when there was a knock on the door. Kate opened it to find an elderly man, in a dark suit and a dog collar, standing there.

'I'm sorry to bother you,' he said in a thick Irish brogue, 'but is this where Woody Forrest lives?'

After Kate confirmed that he did, the man said, 'Well now, my name's Dominic Monaghan, and I wanted to speak to your husband about the late Frank Ford.'

'Oh,' said Kate, almost at a loss for words, 'do please come in, er, Mr... Father Monaghan!'

'Oh, Father Dominic's fine,' he said with a smile.

Kate led him into the sitting room. 'Can I get you a drink, Father?'

'Oh, a cup of tea would be very welcome,' he said, 'and with three sugars, if you wouldn't mind.'

'Three sugars it is!' Kate said, disappearing into the kitchen, where Woody was sitting at the table, raising an enquiring eyebrow. 'Father Dominic would like a word,' she said quietly as she switched on the kettle.

'What the hell...' Woody got to his feet and went hesitantly into the sitting room.

As Kate made the tea, she heard Woody and the priest discussing the weather, the view of the sea from the window and how long it had taken to drive here from Exeter, and wasn't this just the prettiest village? Woody agreed it was and, after Kate appeared with the tea, Father Dominic said, 'Well, you must be wondering what on earth I'm doing here!'

Kate offered him a biscuit.

He took a chocolate digestive, dipped it in his tea and had a large bite. 'I do love a biscuit,' he said happily. He took a gulp of tea. 'I phoned him, you see, to find out how he was getting on. And I got one of his sons informing me that he'd passed on, murder suspected. I got the shock of my life because I got to know Frank when he was in prison.' He dipped the biscuit again and ate some more. 'Frank had decided to be taken into the Catholic faith.'

'I did hear rumour that he'd "got religion",' Woody said, 'but I wasn't too sure which one.'

The priest dipped the final piece of his biscuit, half of which fell into his tea. This didn't appear to bother him. 'He was a man looking to find God, you see.' He was eyeing the remaining biscuits on the plate, which Kate immediately offered. He took another chocolate digestive. 'I'm very partial to these,' he said, patting his paunch, 'but, of course, I *shouldn't*, you know. Never mind.' He dipped the biscuit. 'Frank found great solace in the Church after he converted about five years ago. And it was then that he confessed to me that he hadn't killed his wife.'

'What? He really *didn't* kill his wife? But he confessed to it in court!' Woody exclaimed.

'But if he didn't kill her, then who did?' Kate asked. 'Why would he make a false confession?'

'He confessed because it was one of his children who'd

done it and he wanted to spare that child the prison sentence. Now, I'm not sure that that was the *right* thing to do, but it struck me as being a very *heroic* thing to do.'

Kate and Woody exchanged glances. Woody blew out a long breath. 'He spent twenty years in jail to spare one of his children? Which one would that be?'

'Ah,' said the priest, wiping some crumbs from his mouth, 'that I cannot tell you.'

'I never did think he was capable of killing anyone,' Woody said, shaking his head. 'But, even so, this is a terrific shock!'

'He said that you had faith in him when no one else did, and that you were a fine policeman. He never forgot you.'

'Did he really say that?' asked Woody.

Kate noticed that Woody looked quite overcome.

He cleared his throat. 'But you say he didn't tell you which of his children killed their mother?'

'No, he didn't tell me,' said the priest, 'but I think he was planning to tell *you*.'

'Why do you think that?'

'Because he asked me to come to see you if anything happened to him, so he must have had his suspicions.'

'How did he know where to find me?' Woody asked.

'Ah, he'd read about you in the newspapers. I gather you've been involved in solving crimes down here which have made it into the nationals?'

'You can say that again,' muttered Woody.

'More tea, Father?' Kate asked, needing an excuse to escape for a moment to digest this information.

'That would be lovely,' said Father Dominic, handing her his mug, complete with a layer of soggy biscuit in the bottom. He hesitated for a moment. 'Would I be able to have a wee drop of something in my tea, do you think? Just a touch, of course, because I'm driving.'

Kate was taken aback for a moment, but Woody came to the rescue. 'A drop of Scotch perhaps?' he suggested.

'Oh, that would be lovely,' said Father Dominic happily. 'Now, getting back to Frank. He gave me the address, but not *this* address. It was a house on the other side of the valley there, by the name of On the Up. There was no one there, but the woman next door directed me here.'

'I'm glad she did,' Woody said. 'Hopefully this information might *finally* get me off the hook. Did you know that Frank's body was found in our garden?'

'No, I didn't. That's very strange indeed because he was very, very insistent that if anything should happen to him, I was to come to see you.'

Kate handed the priest his refilled and fortified mug of tea and offered the biscuits again.

'Oh, thank you, dear. Maybe I'll just have a wee custard cream!' He dipped the custard cream into the tea.

'So you think then that he suspected he might be murdered?' Woody asked. 'I mean, it was a strange thing to say, wasn't it?'

'Sure it was, and I thought it was odd at the time.'

'Did he seem afraid or anxious?' Kate asked.

'No, he didn't; he seemed quite resigned.' Father Dominic cast his eye at the biscuit plate again.

Kate was becoming concerned about the man's appetite. 'Can I make you a sandwich or something, Father? Have you had anything to eat?'

'No, no, thank you. You're very kind. I wouldn't say no to another biscuit though.'

As he helped himself to another custard cream, Woody said, 'Charlotte Martin needs to hear this. She's the detective inspector in charge of the case, and she's at Launceston.'

'Oh, I shall go back that way,' he said. 'I'm staying in a seminary near Exeter tonight. I hired a little car to come here because I was none too sure about buses and things.'

'Very wise,' Kate murmured. 'But you'd be most welcome to stay for supper, and we could even give you a bed for the night.'

'Most kind, my dear, but I'll stick to my schedule. I only wanted to carry out Frank's wishes; that I was to contact you if anything happened to him, God rest his soul. He was a good man and he didn't deserve to die in the way he did.'

'And you've no idea, no clue at *all*, as to which of his children he took the blame for?' Woody persisted.

'No idea at all.'

Woody looked thoughtful. 'I think it's fair to say that whichever of them did kill their mother is now most likely the killer of their father as well, to stop him coming out with the truth.'

'Well, 'tis a very sad state of affairs indeed,' said Father Dominic. 'I don't know any of his family personally, but I would appreciate you letting me know who did kill Frank when the person is found.'

'Do let us know where to contact you, and I promise I'll write to you,' said Kate, producing a piece of paper.

As the priest scribbled on the paper and handed it to Kate, he said to Woody, 'You have a very difficult job, Woody.'

'I *did* have a difficult job,' Woody said with a smile, 'but I'm supposed to be retired now. Trouble is, I've had almost as many crimes to solve since I came down here as I did at the Met! It just goes on and on!'

As they all stood up and Father Dominic prepared to leave, Kate said, 'Thank you so much for making this trip, Father. I promise we'll do everything we can to bring the real killer to justice. At least now the list of suspects has been narrowed down a little.'

'Can there be any greater love than that of a parent who takes such a punishment in order to spare his child?' The priest hesitated as he got to the door. 'Only the love of God.' He gave a little bow and a wave before heading towards a small blue Ford. 'I wish you farewell. I'm off to Launceston.'

'Father Dominic, before you go, do you know of anyone else that Frank could possibly have given this information to?'

'Only one person I can think of,' Father Dominic replied.

'Who would that be?' Woody asked.

'The woman he planned to marry.'

'*What?*' Kate and Woody both stared at him in disbelief. 'Who was that?'

'Oh, I can't be telling you that,' said the priest, shaking his head sadly as he opened the car door. 'I promised not to.'

Without further ado, he gave a little wave, got into the driving seat, switched on the engine and was gone. And Kate's mind was whirring. How were they going to find the mystery woman that Frank had been in love with?

NINETEEN

Shaking his head in disbelief as he sat down again, Woody said, 'I cannot take in what's just happened!'

'He certainly confirmed what you thought,' said Kate, 'that Frank Ford wasn't a man capable of murder.'

'What I really want to know is: who the hell is this woman that he was planning to marry?' Woody asked.

'How on earth could he have met somebody if he was in prison?'

'It happens all the time,' Woody said. 'You get these women, often religious women, who are fascinated by murderers. It's as if they have a mission in life to redeem these men.'

'I know what you mean,' Kate said, 'because I've seen documentaries about women marrying killers on Death Row in the States.'

'Well, he didn't get that far, but we need to find out who she is, and when we get to the bottom of this, we'll send Father Dominic a note. *And* a box of biscuits,' Woody said.

'What was interesting was that the priest referred to one of his "children", as opposed to one of his "sons", so that wouldn't exclude Sharon, would it?'

Woody heaved a sigh. 'Who knows, Kate?' He glanced at his watch. 'Very shortly he should be talking to Charlotte, and it will be interesting to hear what she has to say on the subject. *Surely* she might now be completely convinced that it wasn't me who killed Frank Ford?'

Before Charlotte was likely to be convinced of anything, they heard the sound of a car draw up. Barney did his usual mad barking.

'Don't tell me Father Dominic's forgotten to tell us something? Or has he come back for another biscuit?' Woody asked and then, as the doorbell rang, 'Who the hell is it *now*?'

Kate, who was rinsing the soggy crumbs out of the priest's mug before placing it in the dishwasher, could decipher voices, including a woman's. Full of curiosity, she made her way to the hallway and was extremely surprised to find herself face to face with none other than Sharon Mason, née Ford.

'I've just introduced myself to your husband,' she said as Woody led her into the sitting room, 'so I hope you don't mind me calling.'

'We appear to be having an open day,' Woody muttered.

'No, of course we don't mind,' Kate said, completely taken aback. What on earth was this woman doing here? And how did she get their address?

'Have a seat,' said Woody, 'and can we get you something to drink?'

She glanced at her watch. 'It's a bit early,' she said.

'I was thinking of *tea* – or *coffee*?'

Sharon shook her head. Not one blonde hair was out of place and, again, she was immaculately made-up. 'I'm here because I came over to visit my brothers.' She rolled her eyes and sighed. 'And I wanted to see for myself where Dad's body was found.' She looked from one to the other. 'I still can't believe what happened to him, and now *Grandpa's gone too*! I just can't work out what the hell's going on!'

'I think the police are having problems working that one out too,' Woody said drily, exchanging glances with Kate.

'I've no doubt they are,' Sharon replied with a sniff, 'and it isn't for lack of questioning *us*! They've been out grilling us *four* times.' She held up four fingers to emphasise the point. '*Four* times! Questions, questions, bloody questions, and what do *we* know? Len's going mad; says I should disown the whole bloody lot of them, but, you know, at the end of the day, blood's thicker than water, and although I don't see my family much these days, I am nevertheless gutted! *Gutted*!' She removed a tissue from the sleeve of her cream sweater and dabbed her nose.

The sweater looked expensive. Kate was sure it was cashmere, and Sharon wore it with a pair of fashionably ripped jeans, which, in spite of the slits and gashes, no doubt cost a fortune because they were a perfect fit. Kate also had to admit that Sharon was another one with a perfect figure. Damnit. She must stop being envious of other women's figures.

'It must all have been a terrible shock,' Kate agreed, unsure of what else to say.

'At least I *saw* Grandpa briefly when he arrived with Jason and Meghan a few days before Wayne arrived with Dad,' Sharon went on, 'but I never got the chance to set eyes on Dad at all.' She dabbed her eyes again.

'Well,' said Woody, 'if it's important to you, we can certainly show you where we found your father, but I'm not at all sure that will do much to assuage your grief.'

'It might just help,' Sharon said, getting to her feet, 'if it's not too much trouble?'

Woody escorted her out into the back garden, and Kate followed behind. Mutely, he pointed to the bed of nettles behind the garage. 'There,' he said, 'is where Kate found him.'

Sharon stared at the nettles as if in a trance, while Woody rolled his eyes at Kate, who shrugged.

'He died *there*?'

'We've no idea if he died there, or if he was killed somewhere else,' Woody replied.

'And what about Grandpa?'

'What about him?' Woody asked. 'I've no doubt you've already been told that he was found near the cliff-tops.'

'Yeah, but that's not far from here, is it?'

'It's walkable,' Woody replied shortly. 'But I can assure you that neither death has anything whatsoever to do with us.'

'But you *are* a suspect,' Sharon said, 'because I'm told Dad wanted to see you.'

'Well he didn't exactly get much chance to meet me,' Woody snapped.

'No, of course not.' Sharon looked almost contrite for a moment. 'But it does seem strange that you found Dad's body *and* Grandpa's, but I'm not insinuating...'

'Are you sure you won't have a drink?' Kate asked, anxious to defuse the situation.

Sharon hesitated for a moment. 'I'm driving,' she said, 'but I could *murder* a Scotch.' She then clapped her hand over her mouth. 'I could have chosen a better word, couldn't I?'

'I think we all have need of a small something,' Woody muttered as he led the way back to the house.

In the kitchen, Kate located the bottle of Glenmorangie again.

Woody, who was filling a jug with water, muttered, 'It would be *rude* not to join her, wouldn't it?'

As Kate placed the drinks on a tray, she said, 'I'm having mine with ginger ale.'

'You sure know how to ruin a good Scotch,' Woody retorted.

'Rubbish!' said Kate. She lowered her voice. 'I didn't think it would do any harm to keep her talking for a bit.'

'Good thinking, Batman,' Woody said, picking up the tray and heading into the sitting room, where Sharon was stroking Barney's tummy.

'Nice dog,' she remarked.

'Yes, he is,' Kate agreed, placing her drink and the jug of water on the table beside her.

'I'd quite like a dog, but they make a bit of a mess, don't they?'

'Indeed,' Kate said, picturing muddy paw marks adorning the floor of Sharon's sterile kitchen. 'How are your brothers coping?'

Sharon rolled her eyes. 'Jason and Meghan are at logger-heads because *she* was supposed to be Grandpa's carer, and she let him wander off from right under her *nose*. I mean, you couldn't swing a cat in them caravans, far less lose a grandfather! They don't get on anyway, and you could cut the atmosphere with a knife in there. Then, Damian and Jackie are moaning non-stop about having to be here when they should be back in sodding Spain, and neither of them seem to care a damn about either Dad or Grandpa.' She sighed. 'Wayne's out all the time, because he can't stand being stuck in his caravan for long, and he's still wailing cos he feels responsible for not waking up when Dad went walkabout. All in all, they're a miserable bloody bunch, and they were doing my head in. If you want instant depression, go visiting my dear brothers!' She gulped her Scotch in one go.

'So who do *you* think, then, might have murdered your father and grandfather?' Kate asked, determined to hopefully extricate *some information* from this woman. She saw Woody giving her a strange look.

'I've no idea. I wouldn't put it past any of my brothers, it could be a passing stranger, it could be this guy at the pub apparently and it could certainly be *you*.' She gave Woody a little smile to soften the remark. 'Is that an American accent I've been hearing?'

Woody nodded.

'I *thought* it was! Where do you come from?'

'California,' Woody answered tersely.

'Oh, *California*!' Sharon's face lit up. 'Len and me, we did this *wonderful* cruise from Miami, all the way down and through the Panama Canal, and then all the way up the Pacific coast to San Diego. It was *fantastic*! I already told Kate here that you two should go on a cruise; it would do you the *power* of good! I could send you the brochure.' She stood up. 'Thanks for showing me where Dad was found, and thanks for the Scotch.'

They both escorted her outside, where she headed for her black BMW and, with a wave, roared off down the lane.

Woody turned to Kate. 'So what do you make of *that*?'

Kate shrugged. 'Not a lot, except I'm beginning to wonder if she's got shares in the cruise company.'

'Let's go in, lock the door and pretend we're out,' Woody said, 'because we sure as hell don't want any more callers today!'

They sat down opposite each other in front of the wood burner, strangely silent, each engrossed in their own thoughts for several minutes.

Finally, Kate said, 'I'm trying hard to make sense of what we've just been told.'

Woody nodded as he chucked another log into the burner. 'I've no reason to doubt the old priest,' he said. 'He was only fulfilling the promise he'd made to Frank. I agree with you that Frank's choice of the word "children", as opposed to "sons", may or may not be relevant. I have to say, of course, that Sharon put on quite a convincing performance.'

'I thought it was rather touching that she wanted to see where her father's body was found,' Kate remarked.

'Unless she put it there,' Woody said drily.

'Somehow or other I just can't believe she did,' Kate said. 'I still think it was one of the sons.'

Woody grinned. 'Perhaps she *did* do it, and then her husband came up to finish off the grandfather in case he blabbed.'

'But what reason could she have to want to stop him talking, unless it was *she* who killed the mother?' Kate asked.

'Well we can't rule that out, can we?'

Kate stared into the flames. 'I suppose not.'

'I can understand that you think Pauline's killer must be one of her sons, but don't be fooled. Think about your own experiences down here. Women are just as likely to wield a murder weapon, are they not?'

'I suppose so. But my money's still on that Damian, the loan, and how keen he is to get back to Spain.'

'Then that would mean presumably that Damian had killed his mother?'

'I don't know. But, as regards Frank's killing, maybe it was just about the *loan*,' Kate suggested.

'That might apply to Frank, but why kill Sid?'

Kate gave a long sigh. 'I've been wracking my brains about that, but I can't come up with a reason. Then there's Wayne, who I've not met yet.' *But I damn well will*, she thought. 'What reason could he have?'

'No idea what reason *any* of them might have had. That's the crux of the problem, Kate.'

'Then there's Jason.'

'Well, Jason openly hated his father for what he'd done, or *said* he'd done,' Woody remarked, 'so perhaps Jason did kill Frank. Maybe the old man was rambling on about the past, and coming out with stuff that could give too much away, and they couldn't risk him saying it to the wrong person. And I certainly wouldn't rule out Wayne.' Woody sighed. 'I might have need of another Glenmorangie!'

'I'd prefer some wine,' Kate said, 'and then I'd better think about what we're going to have for dinner.'

'Relax!' said Woody. 'We'll order a takeaway pizza from Hot Stuff tonight.'

A pizza! Kate worried about her so-called diet, then she

worried about the fact that she hadn't a clue who might have killed whom, and she then worried about how much danger she might be in if she tried to question all of Frank Ford's offspring individually. And how exactly did she plan to do that?

She decided she needed that glass of wine. Even if Woody's reputation was about to be cleared by Father Dominic, she was too involved in the case now. She must find out who killed Frank and Sid.

TWENTY

After Kate had walked Barney up on the cliffs on Thursday morning, she decided to have a coffee and catch up with Angie again. After all, now that Angie owned The Old Locker, it would be rude for Kate not to make the most of it.

The place was empty apart from three elderly ladies drinking tea and eating buns at a table by the window. They were making a fuss of Maximus, who'd parked himself on the windowsill alongside.

Kate found her sister making sandwich fillings in the little kitchen tucked behind the bar.

'Oh, hi!' said Angie, chopping hard-boiled eggs. 'How goes it?'

'You would not believe,' Kate replied.

'Try me. Fancy a coffee or something stronger?'

'Coffee's fine. Where's Fergal?'

Angie raised her eyes heavenwards. 'We've had a bit of a *difference of opinion*, I suppose you'd call it.'

'About what?'

'Oh, you know what Fergal's like. What's sauce for the gander apparently is *not* sauce for the goose!'

'In other words, he's jealous of you flirting?'

'Listen, Kate! All summer he's flirted with everything in a skirt. And, you'll remember, he went off back to that woman's hotel with her not so long back, and the only reason he wasn't actually unfaithful was because he was so drunk he couldn't perform! I mean, who is *he* to talk!' Angie was quite pink-faced with fury.

Kate remembered the incident only too well. Angie had chucked him out and then had second thoughts and went off to find him, leaving Kate and Woody to run the bar. 'So what happened last night? Need I ask?'

'Clint came in again, and he brought me some *gorgeous* yellow roses. Look, they're just out there, on the bar top!' Angie packed away the sandwich fillings into their Tupperware boxes and placed them in the fridge. 'Come on, I'll make us a coffee.'

As Kate went back round the bar and climbed onto her usual stool, she duly admired the roses. 'It might have been worse if he'd brought you red ones,' she remarked. 'So Fergal's upset because Clint brought you *yellow* roses?'

Angie placed a cappuccino in front of Kate. 'He was going on and on about what he called my blatant flirting. *Me* – I ask you! And do you know what?'

Kate shook her head and sipped her coffee.

'It's because he says it makes him look like a *fool*! Him and his bloody ego! It's not even as if we're married, for God's sake!'

Any minute now, Kate thought, *I'm going to hear about how she rescued him from having a hand-to-mouth existence in Plymouth, and how she's not only given him a job but put a roof over his head.*

'I mean, where would he be without *me*?' Angie asked crossly. Then, remembering the three ladies were still sitting at the table a few yards away, she lowered her voice. 'I'll *tell* you where he would be! He'd be living hand to mouth in that tacky caravan, *that's* where he'd be! Who put a roof over his head and made him a partner in the business, eh? Tell me *that*!'

Kate nodded obediently.

'So he slept on the sofa last night.'

Kate sipped her coffee. 'Well, you'll have problems if he decides to leave.'

'He won't leave! He knows which side his bread's buttered on! Anyway, it's quietened down a lot now, so I could manage perfectly well on my own, for a time anyway. More coffee?'

Kate glanced down at Barney, who was fast asleep at her feet. 'OK, why not?'

'Anyway, that's quite enough about us.' Angie refilled Kate's cup. 'What's happening with you? Found any more bodies recently?'

'You wouldn't believe it,' Kate replied, thinking of the previous day and their two unexpected visitors. She told Angie the salient points.

Angie digested this information for a moment. 'Of course it has to be the sister then, doesn't it? I mean, otherwise the priest wouldn't have said "children", wouldn't he? He'd have said "sons" surely?'

'I'm not sure it's quite as simple as that,' Kate said.

'Perhaps the priest's memory's not too good,' Angie suggested. 'I mean, you said he was old. And if this conversation took place some years ago, he could have forgotten which words were actually used.'

'He seemed very definite,' Kate said thoughtfully.

'At least you know it's *one* of them now, and Woody can hopefully sleep soundly at night.'

'It remains to be seen if Charlotte is convinced. Father Dominic was calling at the police station on his way back to Exeter.'

'So how are you going to apply your sleuthing skills now,

Miss Marple? Are you going to grill each of them independently?'

'I haven't worked out how to do that,' Kate admitted, 'but I'm going to have a damn good try!'

'Be careful, Kate. One of that family must be dangerous, and you don't want to become the next victim, do you?'

'Not particularly, no.' Kate looked down at the dog. 'Come on, Barney – time we were going home.' She finished off her drink. 'Thanks for the coffee, Angie. I hope you and Fergal will make up soon – if that's what you want.'

Angie shrugged. 'But there's always the lovely Clint!'

'You know little about him. Just be careful!'

'You be careful too, Kate!'

'Oh, I will,' Kate said as she and Barney departed.

When Kate got home, she found Woody chopping logs outside the garden shed. 'Charlotte's on the way,' he said.

'What can she possibly want to know *now*?' Kate asked crossly.

'I'm just hoping she's removed me from her list of suspects,' Woody said, laying down his axe and gathering up an armful of logs.

Kate picked up some logs as well and followed him into the sitting room, where they deposited the logs into the basket. As she went into the kitchen to refill the dog's water bowl, she heard the doorbell ring and Woody escorting Charlotte into the sitting room.

As Kate joined them, Woody said, 'I imagine you had a visit from Father Dominic yesterday afternoon?'

Charlotte sighed as she sat down. 'Yes,' she said, 'although it doesn't prove or disprove anything very much.'

'Surely,' Woody said, 'it narrows down the killer to one of the Fords?'

'Yes, but *only* if we *assume* that one of them murdered their mother and has now had to see off their father and grandfather,' Charlotte replied.

'That *must* be the case!' Kate exclaimed. 'You *know* what the priest told us!'

'Not necessarily. There could be another reason for killing Frank and his father-in-law. We can't *assume* anything. As far as the police are concerned, Frank served a sentence for killing his wife, so that's done and dusted, and may have nothing at all to do with this case.'

Kate could hardly believe what she was hearing. 'But the priest said—'

'I know what the priest said, Kate, and I'm sure it's true, and everything points to the four Ford offspring. But we've interrogated them all very thoroughly and come up with *nothing*.'

'We've also had a visit from Sharon Mason,' Woody said.

'What did *she* want?' Charlotte asked.

'She wanted to see where we found her father's body,' Kate replied.

Charlotte grimaced. 'Really? Had she forgotten where she dumped it? OK, OK, I'm kidding! I don't suppose she came up with anything other than telling you how awful her brothers were? Sometimes I think that lady doth protest too much.'

'But surely you can remove Woody from your list of suspects now?' Kate asked.

'Personally, I might. If I thought he had any part in this, I wouldn't be speaking to you so freely. But as far as police procedure is concerned – and *you* know this, Woody – you must remain on the list until the killer or killers are found. After all, you've been acquainted with that family for more than twenty years, Frank Ford was coming down here to see *you* and his body was found in *your* garden. You also found Sid Kinsella's body not that far from here. So, no, I can't officially remove you from the list yet.'

At least I've removed him from my *list*, Kate thought, feeling resigned as she went back into the kitchen. She could hear Woody chatting with Charlotte as he was ushering her out.

After she'd gone, he came into the kitchen and shrugged.

'Woody, I cannot believe she can still suspect you!'

'You heard what she said, and she's right. But I just thought I'd ask anyway.'

'But we have alibis, as does Steve. We must all have been in the pub at the time Frank was murdered.'

'Perhaps Charlotte doesn't believe us. She probably thinks we're a tight little clique, helping each other out.'

'But that's ridiculous! And *we* are going to find out who did this,' Kate said firmly, 'because Charlotte is plainly getting nowhere.'

Woody put his arm round her. 'I know you mean well, darling, but you are not – *not* – going anywhere *near* that family!'

Kate, who intended to do just that, nodded but said nothing.

TWENTY-ONE

On Friday, at three o'clock in the afternoon, Kate set off down the lane with Barney for a walk on the beach. As she was passing The Greedy Gull, Damian Ford came out, alone.

'Oh hi!' he said cheerfully. 'As you can see, I'm becoming quite a regular here!'

'Is Jackie not with you today?' Kate asked.

'No, she's stayed behind to give the caravan a good clean while I'm out. We've been told that all the summer cleaners have gone and, apparently, no one else wants the job. Bloody cheek! If we've got to stay here much longer, I want to be in a decent hotel.'

For a brief moment, Kate wondered if she could possibly fit in some caravan cleaning with her other commitments, because what a great opportunity it would be to have a good old scout around! It only took another split second to dismiss the idea.

Damian was looking down the lane. 'I've ordered a taxi because I wanted to have a few drinks, but nothing happens in a hurry round here! He said he'd be here directly.'

'Oh, you'll have to get used to the Cornish "dreckly",' Kate said with a laugh, 'because it means any old time that suits them.'

Damian sat himself down at one of the rustic outdoor tables. 'Can I buy you a drink?'

Kate wondered how long the taxi would take to come, but this was surely an opportunity to speak to at least one of the Fords. Or should she offer to drive him home? Probably not, since he'd already ordered the taxi. And he might be the killer.

'No, thank you, I won't have a drink,' she replied, 'I was just walking the dog...'

'Well, he can wait, can't he?' Damian asked, eyeing Barney.

'I won't have a drink,' Kate repeated, 'but I'll keep you company until the taxi comes. And I wanted to say, I'm so sorry about your grandfather.'

Damian screwed up his face. 'He was nutty as a fruitcake but harmless. Why would anyone want to kill him? Poor old Grandpa Sid!'

'Have you any idea who could have done that?' Kate asked. 'I mean, it might be the same person who killed your father, mightn't it?'

'Who knows?' He shrugged. 'I know you're being loyal and all that, but let's face it, it was your husband who found *both* bodies! Isn't that quite a coincidence?'

'I can assure you – because I was with him all night when your father was killed, and I was with him when we found your grandfather's body – that he did not kill either of them.'

'Well, I'm sorry, but you're his wife, so you *would* say that, wouldn't you? All I know is that we want to get out of this bloody place before someone else gets killed.'

Kate hesitated for a moment, trying to suppress her anger. Then she asked, 'Why do you think your father wanted to see Woody?'

'No idea. Apparently, before he left London, he didn't say anything to anyone about going to see Woody. As far as we were concerned, this was a family reunion, to include my sister, who lives near here. It was only when we got here that Dad said something about Woody. I suppose they'd known each other a helluva long time, and Dad thought a lot of Woody, but maybe Woody didn't think that much of Dad, eh?'

Kate counted to ten before she spoke. She didn't want to sound as angry as she felt. 'It must have been awful for you,' she said, 'losing your poor mother like that?'

'Oh, it was, believe me. But it was a crime of passion, see?' Damian was in for the full confessional now. 'Our mum had been messing him about and threatening to leave, like. Dad's got a hot temper and he got a bit carried away. Awful it was. like I said—'

Kate took a deep breath. 'Are you really sure it was him who killed her?'

Damian looked genuinely astonished. 'What a very weird question, Kate! Who the hell else would it be? We all loved our mum and, at that point, we didn't know that she'd found someone else. Why did you ask that?'

Now, thought Kate, *do I tell him what Sid said in the car? Or what the priest told us?*

At that moment, the taxi came lumbering up the lane and Damian got to his feet.

'I don't know where you got that idea from,' he said. 'Much as I'd like to know, I'm not going to keep that taxi waiting. Next time you're up at Sunshine, or we're in the pub at the same time, perhaps we can continue the conversation? I'm intrigued.'

'I'll bear it in mind,' said Kate through gritted teeth.

He got into the taxi and gave a brief wave as it set off down the lane.

Kate wondered if that was as good as an invitation.

She was about to pick up Barney's lead and set off for their walk when Steve came out to clear the glasses still on the tables.

'Kate,' he said, as he placed glasses on a tray, 'can I have a word?'

'Yes, of course,' Kate replied.

'I saw you chatting with that Damian Ford just now. Do *not* trust him; don't trust *anyone* in that family! Or their wives! They are *bad* news!'

'Do you *know* them all then?' Kate asked, mystified.

'I know enough. Take my word for it.'

'Did you know them in London?'

Steve tapped his nose and pursed his lips.

'But, Steve, Damian's a good customer surely?' Kate said.

'Being a good customer's got nothing to do with it. They're a bad family, Kate. Don't go near them!' He picked up his tray, shook his head and disappeared inside.

Kate was astounded. What a peculiar thing to say! How on earth could he know so much about them? He must *surely* have known them from London! She considered going into the pub and questioning him, but she had a feeling that he was going to give nothing away.

Later, she would wish that she had.

She looked down at Barney, secured his lead and walked down the lane.

That evening, as she was preparing dinner, Kate asked Woody, 'What do we know about this Steve at the pub?'

Woody, who was struggling to remove an obstinate cork from a bottle of wine, shrugged. 'Not much. He's a good enough barman. Des thinks he's got a cocaine habit, but it certainly isn't very obvious. Why do you ask?'

Kate told him about her meeting with Damian and the ensuing conversation, and then Steve's warning about the family. 'I wondered if he might have come across them in London,' she added.

Woody chewed his lip. 'I'm trying to recall a chat I had with him and Des in the pub shortly after we found Frank's body here, when I popped in one lunchtime.'

'Did he say anything that might be relevant?'

'I'm trying to think.' Woody finally succeeded in removing the cork. 'Everyone in there was talking about it, as you can imagine, but I'm damn sure he didn't say anything about knowing any of the Fords. I think I'd remember if he had.'

'I wonder why he might have been warning me like that?'

'I don't know,' Woody said. 'Maybe he's just concerned for your safety. As I am. Maybe he thinks ladies shouldn't get themselves tied up with criminals.'

'Depends on the lady,' Kate said with a smile.

On Saturday afternoon, while Woody was at the allotment persuading his vegetables to grow, Kate took Barney for a cliff-top walk. They got as far as Penhallion Cliff, where, as usual, Kate sat down to get her breath back and look out at the choppy grey sea. Autumn had well and truly set in now and there was a chill in the air. Kate found that gazing out to sea was doing little to soothe her soul today because she was having a difficult job removing the current problems from her mind. What had Steve meant by warning Kate away from the Fords? Was it purely because Damian was a murder suspect? For that matter so was Steve!

Her thoughts came back to Woody. She could see why he was considered to be a suspect and there were times when – and she hated herself for thinking this – she wondered if he *had* got out of bed in the middle of the night when she'd been fast asleep? Except that, timing-wise, there was no way he could have killed Frank, unless Forensics had made a mistake. No, Forensics didn't make mistakes. And Kate even began to wonder if he *could* have murdered Sid, while everyone was out looking for him? After all, he'd found Sid's body quite easily when they'd walked up on the cliff. It was almost as if he knew where to go!

Then she felt utterly ashamed. She knew in her heart of hearts that Woody was innocent. The only way to clear him, though, would be to find the real killer or killers, but neither she nor the police were having much success at the moment.

Kate realised with a start that, while she'd been lost in her thoughts, someone had sat down alongside her. When she turned to see who it was, she was bewildered for a moment before she recognised the red hair and the very blue eyes. Meghan Ford!

'What...?' Kate spluttered.

'I didn't mean to scare you,' Meghan said with a smile, 'but, as I was walking by, I *thought* it was you!'

Kate regained her composure. 'But what are you doing here?'

'Well, I've got the car for a few hours, I've done my shopping, and then I thought I'd have a look at Lower Tinworthy – which is lovely. I wanted to see the view along the coast so decided to climb up here. It's quite something, isn't it?'

'Yes, it is,' Kate agreed.

'Not only that, I really wanted some exercise because I feel I've been cooped up in that caravan for ever.'

'I'm so sorry about Mr Kinsella,' Kate said politely.

Meghan sniffed. 'He was ninety, so he had a good innings. We miss him though; don't know what to do with ourselves now.'

She didn't appear to be overly grief-stricken.

'It's just so awful that there's been two brutal murders at what was supposed to be a nice family reunion,' Kate said. 'You must all be devastated.'

'Yes, yes, we are,' Meghan said hastily, 'but I just wish that detective woman would quit asking us the same questions over and over. If I knew who the killer was, I'd bloody well tell her so we could all get out of here! You want another murder at Sunshine Caravan Park? That'll be me throttling Jason, or Jackie knifing Damian, because we're all so *bored*!' She snorted.

'At least Wayne seems to get out and about,' Kate remarked, hoping to get some reaction as to the whereabouts of this elusive man.

'Yeah,' Meghan said, 'he does. He doesn't like being cooped up in that caravan on his own. Unlike the rest of us, who're desperate for some time on our own! We lead quite separate lives in London, you know.'

Kate was unsure how to respond to this. Finally she said, 'Well, for everyone's sake, let's hope they catch the killer soon.'

'Or killers,' Meghan said, with an enigmatic smile, as she got up from the seat.

'You think there may have been more than *one*?' Kate asked.

'Who knows?' said Meghan mysteriously as she waved and set off down the coast path to the village.

Two of them? Kate hadn't seriously considered this possibility. But *which* two? Jason and Damian in league perhaps? Or two warring couples? Meghan and Jason? Jackie and Damian? Wayne and... Wayne and who? Could it possibly be Steve? Is that why he was warning her off?

As if this case wasn't complicated enough already!

After a few minutes, Kate got up, called out for Barney and they retraced their steps back along the cliffs and down to the village. Kate needed to think about something else. She wondered how Angie and Fergal were getting on, so decided she may as well have her coffee in The Old Locker instead of at home.

As she positioned herself on the bar stool, she saw Angie serving a queue of customers, and there was no sign of Fergal.

After a few minutes, when everyone had been served, Angie wiped her brow and poured herself a gin. 'Same for you?' she asked Kate.

'No thanks. I'd fancied one of Fergal's Irish coffees, but I'll settle for an Americano.'

'Tell you what I'll do; I'll put a shot of brandy into it. You look like you need perking up,' Angie said, adding a generous splash of Courvoisier.

'I'm fine really. Just a bit worried about everything. So where *is* Fergal?'

'I haven't a clue, and I don't damn well care. We had another row at lunchtime and he swanned off out.' Angie sniffed. 'He'll expect me to beg him to come back, because it gets busy on Saturday nights, but I'm damn well going to manage!' Angie took a large swig of her gin.

'Did the lovely Clint come in again with more roses?' Kate looked around but could only see the yellow ones, which were beginning to wilt slightly.

Angie rolled her eyes. 'Unfortunately he didn't. But I'm hoping he'll be in tonight.'

'Well I'm not going to lecture you, Angie, but, for all his faults, Fergal's a hard worker, and he does think the world of you. That's why he's jealous.'

'It's high time I got someone in to help now and again anyway,' Angie remarked. 'We never get a night off, and that's likely half the problem. We need to get away from here occasionally.'

'He's an attractive man, Angie, and, as you know, women are very partial to his blarney, so don't take Fergal for granted. Nothing wrong with either of you having a little flirt, as long as that's *all* it is.' Kate realised she was sounding very schoolmistressy but felt she had to get the message across. At least it had taken her mind off the Fords for a time, and the coffee had revived her spirits.

'I must go,' she added as another group of people came in.

What a pair, Kate thought as she made her way up the lane.

There was no sign of anyone as she passed The Greedy Gull.

TWENTY-TWO

It was after midnight on Saturday when they heard the police sirens – a sound that was becoming all too familiar. They'd watched a late-night movie, and Kate was cleaning her teeth while Woody was already in bed, engrossed in his Ian Rankin.

'What's all that noise about?' he asked crossly, laying down his book.

Kate rinsed her mouth. 'No idea.' She heard Woody pad into the bedroom at the back, which had a window looking down the lane.

'It's something to do with the pub,' he said, 'because the sirens are still blaring and there's flashing lights down the lane.'

'Probably just a brawl,' Kate remarked, climbing into bed.

'They don't normally give this much attention to a brawl,' Woody said, beginning to get dressed again.

'Where are you going?' Kate asked, surprised.

'I'm going to see what all the fuss is about. I'm taking my key, and I want you to stay inside and keep the doors locked, just in case.'

'Just in case of *what*?'

'Please, Kate, just do as I say.' He was pulling on jeans and a sweater. 'I'll be back before you know it.'

Kate got into bed knowing she wouldn't sleep a wink until he was back safely. It wasn't unheard of for there to be an occasional brawl on a Saturday night, but she'd never heard sirens down at The Greedy Gull before.

Half an hour later, she was still lying, worrying and wondering if she should disobey Woody and go down the lane herself to see what was going on. Because something *must* be going on, otherwise surely Woody would be back by now?

With a rising sense of panic, Kate got out of bed again and had begun to gather her clothes together when Woody came in at last.

'Woody! I was getting so worried! Is everything OK?'

He sat down on the edge of the bed. 'No,' he said, 'everything is not OK. Steve's been killed in a hit-and-run, just as he was leaving the pub.'

'S*teve*?' Kate asked, trying to digest this news. '*Killed*?'

Woody nodded mutely.

'But who... I mean, do they know what...?'

'No, they don't. Apparently, the last customers had all gone home and Steve had done his usual midnight round of clearing up the glasses and rubbish from outside, put his jacket on, locked up and was beginning to head up the lane when he was struck down by a car.'

Kate was horrified. 'It must have been an accident surely?'

'It might not have been an accident.'

'What makes you say that?' Kate asked.

'It looks like the car hit him, then reversed over him, did a speedy turn and raced off down the road, back the way it had come.'

'If that's the case, it's awful! Who would want to kill Steve, for God's sake? What had he done to anyone?'

'Good question. Thing is, none of us knew a great deal

about him. Poor old Des is in shock. He was getting ready for bed when he said he heard "a funny sound", as he put it. He looked out the bedroom window and saw Steve sprawled flat a few yards up the lane.'

'Didn't Des see or hear a car?'

Woody shrugged. 'Apparently not. He rushed up the lane, found Steve dead as a dodo and phoned the police.'

'Are they *sure* it was a hit-and-run?'

'I'm not going to be graphic, Kate, but there were two sets of tyre marks on his body, making it pretty obvious the car reversed over him. The same car tyres can be seen reversing into The Gull's car park before it drove off.'

'And nobody heard *anything*?'

'No, and neither did we. Let's face it, it would have been about the time we were getting ready for bed, so we would almost certainly have heard something even three or four hundred yards away. You know how silent it is up here at night.'

'So how could anyone run over him without us hearing anything?'

'Well there's only one explanation I can think of,' Woody said.

'An electric car?'

'Almost certainly,' Woody replied. 'Now they'll be searching the area for anyone who's got an electric or a hybrid car, and checking the tyre treads.'

'Poor, poor Steve! What have they done with his body?' Kate asked.

'When I left, he was still on the road, and they were taking photographs and measurements. Charlotte wasn't there, but Pete Davis was in charge and I've known Pete from old. He said they'd probably move the body in the next hour or two.'

Kate put on her dressing gown. 'This is just horrendous. And it's exactly four weeks since we found Frank's body in our garden. What on earth is going on?'

'I've no idea, Kate. But at least they can't pin this one on me.'

'Well I'm not going to be able to sleep tonight, are you?'

'Probably not,' Woody admitted. 'Let's go downstairs and have a cup of tea. Or something.'

Kate had never seen The Greedy Gull so full as it was the following evening.

'Where have they all come from on a Sunday evenin'?' Des asked irritably as he struggled to serve everyone. Kate thought he'd aged overnight. 'I should've stayed shut all day,' he said, 'instead of just closin' at lunchtime.' He looked around. 'But I need to be earnin' a livin'.'

'People can be very ghoulish,' Kate remarked.

As they'd walked down the lane, on the way to the pub, they'd passed groups of press and other people gazing at the taped-off spot where Steve's body had been found. Then they'd poured into the pub to quiz poor Des. Word had got round fast. Even for this little Cornish village.

'I'm not sayin' nuttin',' Des announced to one and all. 'Police orders.' He turned to Kate and Woody and lowered his voice, 'Mind you, Steve was on drugs, you know. Told me himself, but I can't see wot that's got to do with it.' He sighed loudly and shouted out, 'Now, who wants a drink?'

Des's long-suffering wife, who rarely emerged from the kitchen, was behind the bar, helping her husband. 'No food tonight!' she yelled. 'I can't be in two places at once!'

There was no sign of Damian Ford tonight.

Once the groups of non-regulars realised that there was little to see or to hear, they began to disperse. Kate and Woody, along with half a dozen other locals, including the domino players, stayed on for a little while.

'Police been in and out of here all day long,' Des said

morosely. 'Questions, questions and more bloody questions! What do *I* know? He was a good enough barman, but, truth be known, I was wonderin' how to get rid of him like, because it's gone quiet now most of them tourists have gone home.' After looking at their faces, he added, 'But it ain't *me* who killed him!'

'We really didn't think it was,' Kate said with a faint smile.

'Well the way the police was questioning me, askin' me over and over if I heard a car,' Des said, 'but I never heard nothin', apart from a funny noise.'

'What kind of funny noise?' Woody asked.

'Well, like a thump and a rattlin'. But by the time I looked out of that window, there was nuttin' to see except poor Steve lyin' there. They must've been quick as bloody lightnin'. Another drink?'

'I don't think so, Des,' Kate said, placing her empty glass on the counter. 'We're going to have an early night, because we didn't get much sleep last night.'

'Make sure you lock your doors then,' Des advised, 'cos you don't know who's out there waitin' to kill you. And I'll tell you somethin' else. I don't care how many glasses and stuff is lyin' outside there at closin' time tonight, I ain't goin' out to get them. They can wait till the mornin', so they can.'

'Quite right,' Woody said approvingly. 'And we shall be watching out for phantom cars as we walk up the lane, won't we, Kate?'

Kate shuddered.

They were getting ready to go to bed when Angie phoned. 'Kate, you'll never believe what's happened!'

Kate, desperate for sleep, groaned. 'What now?'

'It's Fergal!'

'What about him?' Kate didn't want a blow-by-blow

account of Angie and Fergal's latest altercation at quarter to eleven in the evening.

'Well, he doesn't know if he should go to the police or not.'

'Why would he go to the police?'

'I told you that we had a bit of a row? Well he stayed away last night. He spent the late evening in The Greedy Gull apparently, and then he fell asleep in his car, which was in the far corner of The Gull car park.'

Kate had become suddenly alert. '*And?*'

'He woke up after an hour or two and saw this car whizzing by, then, after a couple of minutes, it reversed into the car park and shot off back down the lane. The thing is, this car was big and white, and completely silent, so Fergal thinks it might have been a phantom. Or else he was dreaming. He'd had a few, you know. Now, in view of what's happened up at The Gull, do you think he should tell the police?'

'Of course he *must*, Angie! First thing in the morning! Is he back with you now?'

'Oh yes, he came back this morning. He was very cramped after being in that car all night.'

'And he saw a white, silent car?'

'He *thinks* he did,' Angie replied. 'But he could have been dreaming. He thinks it was something like a Land Rover, because it was quite big, but it didn't make a sound.'

'That could be very important, Angie. I repeat: he must go to the police station tomorrow morning.'

Kate switched off her phone, exasperated by the goings-on with this silly pair. Surely it was time they started to act their age? But providing Fergal wasn't too inebriated, this could be a very relevant piece of information.

'What was that all about?' Woody asked as she came back into the bedroom.

'You know I told you that Angie and Fergal have been having one of their many squabbles? Well, apparently Fergal spent Saturday night in his car in The Gull car park, having had a few too many as usual. He says he saw this large white car race up the road and, after a few minutes, reverse into the car park and race off down the lane again. But he thinks he *may* have been dreaming.'

'*What?*'

'Not only that, he thinks it might have been a ghost car because of it being white and completely silent! But surely the police would have checked the car park and would have seen Fergal's old black Mondeo?'

Woody collapsed onto the bed. 'They obviously didn't check very thoroughly. As you know, there are lots of odd nooks and crannies in there. Maybe they just quickly beamed a torch around and were more concerned with what had happened out on the road.'

'Yes, but you said that the killer car's tyre treads indicated that it had turned into The Gull's car park before it headed off, so that would tie in with Fergal's story. And if it was electric, *that* would tie in with Fergal's story too.'

Woody sighed as he climbed beneath the duvet. 'As long as you told him to go straight to the police station in the morning?'

'I did.'

'Fergal might have been three sheets to the wind and/or dreaming, but it ties up. Either way, I'm exhausted and I am not going to let anything disturb my sleep tonight!'

By the time Kate finished undressing and got into bed beside him, Woody was already fast asleep.

TWENTY-THREE

Kate lay awake for almost an hour before, finally, falling deeply asleep. She was in the throes of a very interesting dream where she and Angie were in a white Land Rover, and on the way to visiting Fergal's castle in Ireland. It was an enormous castle, bigger even than Windsor, and was the Donnellys' ancestral home. They'd just pulled up in front of the massive door when the alarm went off.

Kate yawned and struggled to open her eyes, annoyed that she'd not been able to get inside Fergal's impressive habitat. Oh God, *Monday morning*! Somehow or other she'd have to deal with the villagers' ailments and, at the same time, fend off yet more questions about another killing! On this occasion, it really had nothing to do with her, apart from being geographically close to the cottage.

The first person she met as she entered the building was Dr Andrew Ross, the senior partner at the practice.

'Ah, Kate,' he said, 'I was hoping to catch you. Are you all right? I heard about this business at The Greedy Gull and I imagine you were aware of some of the action?'

'Oh, we were, Andrew,' Kate replied.

'Are you sure you're OK to work today? You've had all these killings more or less on your doorstep, and I imagine you must be very stressed.'

Kate was touched by his concern. 'To be honest, when the alarm went off this morning, all I wanted to do was turn over and go back to sleep and forget everything! But now I'm here, I'm feeling fine. Honestly!'

He squeezed her arm. 'Any time you feel exhausted, you let me know and we can get an agency nurse in.'

'Thanks so much. I'll remember that,' Kate said as she headed towards the reception desk, where Sue and Denise were deep in conversation.

'More fun and games up Lavender Lane!' Sue quipped.

'Don't ask!' Kate picked up her list of patients from a cheerful-looking Denise, who said, 'I never met that Steve fellow. What was he like?'

Kate confessed to knowing little about him and tried rapidly to change the subject. Fortunately, Denise had other things on her mind.

'I've been telling Sue about my friend, Lloyd Bannerman,' she said.

'Ah yes,' Kate said. 'How's the big romance going?'

'Oh, it's great!' Denise replied happily. 'We had a lovely dinner at the Atlantic Hotel on Friday night. He is just *gorgeous*!'

'How's he getting on with his book?' Sue asked.

'Really well. And do you know what? He's planning to set up his own publishing company when he gets back to London. Isn't that exciting? "Bannerman Books" he's going to call it. Of course, it costs a lot to set it all up, what with premises, equipment and everything. At the moment, he's looking for investors, and it seems like a good deal to me because he says that all investors will get their money back, a hundred times over, within a year or so. Isn't that wonderful?'

There was a moment's heavy silence.

Then Sue said, 'I hope you're not planning to put your hard-earned money into this, Denise?'

'Well, I can afford to invest a *little*,' Denise replied.

'But you know practically nothing about him!' Kate exclaimed.

Denise bristled. 'Rubbish! I've got to know him really well, and I'd trust him to the ends of the earth!'

Kate groaned. 'Oh, Denise! You read about this sort of thing in the papers almost every day! He could take your money, scarper, and you'd never see him or your cash again.'

'Is it because you're married to a detective that you've got such a suspicious mind?' Denise snapped. 'I know this man and you *don't*!'

'OK, Denise,' Kate soothed, hoping to defuse the situation before the first patient arrived. 'All I ask is that you don't give him all your savings.'

She exchanged glances with Sue as they moved away from the desk towards their respective treatment rooms.

'She's nuts,' Sue said, 'and she's man-mad, falls for every guy she meets and believes every damn thing they tell her.'

'We've got to try to stop her handing over her savings,' Kate said.

Sue shrugged. 'I guess all we can do is keep nagging!'

As Kate sat down at her desk, she wondered how she could contrive to meet this Lloyd Bannerman, and try to suss out how genuine he might be. She liked Denise but knew only too well how susceptible she was to any man who paid her a compliment.

But did she *really* need to worry about Denise as well as everything else?

Kate sighed, picked up her list and went out to the waiting room to call her first patient.

The shift was predictable, with most of her patients agog at 'all the goings-on up at your place'. Kate managed to ward off the usual questions from the usual patients, some of whom had come in on the pretext of some ailment purely to find out anything they could.

Kate, getting into her car, remembered that they were short of milk so decided to call in at Bobby's on the way home.

Bobby's Best Buys was the one and only grocery in Lower Tinworthy, and it occupied a prime spot, near Angie's, just a stone's throw from the beach. Bobby himself was well into his seventies, cranky and saw no reason whatsoever to move into the twenty-first century. He had turned down countless offers for his shop, which needed complete modernisation and refurbishment, but Bobby wasn't selling.

'I'll serve the folks around here until I drop,' he informed one and all, regardless of the fact that most of his 'folks' hotfooted it to the supermarkets these days, as Bobby only sold the basics. 'If I can't spell it, I won't stock it' was Bobby's motto. It appeared that his vocabulary was very limited, as was his stock. He had the one and only window jammed full of buckets, spades and windbreaks all summer, and was now about to do his annual tribute to Halloween, which involved piling up dozens of pumpkins and adding a few scary masks. All of which darkened the already gloomy shop and left Bobby standing underneath the solitary strip light. Which is where he was today.

'Ah, Nurse Palmer, what can I do for you?' he asked, bending down to shoo a large ginger cat into the back of the shop.

'Just a couple of pints of milk please, Bobby.'

Bobby leaned forward, both hands on the counter. 'What's goin' on up that lane of yours?'

'You may well ask,' Kate said drily.

'I hear you found that barman's body up near your place? Who was he anyway? Never known him to come in here.'

'No,' Kate said, 'I did *not* find the barman's body. And I know nothing about him.'

'Well someone didn't much like him, did they?' Bobby was still showing no sign of fetching any milk. 'So he must've been doin' somethin' dodgy, don't you think?'

'Perhaps,' Kate replied vaguely.

'But you don't know what?'

'No,' she confirmed, 'I don't.'

Kate was just about to remind him about the milk when the ginger cat reappeared.

'Get out!' Bobby shouted at the cat, who paid no notice whatsoever.

'That,' said Kate, 'looks very much like Maximus, my sister's cat.'

'Well, he be comin' in here every damn day when I'm cuttin' up my big blocks of Cheddar, and then he licks up all the crumbs afterwards. He don't half like cheese! But I shouldn't be havin' him sittin' on the counter when there's folks around, I suppose. Anyway, that's just where I cuts the cheese each mornin'.'

Kate made a mental note *never* to buy cheese again from Bobby's. Maximus, in the meantime, had settled himself on the cheese-cutting counter and was looking hopefully around.

'I'll let him stay, seein' as it's just you,' Bobby conceded, 'but you can tell that sister of yours that she needs to take control of her bloody cat.'

'I will, Bobby. Now, how about some milk please?'

'Milk?' Bobby looked astonished. 'Ain't got no milk. All sold out by lunchtime, it was.'

Kate sighed. 'OK, Bobby, I'll be off then.' She turned to go, hoping Angie might have a spare pint.

'How about a nice bit of Cheddar?' Bobby produced one of his 'cuttings', all neatly wrapped in cling film.

'No thanks, Bobby,' Kate said, watching Maximus groom himself on the countertop.

'Did you know that your Maximus is sitting on Bobby's counter looking for cheese?' Kate asked Angie a few minutes later. 'And do you have a spare pint of milk?'

'Yes, yes,' Angie answered impatiently, 'but did you know that Fergal went up to the police station this morning?'

'How did it go?' Kate asked.

'They don't think he was dreaming,' Angie said.

'So where is he now?'

'He thought he'd have a chat with Des, so he's gone up to The Gull. I daresay he'll be having a pint or two.' She rolled her eyes.

'I daresay he will,' Kate agreed.

'You see, Fergal forgot about electric cars, and that must have been what he saw. Apparently, the treads they found do match tyres that would be on an off-road vehicle, and they're searching for Land Rovers and things like that all over Tinworthy.'

'A *white* Land Rover?' Kate prompted.

'He *thought* it was white. It *looked* white in the dark, you see. But, according to the police, it could have been silver or any pale colour.'

'Well let's hope they come up with something,' Kate said. 'Are you and Fergal OK again now?'

Angie gave a long sigh. 'As much as we'll ever be, I suppose. Anyway, just as well we did fall out, otherwise he wouldn't have spent the night in his car and seen that Land Rover up at The

Gull. And Clint's not been in all weekend, so there's been no cause for friction. I think Clint said they might be doing some late filming, so I expect that's what he's been doing.' She looked wistful. 'But, you must admit, Clint is very dishy!'

Kate grinned. 'Yes, he's not bad. Now, how about that pint of milk?'

TWENTY-FOUR

On Wednesday morning, when Kate was on her way back from the supermarket in Wadebridge, she had to slow down just as she approached Higher Tinworthy, due to a cock pheasant meandering along in the middle of the road. As she crawled along behind him, Kate espied the sign for the Boscastle road, and Sunshine Caravan Park, and pulled into a lay-by to have a think. Luckily, she hadn't bought any frozen food, so there was no need to panic about getting home in a hurry. She'd got round the supermarket in record time, so Woody – if he was still at home and not at his beloved allotment – wouldn't be expecting her back just yet.

Kate was a great believer in omens, and surely this pheasant slowing her down – right here at the turning to Sunshine – was some sort of sign?

The pheasant decided to move into the hedge, and Kate decided to move onto the Boscastle road.

It irked her that she hadn't yet set eyes on Wayne Ford, and she felt it was high time that she tracked him down. Surely he'd be around this morning?

Sunshine Park looked bleak and unlovely on this grey

November day. Kate turned into the car park, which was completely empty, and locked the door of her car when she got out this time, although it was highly unlikely anyone would now be around to park themselves in the passenger seat. She felt a moment of sadness; she hadn't known Frank at all, but she had had brief contact with Sid, who'd seemed to be a confused and harmless old man.

As Kate strolled into Bluebell Road, there was no sign of life at any of the three Ford-occupied caravans. Surely they couldn't have gone far, since the whole family were forbidden to leave the Tinworthy area?

The curtains were closed across at Wayne's caravan, just as they had been on her previous visit, and Kate wondered for a moment if he might still be asleep. She glanced at her watch: quarter to eleven – so, unlikely. Unless he had very late nights of course, although she couldn't imagine many places where he could burn the midnight oil in Tinworthy. In any case, she was here now and, if need be, she'd wake him up.

She rapped on the door and listened for any reaction, but there was no sound from within. She knocked again, louder this time. Then she jumped as she heard a male voice behind her shout, 'What do *you* want?'

Kate spun round to see Jason Ford standing in the road.

'Oh, hello,' she said, feeling embarrassed. 'I was hoping to see your brother, Wayne.'

He was staring at her. 'I *know* you, don't I?'

'Um, yes, I—'

'*You* were here each time Grandpa went missing,' he interrupted, continuing to stare at her. 'Who *are* you?'

Kate moved away from Wayne's caravan to face his brother.

'Yes,' she said, 'I was here. My name is Kate Palmer.'

He frowned. 'That rings a bell. You gave me your phone number, didn't you?'

Kate decided she might as well get to the point. 'Yes. My

husband's name is Woody Forrest and your father's body was found in *our* garden.'

'Blimey!' He looked genuinely shocked. 'So why were you here when Grandpa went walkabout?'

'I'm a nurse. The first time we met I'd come to deliver medicine to the warden, which is when I found your grandfather sitting in my car. The second time I came was when I was walking my dog nearby and decided to check to see how your grandfather was. That time, you were all rushing around because he'd gone missing again.'

'When he was *murdered*,' Jason said sharply.

'I'm well aware that he was murdered, because Woody and I found his body later in the day, when we were walking up on the cliffs.'

There was a moment's silence while Jason digested this information. 'So you found Dad's body *and* Grandpa's body? Are you *kidding* me?'

'Unfortunately not. It's the stuff of nightmares and I very much wish we weren't involved.'

'Bloody hell,' said Jason.

'Yes, quite,' agreed Kate.

'So *why* are you here now?' He narrowed his eyes.

'I was hoping to see Wayne. I met Damian in our local pub, and I've met you briefly, but I've not yet set eyes on Wayne.'

'Why do you want to meet Wayne?' Jason asked.

'I thought he might be able to answer a few questions,' Kate replied.

'What sort of questions?'

Before Kate could answer, Meghan had emerged and shouted, 'Hi there! What's going on?'

'You wouldn't believe,' Jason shouted.

'It's cold out here,' Meghan said, 'so why don't you come inside?'

Having given up again on finding the elusive Wayne, Kate

decided she might ask Jason a few questions instead. She recollected Woody's warnings and knew that she could be in danger, so she'd have to be very careful with what she said.

'That's very kind of you,' she said to Meghan, glancing at Jason as she spoke.

He shrugged. 'Yeah, why not?'

Meghan led the way and said, 'We've met a few times now, haven't we?'

'On the cliff-top recently,' Kate reminded her.

'Yes, of course.' She turned to her husband. 'Jason, this kind lady looked after your grandpa when he wandered off and sat in her car, so the least we can do is offer her a cup of tea.'

Jason merely shrugged again.

As Kate stepped into the caravan, she found the interior surprisingly bright and warm. The living room featured a large built-in sofa which wrapped round three walls, a coffee table and an enormous television set.

'Take a seat,' Meghan commanded from the open-plan kitchen area, 'and I'll put the kettle on.'

Kate wondered what people did in non-tea-drinking communities in awkward situations. Perhaps they offered wine instead, which wasn't such a bad idea.

As she sat down, she could hear Jason quietly informing his wife about their visitor.

Meghan emerged from the kitchen round-eyed. 'Oh my God! I can't believe this! Jason says you found both Frank *and* Grandpa!'

'I'm afraid so,' Kate confirmed.

'But that's *unbelievable*!'

'Everyone says that,' Kate replied, 'but it's not so unbelievable when you consider that Frank's body was placed in our garden, and shortly afterwards Mr Kinsella was found not that far from our home.'

Jason appeared to have taken over the tea-making duties

and Meghan had parked herself on the sofa. 'That can't be just a coincidence *surely*?' she asked.

'We certainly didn't plan it,' Kate replied, then confirmed to Jason that she'd just like a drop of milk in her tea.

As Jason appeared with her mug and laid it on the coffee table in front of her, Kate said, 'There's just a couple of things I wanted to ask you all, in connection with this.'

Jason sat down next to Meghan, and Kate was aware that he was studying her intently. 'What exactly do you want to know then?' he asked.

Kate took a deep breath. 'The day your grandfather wandered off, the day he was killed, four of you set off to look for him.'

'Yes, we did,' Meghan confirmed, 'but we obviously didn't look in the right place.'

'After I'd walked around the site, like you asked me to,' Kate said, 'I could only see three of you heading in the direction of Higher Tinworthy.'

'Well, we split up and went off in different directions,' said Jason. 'I can't remember who went first or where.'

'So you *don't* know who went where?'

'Why are you asking these questions?' Jason asked. '*You're* not the bloody police!'

'No, but you now know how involved we are. I wondered why none of you headed towards the cliffs?'

The couple looked at each other and frowned.

'I *told* you what I know,' Jason said with mock patience. 'We didn't manage to find him, and I see little point in this interrogation.' If he'd been reading a book, he'd have snapped it shut at this point, Kate thought.

She was getting nowhere fast on this subject, but she decided to ask one more question. She looked Jason straight in the eye. 'Why do you think your father wanted to see my husband?'

'I don't know what you're talking about.'

'Your father wrote to my husband, Detective Inspector Forrest, now retired, some time ago, saying he wanted to see him when he came to Cornwall. I'm sure you remember that Woody was involved at the time of the hearing about your mother's death all those years ago?'

Jason didn't react at all. 'I didn't know he'd written to your ex-detective husband, and I haven't got the faintest idea why he might have wanted to see him.'

Kate sighed. 'Well, it might have been a coincidence when we found your grandfather's body, but it was no coincidence that your father's body was dumped in our garden. As a result, my husband is also a suspect, and all I want to do is to clear his name.'

'I can understand that,' Meghan said. 'It must have been one hell of a shock.' She paused. 'In a way, I blame myself for Grandpa wandering off. I went into our bedroom to change, Jason was watching TV and I was sure Grandpa was asleep on the bed in his little room. But he wasn't of course, and by the time I checked, he'd been gone some time.'

'You were *supposed* to be his carer!' Jason snapped nastily.

'Well you had the television blaring or else you'd have heard him going out.' Meghan turned to Kate. 'These partition walls are paper-thin. I could hear the TV right down at the far end of the caravan, so poor Grandpa was probably deafened and decided to find some peace.'

'Everyone's to blame except you,' growled Jason.

At this point, Kate stood up, unwilling to be involved in a domestic. 'I'll go now,' she said, 'but I hope you can both understand why I'm so concerned. I just want to clear my husband's name.'

'*Your precious bloody husband!*' Jason stood up and, for the first time, Kate felt some fear. 'Your precious bloody husband's the main *suspect*! Dad wanted to see him, so you tell me *why*,

Mrs Know-All! My guess is that your precious bloody husband didn't like whatever it was Dad said to him and finished him off.' He was breathing heavily now. 'And *where* was he when Grandpa was murdered, eh? Tell me that!'

Kate was speechless for a moment. When she found her voice, she said, 'Woody was at his allotment! *That's* where he was when someone murdered your grandfather!' She wondered if he *had* gone to the allotment that day; she couldn't remember.

'Oh yeah?' Jason was standing dangerously close now. 'And you can prove that, can you?'

'I'm sure he can,' Kate said, aware of the menacing tone in Jason's voice. 'And I can certainly vouch for the fact that he was in bed fast asleep on the night your father's body was dumped in our garden!'

'Of course you can!' Jason edged ever closer. 'You're the obedient little wife! Of *course* you'll give him an alibi!'

Obedient little wife! How Woody would laugh at that! Particularly as I disobeyed him by coming up here in the first place!

Nevertheless, Kate was becoming increasingly nervous. Meghan was still sitting opposite, saying nothing but staring straight at her while Jason was ranting on. It was high time to get out of here, Kate thought.

'My husband is innocent,' she repeated, hoping her voice didn't sound too shaky, 'and I'm going to prove it.'

'Well good luck with *that*! And while you're at it, tell your precious ex-copper husband to pull some strings with that detective woman to see about us all getting out of this bloody place. Now get the hell out of here and do *not* come back!' With that, Jason plonked himself back on the sofa and picked up a newspaper, while Meghan got to her feet and accompanied Kate to the door.

'You must understand he's still grieving,' she said quietly, 'so maybe you coming here today was a bit insensitive.'

Kate was relieved to step out into the fresh air. 'I'm sorry, but I only wanted to find some answers.' She hesitated. 'Have you any idea when Wayne is likely to be in? I'd really like to talk to him.'

Meghan shrugged. 'He's a law to himself. He's very keen on birdwatching, and he goes out at all hours of the day and night to take photographs. I expect you'll bump into him sooner or later. But you'd be wise not to come back here,' Meghan said with what Kate took to be a rueful smile as she closed the door.

Kate drove home, deep in thought. Was a wife's alibi really worth nothing? With a start, she realised that she hadn't been there when Woody was originally questioned, but he must surely have had an alibi for his movements at the time Sid Kinsella had wandered off and got killed. *Of course* Woody was at the allotment! And he was bound to have an alibi because surely there would have been other gardeners there who could verify that? At least she hoped there were.

Why on earth would her lovely husband want to kill anyone? Or *did* something happen twenty years ago when Woody knew the Ford family in London? Could Woody have done something he shouldn't have done back then? And so had to silence Frank and Sid?

Kate pulled into a farm gateway and looked down, past the peacefully grazing sheep, at the sea in the distance. Thoroughly ashamed at her thoughts, she began to cry. How could she *possibly* doubt Woody? She was an idiot. She'd managed to antagonise Jason, she couldn't find Wayne at all and she'd been warned against Damian. How was she ever going to be able to make sense of this? Not only that, but there was no way she could admit to Woody that she'd been up here today, because he'd go crazy.

Kate blew her nose, dried her eyes, took a deep breath as she started up the car again and headed for home.

TWENTY-FIVE

There was a bevy of reporters outside the gate of Lavender Cottage when Kate got home, including little Eddie, who, today, was wearing the tartan scarf again.

'Hey, Mrs Woody!' he yelled cheekily. 'You've got a reputation for solving crimes, we hear, so what do you make of this latest one? Were you friendly with Steve Morley?'

So *that* was his last name!

'Did you know he was a druggie?'

As always, Kate shook her head, smiled and headed indoors.

Woody was looking out of the window and stayed there until such time as the reporters had dispersed before he helped Kate to unload the shopping. 'Charlotte's on her way here again.'

Kate's heart sank. 'What does she want now?'

'No idea.'

'I don't suppose it's good news,' Kate said, still feeling guilty at where she'd been and what she'd been thinking. Surely this visit wasn't anything to do with Woody still being a suspect?

'We'll find out soon enough,' he said with a sigh, 'because I can hear a car approaching.'

. . .

Today the detective inspector was wearing a skirt, a knee-length denim one, with a white polo-necked sweater and a tailored navy-blue blazer. As always, she looked immaculate. As always, Kate felt a mess.

Charlotte refused the offer of coffee as she sat down at the kitchen table and removed some papers from her briefcase. 'I've only come to update you on what's going on.'

Woody grinned. 'Still not arresting me then?'

'Not yet. No, we've had a problem with Damian and Jacqueline Ford, who tried to do a runner.'

'*What*?' Kate and Woody chorused together.

'They decided they wanted to go back to Spain,' Charlotte continued. 'Seemingly, they'd had enough of both their family and the bracing Cornish weather.'

'So where did they go?' Kate asked.

'They got as far as Exeter Airport before we discovered that their hired Vauxhall was no longer in the Sunshine car park. We do check each day, you know. Anyway, the older brother – Wayne – was around and he confirmed that Damian had told him that they'd had enough, they hadn't killed anyone and they were going home to Spain.'

'Where are they now?' Woody asked.

'Bluebell Road, Sunshine Caravan Park,' Charlotte replied, 'minus their car and minus passports. And that is where they're staying until we solve this thing.'

'I don't suppose they're too pleased?' Kate asked.

'No, they're not. But we have to take precautions obviously. None of the Ford family are now allowed to leave Sunshine Park without our knowledge. We've moved their cars into the police compound, and that's where they'll stay until such time as, and if, they're free to go home. In the meantime, they are permitted to go into any part of Tinworthy – *only* Tinworthy –

for groceries, the hairdresser, even the pub, by bus – or by taxi, to be organised by us and paid for by them.'

'Whew!' Woody exclaimed. 'I don't suppose that went down too well?'

'Like the proverbial lead balloon,' Charlotte replied. 'Now, the only other suspect, aside from the Fords, is yourself of course. So, I need to stress that you must not leave Tinworthy either, and certainly you must not make any visits to Sunshine Park, supposing you felt any desire to go there. You can use your own car because I don't honestly think you'd do a runner, Woody, but otherwise the rules for you must be the same as the rules for them.'

Woody bristled. 'What about my allotment? I've been going up there most days and it's right on the edge of the village.'

Charlotte thought for a moment. 'That should be OK because it's just within the Tinworthy boundary.'

She turned to Kate. 'I know you have a flair for criminology, Kate, but you must keep well away from Sunshine Park. You are the wife of a suspect, as are Jacqueline and Meghan Ford, and so I must apply the same restrictions.'

Kate was staggered at this information. 'So I'm not allowed to go anywhere outside of Tinworthy?'

'I didn't say that, but you must *not* go visiting Sunshine Park. That's strictly out of bounds. I'm bringing Damian Ford in for questioning, as we want to know why he was so determined to get away. We've also been examining his assets, and his debts, down in Malaga, and he has a lot of explaining to do.'

Charlotte dug some more papers out of her briefcase and then turned back to Woody. 'Now, I'd like you to run over again your movements during the day when Sid Kinsella met his death. We've established that you were at your allotment?'

'Yes, I was.' Woody sounded weary.

'And you were going to find another gardener, who would have been there at the same time, to confirm that?'

'I was, and I am,' Woody replied, 'but there was only one other guy there at the same time as me that day, and I haven't seen him since. I think his name is Dave, but I've no idea where he lives. I look out for him each time I go up there.'

'Well we do need confirmation,' Charlotte continued, 'so I'll get my sergeant to contact whoever's in charge of the allotments, and we'll get a list of names and addresses, and try to confirm your alibi that way. I'm sorry, Woody, but you know I have to do this by the book.'

'Yes, I know.'

'OK, so I'll be off.' Charlotte replaced the papers into her briefcase. 'I think we'll *all* be very relieved when this thing is solved.'

When she got to the door, she said to Woody, 'In the meantime, if you do manage to find that allotment guy, do let me know, because it will save us some time.'

'I will, I will,' Woody said.

Knowing that she was prohibited from going to Sunshine Caravan Park, Kate now felt guilty about her earlier visit. She was worried for Woody and thoroughly ashamed of her own doubts. Charlotte's visit hadn't helped her anxieties.

'You've got to find that Dave, or whatever his name is,' she said when Woody came back into the kitchen.

'Yes, I know.' He sat down and drummed his fingers on the kitchen table. 'God, how I wish I'd never set eyes on that damn Ford family!'

'We're in this together,' Kate said, squeezing his hand.

'Well we can't go visiting Sunshine Park,' Woody said, with the semblance of a smile, 'which is a great shame, as I'd really like to know what they're all doing up there.'

For a brief moment Kate was sorely tempted to tell him of her visit. Not that she'd found out anything which was in the slightest way helpful.

No, she'd say nothing.

TWENTY-SIX

'We've had loads of reporters in here,' Angie said accusingly when Kate popped in next morning. 'They've got wind of the fact that I'm your sister. Now how would they know that?'

'Perhaps they read Sally Brand's article about sisters that we featured in earlier this year, but, in truth, I've no idea,' Kate admitted. 'Unless they've been talking to Des or Bobby because they've been hanging around The Gull and Bobby's shop for weeks, looking for snippets of information.'

'Well they've been hanging around this place too, but they're not likely to find much here,' Angie said. 'Although Fergal has been free with the blarney while he's been selling them drinks, and God only knows what he's been saying to them.'

Kate grimaced. 'What have they been asking?'

'Oh, all sorts of daft questions. How well do I know my brother-in-law? Did I know he was a suspect? They're *very* interested in Woody. And they're from the nationals, not the local rags. They even asked how well you knew *Steve*! Was there a *relationship* going on there? Did Woody kill him in a fit of jealousy?'

Kate stared at Angie horrified. 'You are *kidding*!'

'No, I'm not. And how well do you know the Fords? Were you particularly friendly with any of the sons? Is Woody a jealous man?'

'That is *unbelievable*!'

'If you tell them nothing, they start making stuff up. I have a feeling you could do with one of Fergal's Irish coffees?'

'After what you've told me,' Kate said, 'I think I could.' She glanced at her watch. 'It's not even *midday* yet!'

'What's that got to do with anything?' Angie shouted at Fergal, who was in the kitchen, 'Kate needs one of your coffees!'

Fergal emerged, hailed Kate and set about concocting one of his specials.

Eager to change the subject, Kate asked, 'Have you seen your toy boy recently?'

Angie beamed. 'Oh yes, he's been in a couple of times this week. He's very interested in what we're doing here.'

'What do you mean?'

Fergal came with the coffee and Angie waited until he'd wandered off again before continuing the conversation.

'Well,' she said, 'I was telling him all about how Polly Lock made this old place into a nice little tearoom, and how we took over and enlarged the area, made the flat upstairs, all that. Now, Clint thinks we should be expanding our premises to include the remaining old workshops, but I told him we just didn't have the money for that.'

'Why would you want to expand anyway?' Kate asked, taking a gulp of the coffee.

'It would be good to have a function room,' Angie replied. 'The only one in Tinworthy is up at the Atlantic Hotel and we'd like to be doing wedding receptions and stuff like that.'

'I had no idea you were both so ambitious,' Kate remarked. 'I thought you wanted to keep it small and cosy?'

'We could still keep this part small and intimate, but it would be good to have an extra string to our bow, wouldn't it?'

'But you can't afford it! You just said that!'

Angie leaned across the counter and lowered her voice. 'Ah, but here's the thing! Clint is interested in investing some money into the project – and taking a share of the profits of course.'

'*Of course,*' Kate repeated, gulping some more coffee.

'Why do you say it like that? Isn't he entitled to take some profit if it's his money that's being invested?'

'But *why?*'

'Why what?'

'Why would he do that?'

'Because he likes this place and thinks we could all do well out of this extension.' Angie glared at her sister. 'Why are you always so suspicious?'

'Sometimes, just sometimes, Angie, you are very gullible. What do you know about this man? How come an actor has so much money to invest in a business and people that he hardly knows?'

'Couldn't it just be that this is a good-hearted, generous man who's looking for a project to invest in? A lovely old listed building, close to the sea, really busy all summer? Couldn't it just be that he *likes* us?'

'In other words,' Kate said drily, 'you think he fancies you, and therefore he must be a man of taste and discretion, so what could possibly go wrong?'

'You are such a cynic!'

'I'm being realistic, Angie. Anyway, it's his money, so let him get on with it if that's what you want. Just make sure it's all done legally. But what about Fergal?'

'What *about* Fergal?'

'Doesn't he get a say in all this? I mean, supposing it comes off, it would mean a lot of extra work for both of you surely?'

'Kate,' Angie said, with a long sigh, 'Fergal is only here

thanks to me. He hasn't put a penny into this business. You *know* that!'

'No, but he's put a lot of hard work into this place, and I think the very least you can do is talk this over with him. Does he even know you've had this offer?'

Angie pursed her lips but said nothing.

'So he *doesn't* know. And you've already had a row on account of this Clint chatting you up. Even Fergal will reach his limit, and he could take off for good next time. What would you do then?'

'I'd have to get extra staff,' Angie retorted.

'You always take him back,' Kate said. 'It's not just business, is it? You'll miss him in your bed!'

'Don't talk rot!' Angie snapped. 'Now, if you've got nothing positive to say, why don't you go home?'

'Good idea!' Kate drained her coffee, picked up her bag and headed towards the door.

As she wandered up the lane, Kate worried about Angie. She'd always been gullible where men were concerned and appeared completely enthralled by this Clint. However, as long as it was *his* money that was financing the project, then perhaps she really shouldn't be worrying. She had more important things to think about at the moment. She'd get out The List again when she got home.

TWENTY-SEVEN

Kate studied The List in despair. So far, only Woody and Steve had been eliminated, and Woody had only been eliminated because Kate just *knew* that he couldn't have done it. So she was still left with Wayne, Damian and Jason Ford, Sharon Mason, and their various spouses. She hadn't even succeeded in meeting Wayne yet, but no doubt he'd have the same stock answer as his siblings: they'd all come down to Cornwall to celebrate their father's release from prison and to visit their sister. No one had any inkling – or so they said – of Frank wanting to visit Woody. And, as regards the spouses, why would any of them want to strangle Frank or batter Sid on the head anyway? Possible, of course, but most unlikely.

There was only one faint glimmer of hope on an otherwise bleak horizon. Who was this woman who was Frank Ford's lady-friend, fiancée, or whatever? Why had Father Dominic mentioned her? There was only one way to find out. It would have to be via Father Dominic, and she had his address.

Kate decided she'd go to London.

. . .

'No, Kate!' Woody's expression was thunderous when Kate brought up the subject later in the day.

Kate sighed. 'But I must because, at the moment, it's our only hope of clearing your name, and that is my main concern!'

'I do not want you going up there on your own.'

Kate grinned. 'I promise to be good.'

'That's not what I mean, and you know it.'

'Listen,' Kate said patiently, 'I'm only going to see if I can find this woman who was Frank's fiancée, because she's the only other person on this earth who might have any idea who Frank spent twenty years in jail for.'

Woody sat, silently chewing his lip. 'And how do you plan to do that?'

Kate had given this some thought. 'Well, I have to visit Father Dominic. I have his address, and all I have to do is persuade him to give me this lady's name. Surely it's worth a try?'

Woody thought for a moment. 'Why did he only mention this woman just as he was leaving here? I wonder if he told Charlotte?'

'I don't think he would have told Charlotte because I have a feeling that perhaps he got this information under the seal of the confessional, which means that he wouldn't be allowed to tell anyone, and that's why he told us about Frank's fiancée, so we can find out for ourselves.'

'Well, if you're determined to follow up on this, then Charlotte mustn't get any hint of it,' Woody said. 'We'll have to come up with a good cover excuse.'

'So, for once, you're not telling me not to get involved,' Kate said.

Woody smiled ruefully. 'If it's to save my skin, my love, you can get as involved as you like, provided you're not in danger, and I'll do whatever I can to help you. I'll get in touch with

Charlotte to make sure they're not keeping a close eye on Father Dominic.'

It was the following morning before Woody finally succeeded in getting a call through to Charlotte after leaving several messages. When Kate came in after walking the dog, he said, 'She doesn't appear to have any new leads. I asked her if she'd talked with Father Dominic again, but she just said there was no need – he was a nice old boy but he hadn't told them anything very useful. She seems to still be of the opinion that Frank served his prison sentence and that his murder is unlikely to be connected to that. She still has Damian in custody, so perhaps she knows something we don't.'

'OK,' Kate said. 'I'm working Monday and Tuesday next week, so I can drive up to London on Wednesday morning, and hope to be back by Saturday at the latest.'

'I'm not sure about that, Kate. If you're going to do it, then I think you should take every precaution – I think you should get the train up, pay for your ticket in cash, so they can't trace you.' He clasped her hand and looked really concerned. 'I only wish I could come with you.'

'I wish you could too. But it's not as if I'm going to be in danger because all the suspects are down here.'

'I know, but...' Woody stared moodily out of the window.

'It's a chance to clear your name, and it's not as if Charlotte's come up with anything, has she? This titbit of information just might be important.'

'I've spent the past three years lecturing you about *not* getting involved,' he said with a wry smile, 'and now I'm encouraging you to do the opposite! Are you going to contact Father Dominic to tell him you're coming?'

'No, I don't think so,' Kate replied. 'I think I'll just land on his doorstep. If he knows I'm coming, he might come up with some excuse or other to avoid me. I shall knock on his door clutching a large box of biscuits.'

'And a bottle of Scotch,' Woody added.

When Kate arrived at work on the Monday morning, she found Sue and Denise having what sounded like an argument.

Sue whirled round when she heard Kate approach. 'Kate, see if *you* can talk some sense into this woman!'

'What's going on?' Kate was shocked by Denise's angry expression.

'What's going on is that this daft woman is about to hand over *ten thousand pounds* to a man she barely knows!' Sue exclaimed.

'It's an *investment*!' Denise shouted, red in the face. 'It's going to make me a lot of money! Anyway, I've come to know Lloyd really well and I think, at my age, I'm a pretty good judge of character!'

'Not where men are concerned,' Sue snapped back.

'Calm down, you two!' Kate ordered. 'Look, Denise, why don't you do some research before you hand over any money? I mean, isn't there some way you can check up on him? Google or something?'

Denise raised her eyes to heaven. 'He's a *writer*, Kate,' she said patiently, 'and he's shown me some books he's had published by a bona fide publisher. Now all he wants to do is start up his own publishing company so he can publish his own books and cut out the middle man, so to speak.'

'When does he want this money?' Sue asked.

'As soon as possible,' Denise replied.

'I'll bet!' Sue muttered under her breath.

'Make him wait,' Kate suggested. 'Make some excuse that it'll take you some time to access the money. You can say it's tied up in some other investment until a certain date, so he'll have to wait. Surely he could understand that?'

Denise looked doubtful.

'Kate's right,' Sue said. 'It can take you a matter of minutes to hand it over and, if he turns out to be dodgy, you might never get it back.'

'I'll think about it,' said Denise then switched on a smile as the first patient of the day approached.

Kate was fond of Denise, but the one thing she didn't need right now was somebody else to worry about.

TWENTY-EIGHT

On Wednesday morning, Angie had been persuaded into giving Kate a lift to Bodmin Parkway station to get an early train up to London, since Woody wasn't permitted to leave the village – a restriction which infuriated him daily.

'*Why* are you going up there?' Angie asked several times on the drive.

'I *told* you. I need to get some more information from the priest who came to visit us,' Kate had replied on each occasion.

'But surely he told you everything he knew?' Angie persisted. 'Why do you have to keep doing this Miss Marple thing? What are you planning to do – give the poor man the third degree?'

Kate was beginning to wish she'd ordered a taxi. The only reason she hadn't was because she was probably going to need one at the other end, and there was a limit to her spending power, even though Woody had given her a generous wad of cash for the trip. He'd felt increasingly guilty because she was having to go on her own and had kept apologising for not being able to accompany her. He had also cursed Charlotte a great deal, so he plainly wasn't seeing her in the same utopian light as he'd done when she first arrived. Which was fine by Kate.

'Will you pick me up again when I get back?' Kate asked. 'It'll probably be evening – late evening.'

'Phone me when you're on the way back,' Angie said, 'and I'll escape for an hour or two.'

'Will Fergal mind?'

'Kate,' Angie said with mock patience and some sighing, 'Fergal is not my *keeper*. I am a free woman, and don't you forget that.'

'As if,' replied Kate.

The train was half-full leaving Bodmin Parkway, but it would no doubt fill up at every stop on the way to London. Kate enjoyed travelling by rail, particularly on scenic routes such as this.

She'd been deep in thought about how she was going to approach Father Dominic, in the hope of extracting some more information, when they approached the Tamar. The River Tamar, which separates Cornwall from Devon, was at its widest here as it approached the sea, and was spanned by Brunel's iconic Royal Albert railway bridge, all 330 metres of it. High above the river, the train sped towards Plymouth in Devon, or, as the more nationalistic Cornish called it, going from 'Cornwall into England'. It was a spectacular and breathtaking view, and Kate, as always, was momentarily distracted from her muddled thoughts.

As expected, the train was crowded out in Plymouth and the seat next to Kate was filled to capacity by an enormous woman with a plethora of plastic bags, most of which contained food. The woman then proceeded to eat, non-stop, all the way to London: sausage rolls, crisps and chocolate bars, all washed down with several cans of ready-mixed gin and tonic.

Kate stared out of the window and tried again to compose what she was going to say to Father Dominic. Then they came to Dawlish and, once more, she was enchanted by this famous stretch of railway track which ran right along the seafront and was constantly affected by storm damage, which roared in every winter from the sea alongside. Dawlish itself was a favourite holiday destination, one of several on this stretch of coastline – known as the English Riviera. This south coast, with its resorts, harbours and beaches, was completely different from the wild, rocky contours of the Atlantic coast to the north.

Kate dozed, ate her sandwich and read her book until, almost five hours after leaving Bodmin Parkway, the train slid into Paddington Station. Paddington was at the opposite side of London from Woolwich, her destination, and so the final part of her journey involved travelling in both underground and overground trains.

More and more these days, she was fascinated and over-awed by the sheer numbers of people, moving at speed and knowing exactly where they were going. As she heaved her roll-along case on and off elevators, Kate realised how much these few years in Cornwall had slowed her down and made her feel like the proverbial country bumpkin.

Kate had a close friend who lived in Windsor, but she decided that Windsor was too distant from South East London to allow for a comfortable commute, possibly over several days. As a result, Woody had booked a room for her in the Premier Inn in Woolwich for three nights, although she hoped to be able to cancel the third night if all went well with her investigations.

As she headed towards Cannon Street on the District Line, Kate continued to worry about whether the priest would see her, or whether he might be away somewhere. Did priests have holidays? Perhaps she should have phoned? And how much information would he be able to give her?

In addition, she worried about Denise, who looked about to hand over her hard-earned savings to a man she hardly knew. Hopefully, Denise would take her advice and make the man wait for his money.

As usual she was worrying about things she could do little about.

Kate wasn't familiar with this part of London, so she had to concentrate on where she was going, even though Woody had written down detailed instructions for her.

Having been travelling for over six hours, Kate was hot, sweaty and exhausted by the time she got to the Premier Inn. She lay on the bed and called Woody.

'I was getting worried about you,' he said.

'Well, I'm here now and I shall go out shortly to see if I can find the little priest.'

'The biscuits and the Scotch still intact?' Woody asked. It was Fergal, in fact, who'd visited the supermarket while she was at work, and, at her request, returned with a box of Fox's biscuits and a bottle of Glenfiddich.

'Yes, they're in my bag and we're ready to go,' Kate replied, smothering a yawn.

Five minutes after she ended the call, Kate was fast asleep.

When she woke up, it was half past five in the evening. Still half asleep, she got under the shower, donned fresh clothing and then studied her map again to see how far Barker Road – where the priest lived – was from the Premier Inn. It appeared to be within comfortable walking distance, which is what Woody had worked out when he made the booking. Time for her next step.

TWENTY-NINE

Barker Road was long and narrow, lined with Victorian terraces, cars parked tightly, nose to tail, on both sides. The walk had taken less than ten minutes. Kate could see a church at the far end of the road, which was presumably Father Dominic's.

The priest's abode was an end-of-terrace, and his little blue car was parked neatly on the strip of concrete which would once have been a tiny garden. The green-painted wooden door sported a gleaming collection of brass door knob, letter box and knocker. Kate was hard-pushed to imagine the little old man wielding a tin of Brasso and a duster, so perhaps he had help.

As she stood hesitantly on the doorstep, Kate wondered if she was overdoing it with the biscuits and the Scotch. She decided she'd start with the biscuits and see how her visit was going to be received before she produced the Scotch. He might not even be in! In which case, what should she do? Should she sit on the little wall and await his return, whenever that might be? She was beginning to wish she'd phoned first.

Nervously, she knocked on the door and waited. Perhaps he might have to take a Mass on a Wednesday evening? Or confession, or something? Perhaps she should wait outside the church?

Kate was relieved to hear footsteps approaching from within. She took a deep breath and waited for the door to open – and there he was! He looked at her questioningly, bewilderment on his face.

Kate cleared her throat. 'Remember me, Father? I'm Woody's wife from Cornwall.'

'Of course, of course,' he said hastily, 'although I never expected to see you on my doorstep!' He smiled uncertainly.

'Well, I just happened to be in London,' Kate said, feeling her face flush, knowing she was lying to a priest, 'and there was one or two things I wanted to chat to you about, so I hope you don't mind me calling?'

'You'd better come in then,' he said. 'Mrs Davis is just leaving.'

Mrs Davis, elderly, with her ample curves firmly encased in an old-style, wraparound pinny, was putting on her tweed coat. She beamed at Kate then said to the priest, 'Now, I'll do the ironing when I come on Friday, Father.'

'Oh, thank you, Mrs Davis,' Father Dominic said, patting her on the arm, 'and I promise to try to keep everything tidy.'

As she went out of the door, Mrs Davis rolled her eyes and said to Kate, 'He doesn't know the meaning of the word!'

'I'm afraid I am a bit messy,' he said, as he led the way into a small sitting room. Mrs Davis had obviously been in here with the Brasso too, because there were gleaming brass and copper pots surrounding the tiled fireplace and hearth, on which rested an electric coal-effect fire.

'Do sit down, dear.' He indicated one of a pair of dark brown leather chairs. 'Now, what can I do for you?'

'I just wanted to ask you a few questions about when Frank Ford was in Belmarsh prison, Father.'

He shook his head. 'I told you all I know when I came to your house in Cornwall.' He hesitated. 'Would you like a cup of tea?'

'That would be lovely,' Kate said.

He pottered into the kitchen, from where Kate could hear the sound of a kettle being filled and cups being placed on saucers. She stood up, wondering if she should help.

As she entered the kitchenette, she said, 'Just a dash of milk for me. And would you like a hand to carry it through?'

'Yes, thank you, my dear. My hands are a bit shaky these days.'

The kitchenette was tiny, with Formica units, a large gas cooker and a washing machine, its contents on a fast spin.

Kate carried the ivy-patterned cup and saucer into the sitting room and sat down again. Father Dominic sat down in the other chair, facing her.

'I've brought you a little gift,' Kate said, burrowing in her carrier bag and withdrawing the box of biscuits.

The priest's eyes widened and a smile slowly crept across his face. 'Oh, my dear, you shouldn't have...'

'Nonsense! I remembered that you rather liked them, and I didn't want to come bothering you empty-handed.'

'This is *so* kind!' He'd got the wrapper off within seconds and was struggling to undo the tape around the lid. 'I should really be sharing these with my flock,' he said, looking a little guilty. He prised off the lid and offered the box to Kate, who took one chocolate biscuit out of politeness.

She watched him gazing at the contents and trying to decide which one to have and reckoned that his parishioners were highly unlikely to see very many.

Kate sipped her tea. 'There were just a couple of things I wanted to check,' she said. 'Did Frank Ford definitely say he was serving the prison sentence for one of his *children*, as opposed to one of his *sons*?'

Father Dominic was busy dunking a shortbread biscuit into his tea. 'I realise I'm becoming rather ancient, dear, and a bit shakier than I once was, but I remember such important conversations very clearly, and this one was very important, and that is what he said.'

'Just as you were leaving you said something about a fiancée?'

'Hmm. I know he planned to ask the lady to marry him, because he told me, but I'm not at all sure he got round to actually placing a ring on her finger. I've not seen her for some time.'

'Can you tell me who she is? Her name?' Kate asked.

Father Dominic shook his head slowly. 'I can't be telling you that, my dear. Apart from anything else, I'm not at all sure I can remember her name.'

Kate let out a long sigh. 'This lady might well know who Frank was serving his sentence for, and it could be crucial in finding out who killed him.'

He held out the box again. 'Another biscuit?'

Kate shook her head. 'No, thank you. Do you think the name might just come to you?'

'I doubt it,' he said, delving into the biscuits again.

'But you said your memory was good!'

'Not so good on names though.' Then he rapidly changed the subject. 'Are you staying around here?'

'Yes, at the Premier Inn.'

'Oh, that's not too far, and the streets round here are busy and well lit. You don't want to be walking alone in dark, deserted streets.'

Kate was aware that they were almost at an impasse. 'I hope I'm not keeping you back from anything important, Father?'

'No, no, my dear. Tonight's one of the rare nights when I don't need to be going anywhere. I did a wedding yesterday and they insisted I stayed and joined in the celebrations afterwards. Would you believe I didn't get to my bed until gone midnight?'

'It was a good wedding then?'

'Oh, it was a lovely wedding! But I'm very partial to a wee drop of Scotch, and I'm afraid I rather overdid it. It's so expensive these days, you know, so I can't afford to go buying it myself.'

Was now the time to play her trump card?

'Funnily enough,' Kate said casually, 'I remembered that you rather enjoyed it, and so' – she produced the bottle of Glenfiddich – 'I thought it might be a good idea to bring you this.'

'Oh, my *dear*!' He seemed genuinely at a loss for words. 'Oh, I can't be taking this!'

'Why not? We were so grateful to you for coming all the way down to Cornwall to see us and wanted to show our appreciation.'

'Oh, but...' He looked longingly at the bottle. 'I shouldn't...'

'Go on, Father! Have a wee drink!'

'Well, maybe just a *taster*. Will you join me?'

'I'm not a big Scotch drinker,' Kate replied, wishing she was.

'Well, I'm not going to drink on my own,' he said.

Kate hoped fervently that some Scotch might loosen up his memory, if he really had forgotten the woman's name.

'Just a tiny one then,' she said. 'Do you have any ginger ale?'

'I'm afraid not,' he said, getting to his feet. 'Would you not take it with water?'

Here we go again, Kate thought, remembering Woody's remarks. 'Yes, of course. Water will be fine.'

Father Dominic headed back into the kitchen, reappearing with two large tumblers. 'I haven't got any smaller ones,' he explained as he laid them on a little side table. 'I'll just get a jug of water now.'

This he did, and then poured out two hefty measures of the golden liquid. 'Get that down you, dear,' he said, handing her one of the glasses.

Kate added a generous amount of water and took a sip. It was nicer than she remembered, but she most definitely would not be having more than one. She noticed Father Dominic was drinking his Scotch straight.

She sipped; he gulped.

'Have you ever been to Ireland?' he asked.

'I went to Dublin once and loved it,' Kate replied. 'My sister's partner is Irish, and he makes the most wonderful Irish coffees.'

'Well, if I had some nice cream now I could make you a Gaelic one, could I not?'

'I daresay you could.' Kate wondered how to bring the conversation back to Frank. 'Do you still visit Belmarsh?'

'Oh, every Friday,' he replied, 'regular as clockwork. I find there's good in most people, even the ones who've committed awful crimes. I never lose faith in them, you know. Are you of the Catholic faith yourself?'

'No, I'm not. My best friend in school was, and I can remember being envious of her devotion, and of the confessionals, and the chanting and the incense...' Kate's voice tailed away. 'I think maybe I should have been Catholic because it's a very emotive religion.'

Father Dominic was busy filling up his glass. 'Any time you want to talk about it, my dear, you know where I am. Are you sure I can't tempt you?' He waved the bottle in her direction. 'It's never too late to convert, you know!'

Kate grinned. 'I think I've left it a bit late. But, Father, can you remember the lady's name yet?'

He shook his head, but he looked thoughtful. 'It might just come to me...' He took a large gulp of his drink. 'My, this is a wonderful whisky! It's a joy to be reminded what a really good malt tastes like!'

'I'm really glad you're enjoying it,' Kate said. 'Is there *anything* you can remember about this woman?'

'Well, now,' he said, staring at the electric flame, 'I know she was one of the Christian Ladies Prison Visiting Scheme. They did a grand job, those ladies, mostly widows.' He took another slurp. 'Some of them fell in love, you know, and actually married men who were unlikely to ever be free.'

'Like on Death Row, in the States?' Kate asked, fascinated.

'Yes,' he said. 'And, of course, it was unlikely some of these marriages would ever be consummated. 'Tis the power of love in a strange world.'

'And this lady came to visit Frank?'

'Oh yes, every week. She knew he'd be getting out of prison of course, and that he'd be having a family reunion when he did. But she was a patient lady was Rose.'

'*Rose*?'

'Oh my, did I say that? Goodness, it's coming *back* to me now! Yes, Rose was her name; *Rose Gerard*. It must be the Scotch, loosening my brain. Yes, of course, Rose Gerard! She was a widow too. Such a nice lady!'

The bottle of Glenfiddich was definitely worth every penny, Kate decided. 'So would you know where this Rose Gerard lives?'

Father Dominic screwed up his eyes. 'No, I'm not sure where she lives. But Betty Lee would know because it's her who organises the visits. Would you like me to have a word with her? She'll be at Mass on Sunday.'

'Is there any way you could see her before then, Father? I want to be back in Cornwall by Saturday at the latest, and I'd dearly like to meet Rose.'

'Well, I'll have a think. It's the least I can do after you bringing me these wonderful presents. Now, Mrs Davis will be in to do my ironing on Friday, and she knows Betty well.'

'Is there any chance you could get in touch with Mrs Davis tomorrow morning? If she could contact the lady who does the organising, and can find out where Rose lives, it means I could perhaps arrange to see her in the next day or two.'

'I'll see what I can do. Give me your phone number, dear.'

Kate happily produced one of her cards. 'My mobile

number's there,' she said, pointing to the relevant figures, 'and I'd really appreciate you finding out anything you can.' She stood up. 'I quite enjoyed that Scotch,' she said, 'but I'll leave you in peace now. I want to get back before it's too late.'

He accompanied her to the door, thanking her profusely with every step, for the biscuits and the whisky.

Kate recalled seeing a curry house on the way to Barker Road and realised that she was very, very hungry. She'd enjoy a curry, followed by a good sleep, knowing she'd done all she could to find this elusive woman.

THIRTY

Kate woke at twenty past five in the morning and immediately began to worry about meeting Rose Gerard, realising that there was no chance whatsoever now of getting back to sleep.

Would this woman even know that Frank Ford was dead? Perhaps Father Dominic had got in touch with her and broken the news already? Or perhaps not.

A long morning stretched ahead of her while she waited for a call from the priest. She wondered how much whisky he'd imbibed last night after she'd left and therefore what time he would be likely to wake up this morning. It was far too early to do anything except make herself a cup of instant coffee from the hospitality tray and watch breakfast television when it came on at six. Kate wondered if there was a shopping mall nearby where she could spend the morning browsing around. Apart from anything else, she needed a new bra.

Kate found a shopping mall where she treated herself to a decent cup of coffee and two croissants. They were hot, buttery and delicious, and she was immediately filled with guilt. A curry last night and now croissants! She was already dreading getting on the scales when she got home.

She was examining the bras in Marks and Spencer when her phone rang.

'Now,' said Father Dominic, 'I haven't been in touch with Rose Gerard myself, but thanks to Mrs Davis, I do indeed have her address, which is 66 Marchmont Road. That's quite near the prison.'

'Thank you so much!' Kate said, replacing a lacy number back on the rack. *Underwired and Miracle Lift*, it said. Well, for sure she could do with a miracle lift but not at this exact moment. For now, her thoughts were on Rose Gerard. Would the woman even be at home this afternoon? Could this be her day for prison visiting? Was Frank one of several, and perhaps she'd agreed to wed them all? Of course not! Kate felt ashamed at even thinking such a thing.

Heading out of Marks and Spencer, she sat down on a seat beside one of the gigantic containers of palms and exotic plants which were sited every fifty yards or so along the length of the shopping mall. She checked the map; Father Dominic was right, because Marchmont Road was situated much closer to Belmarsh than Barker Road was. This meant a longer walk, which she'd certainly want to do in daylight. Kate wondered about going back for the miracle uplifting bra but reckoned she'd be uplifted to the heavens if she could only meet this lady and glean some information.

Kate ate two apples and a banana for lunch before leaving the hotel. She'd consulted the map and decided on her route to Marchmont Road. The walk took nearly twenty-five minutes, which, she hoped, might counteract the effects of the croissants, if not the curry.

Marchmont Road wasn't dissimilar to Barker Road, but

with semis and a few detached houses as well. Sixty-six was a three-storey semi with a neat front garden and a black-painted wooden door with decorative glass panels.

Kate rang the bell and waited. And waited.

After five minutes of waiting, it was obvious that no one was in. Now what? Come back later? Come back tomorrow? What if Rose Gerard had gone on holiday!

Just as she was trying to decide what to do, a young woman emerged from the adjoining house.

'You looking for Rose?' she called out to Kate.

'Yes, I am.'

'She does prison visiting on Thursday afternoons, and sometimes on a Friday, I think, so you'd be best to catch her in the mornings.'

'Thanks so much,' Kate called back. 'I'll remember that.'

'I have her name and address,' Kate said to Woody on FaceTime later, 'so I'll try again tomorrow morning.'

'You're doing great, Kate. Give me the address you've got and I'll see if I can find a phone number for her on Directory Enquiries or somewhere. But I sincerely hope you can find her and only wish that I could be with you, my love.'

'Oh, I so wish you could,' Kate said, feeling emotional as she pictured another evening of solitary dining, television and early to bed. Perhaps, just perhaps, she could meet Rose Gerard tomorrow morning and then she could be on her way home to Cornwall in the afternoon.

Maybe she'd make a quick visit to the mall though. If nothing else, at least she'd go home with a new bra.

On Friday morning, the heavens opened. Kate thanked her lucky stars that she'd thought to stick her hooded raincoat in her case. She put it on and headed off towards Marchmont Road, praying that Rose would be at home. She splashed through puddles and tried to avoid being poked in the eye by the sea of umbrellas. Finally she stood, dripping, at the door of number sixty-six and crossed her fingers. *Please be in!*

Then she saw some movement through the patterned glass panels and breathed a sigh of relief. *Someone* was in there.

The someone turned out to be a tall, thin elderly woman with a mop of white hair and a kindly face.

'Are you Mrs Rose Gerard?' Kate asked when she opened the door.

The woman nodded, looking suspicious.

'My name is Kate and I've come up from Cornwall. I wondered if I might have a word with you about Frank Ford?'

'*Frank?* What about him? Have you seen him?'

'Um, yes,' Kate replied. She had seen him of course, but perhaps not in the way that Rose Gerard meant. 'I have something to tell you, Mrs Gerard, and wondered if I might come in for a moment?'

Rose hesitated but then stood aside. 'All right. You're soaking! Let me take your coat.'

Kate gratefully removed her coat and let the woman hang it up on a coat stand in the hallway, where it dripped onto the tiles. 'It's a horrible day.'

'Yes, it is. Have you come all the way from Cornwall this morning?'

'Oh no,' Kate replied, 'I'm staying locally for a couple of days.'

She followed Rose Gerard into a sitting room at the back of the building. On a nice day, it would be a bright room, she thought, with a view of a well-tended back garden. There was a sofa, chairs, a piano and a large cross above the fireplace.

'Do sit down. What did you say your name was?'

'Kate. Kate Palmer.'

Kate sat down on a green armchair, trying to remember what it was she'd planned to say in the event that Rose wasn't aware of Frank's death.

She took a deep breath. 'I'm afraid I have some very bad news for you, Rose.'

Rose sat down opposite and stared at Kate.

'It's about Frank,' Kate explained.

'What's he done? Is he ill, or...' Her voice tailed away.

'I'm so sorry to be the bearer of such awful news, but I'm afraid he's dead.'

'*Dead?*' Rose's eyes widened in horror.

'Yes, I'm so very sorry,' Kate repeated.

Rose continued to stare for a moment, as if in disbelief, then shuddered and began to sob.

Kate couldn't decide what to do. Should she hug her? Find her a tissue? She leaned across and squeezed the woman's hand.

But Rose Gerard was made of strong stuff. She wiped her eyes, sat up straight and asked, 'Where do *you* come into all this?'

Kate told her about Woody, about Frank's letter, about Frank being found in the garden and about Father Dominic's visit. All the time she was speaking, Rose was gazing at her as if in a trance. 'Father Dominic said he had a fiancée and it was through him that I managed to find you,' Kate concluded, slightly surprised the priest hadn't told poor Rose the news about Frank already.

'Frank was very close to Father Dominic of course.' Rose blew her nose. 'I wasn't really his fiancée, although he did ask me to marry him.' She sobbed again. 'Poor, poor Frank!'

Kate remained silent; there was so little she could say of comfort.

Rose blew her nose again. 'I was worried about him,' she went on, 'when I knew he was going down there with his family, but he was so determined to go – and to get the whole clan together. But I've been worried because I couldn't understand why he hadn't contacted me.'

'Well he did get most of them together, except for the daughter. He didn't manage to see her before he was killed.'

Rose shook her head. 'At least she had the decency to visit him in prison, which is more than the others did.'

'So I believe.' Kate realised it was going to be insensitive to try to interrogate this grief-stricken woman, but she did need to find out what she might know. 'He was obviously fond of his family, wasn't he, in spite of everything?'

Rose shrugged. 'Yes, but he knew what they were like. He'd been brought up in an orphanage, you see, and so family was important to him, but he deserved better than that. At least he was accepted into God's family before he died, and he vowed to lead a good and blameless life, God rest his soul. But as for his children, what can I say?'

'Rose, have you any idea why he might have wanted to see my husband?'

Rose wiped her eyes again. 'I remember him saying what a decent copper your husband was. Yes, that was the phrase he used, "decent copper". And I think he wanted to wipe the slate clean.'

'Which meant telling him what?' Kate pressed.

'We'll never know,' Rose replied firmly.

'Now someone has killed him and it certainly wasn't Woody I can tell you that. And his father-in-law, Sid Kinsella, was also murdered shortly afterwards. Did you know him?'

Rose shook her head. 'No, I didn't know any of them, only Frank. But I know he was fond of his father-in-law. I can't get my head round this – it's a terrible business!'

'Can I make you a cup of tea or something?' Kate asked, feeling guilty at her questioning.

'I think I might need something stronger, dear. Would you mind if I poured myself a whisky? What can I get you?'

'Oh, tea is fine,' Kate said.

'Or a glass of wine? I've got some Pinot in the fridge.'

Why not? She wasn't going to be driving. 'That would be lovely.' She needed to keep Rose talking in the hope that she might be able to provide some clue about Frank's incarceration.

Rose got to her feet slowly. 'Don't worry, dear,' she said as Kate began to rise from her chair, 'I'm OK now, and I know where everything is.'

She disappeared for a few minutes before reappearing with a bottle of Pinot Grigio, three-quarters full, and a hefty-looking Scotch for herself, which, as far as Kate could see, was neat. She wondered if Rose and Father Dominic should get together to see off the Glenfiddich.

When she'd settled herself back in her chair and had a couple of gulps, Rose said, 'I begged him not to go to Cornwall.'

'Why?' Kate asked.

'Because he was so vulnerable. That family of his are all crooks, you know, particularly the one in Spain.'

'The sister said that Damian – that's the one in Spain – had borrowed a lot of money from his father and never paid him back. She insinuated that he could well be guilty of his father's murder.'

'Frank didn't want it back,' Rose said in a very firm tone.

'But I thought he might have wanted to buy himself somewhere to live, a car, whatever...'

'He was going to move in with me. He wasn't bothered about that money.'

'So Damian would have no reason to want to kill him?'

Rose shrugged. 'No reason that I'm aware of. And Frank wasn't a killer.'

Kate sipped her wine. 'So you do know that Frank had

admitted to his wife's murder but that he was, in fact, protecting one of his children.'

'That's true enough,' said Rose. 'More fool him.'

'Oh.' For a moment, Kate was at a loss for words.

'None of them deserved such loyalty,' Rose added.

Kate cleared her throat. 'Do you know which of his children it was that Frank spent twenty years in jail for?'

Rose took another gulp of her drink. 'Yes, I do.'

'Can you tell me?' Kate was now holding her breath.

'No.'

'Why not, Rose?'

'Because I promised him I'd never tell.'

Kate thought for a moment. 'That was while he was *alive*. It's different now, and it's highly likely that whichever one of his offspring killed their mother killed Frank too. I truly believe he was coming to tell Woody which one of them it was, but he was killed to stop him saying anything. Do you think that Sid, his father-in-law, might have known as well? And been killed for the same reason?'

'Yes,' Rose said, deep in thought, 'I do seem to remember that his father-in-law had found out about it all somehow or other, but I don't know the details.'

'You see, Sid was suffering from dementia.' Kate went on to tell Rose about Sid finding his way into her car and what he'd said about 'Frank not killing his little girl'.

Rose remained silent.

'He too could have been murdered to prevent him from saying anything.' Kate paused. 'We need to know who killed Frank and Sid, Rose, or who would have been most likely to kill him.'

'It's just that I promised Frank...' Rose gulped some more of her drink.

'I know you did, and that was understandable – while he was alive. But surely you want to know who killed him? Surely you owe it to Frank's memory to help with this inquiry? The police certainly need information, and so do Woody and myself. Who was he shielding, Rose?'

Rose sat, head bowed, for a moment and Kate wondered if she was praying. Then she looked up and said, 'All right, I'll tell you... It was his oldest son, Wayne.'

THIRTY-ONE

'Wayne?' Kate repeated slowly.

'Yes, Wayne. Wayne was high on drugs at the time, and he'd got himself a druggie girlfriend who he wanted to bring in to live with him at home, but his mother refused. She was having enough problems with Wayne, and she didn't want *two* of them in the house.'

'You can hardly blame her.'

'No, but Wayne got nasty. She still refused to change her mind and...'

'Wayne killed her?' Kate asked in horror. She needed to be sure she'd understood this properly.

'Yes.' Rose sighed. 'Frank said Wayne wasn't in his right mind at the time because he was so high on drugs.'

'Poor Frank. What a heroic thing to do for your child though.'

Rose shook her head. 'I'm not so sure about that. Frank ruined his own life, and a lot of thanks he got from Wayne. Misplaced justice.'

'I suppose so,' Kate agreed, 'but thank you, Rose. Thank you for telling me. I know you feel you've broken a promise, but

Frank would surely have wanted you to help find who killed him. With this information, it all does point to Wayne, I guess. I've met his two brothers, but I haven't actually set eyes on Wayne himself yet.'

'I've never met any of them,' Rose retorted, 'and I never want to. All I know about Wayne is that he deals in drugs and likes the ladies.'

Kate drained her wine. 'Again, I apologise for having been the bearer of such bad news, but thank you so much for the information about Wayne.'

Rose gave a glimmer of a smile. 'Will you let me know what happens? I expect it'll make the national press, but just in case...'

'Yes, of course I will,' Kate replied. 'We all need closure on this.'

She hugged Rose as she left and promised to be in touch.

All the way back to her hotel, Kate considered how she was going to handle this.

By two o'clock, Kate was in a taxi on the way to Cannon Street station to get the Circle Line back to Paddington. All the way on the Tube, and all the way on the almost five-hour journey back to Bodmin, Kate continued to consider her options. She *had* to find Wayne Ford. He was, without any doubt, the main suspect for both murders. Should she go straight to the police? Then again, Charlotte had dismissed Pauline Ford's killing as 'done and dusted', with Frank having paid the price, whether he was guilty or not. So would she even be interested? Surely now she'd have to listen!

By the time the train was crossing the Tamar Bridge again, bringing her back into Cornwall, Kate had decided. She would track down Wayne Ford before she did anything else.

.   .   .

'Well,' said Angie, chauffeuring Kate home to Tinworthy, 'did you manage to find out anything? Did your priest suddenly have a memory recall?'

'Believe it or not, he did,' Kate replied, smothering a yawn. It was dark now, and her instinct was to close her eyes and doze. She felt exhausted after her morning with Rose, then navigating her way across London, and finally the long train journey home.

'So, are you now ready to arrest one of the beastly brothers? Are you going to show Charlotte Martin how brilliant you are and how inefficient her police force is?'

Kate was too tired to rise to the bait. 'What I've discovered may help,' she replied. 'So let's just say it was well worthwhile going up to London. Now, can we change the subject? How's the wonderful Clint?'

'Oh, he's lovely! He's been in a couple more times since you left with a plan for our proposed extension. He certainly doesn't let the grass grow under his feet! And even Fergal agreed the plan looked good, although he keeps going on about money.'

'Who keeps going on about money?' Kate asked.

'Fergal does. Not that he has any of course, so it will have to come from me, and only because Clint will need some deposit.'

Kate was suddenly wide awake. 'Oh, *does* he now? How much cash does your friend Clint think you should deposit?'

'Well, it would be an investment, wouldn't it? We don't expect him to pay for the whole thing and then only take a percentage of the profits.'

'The last I heard, he was planning to invest in all of it, because you made it clear that you didn't have any money,' Kate said, bells jangling in her head as she stared out at the headlights on the dark road ahead.

'It's going to be a little more than we anticipated,' Angie replied, 'that's all.' She sighed loudly. 'Why are you always so suspicious?'

'Strangely enough, Angie, I get mildly suspicious when a

man you know nothing about starts talking about extracting money from your bank account. Exactly how much money are we talking about here?'

Angie sighed in exasperation. 'Honestly, Kate! Don't you realise that making these tatty old storage areas into a desirable venue for weddings and such does not come cheap? Clint reckons something in the region of thirty thousand pounds, and he plans to finance twenty thousand of that.'

'So, in a nutshell, he's asking you to pay up ten thousand pounds?'

'I still have some money left, I'll have you know,' Angie said witheringly, swerving to avoid a fox which had crossed the road in front of them. 'And *I* decide what I do with my own money!'

'Whatever else you do with your money, Angie, don't give him a penny of it.'

'I haven't yet, but he wants it as soon as possible. I see no reason whatsoever not to invest in what is going to be beneficial not only to us but to the community as a whole.'

Kate let out a low whistle. 'OK then. Take him along to a solicitor's office and get a proper legal agreement drawn up.'

'That costs money,' Angie snapped, 'and we have to watch every penny. Clint says there's no need whatsoever to have a middle man.'

'I just *bet* he does!' Kate knew how gullible Angie could be when she wanted something, and the fact that Clint was such a good-looking charmer only exacerbated things. 'Don't hand over any cash until you've thoroughly sussed him out. Have you ever been to see where he's living, or where he's filming?'

'I haven't got the time to go gallivanting around the country-side,' Angie snapped. 'I have a business to run. It's all right for *you*, only working a couple of days a week.'

They'd come through Middle Tinworthy now and were heading down to the coast, and home, and the last thing Kate wanted now was an argument.

'Promise me something, Angie. Don't give him any of your cash for a week. Just one week.' Had she not said something similar to Denise? What was going on with these daft women?

'Why?'

'Because I have a bad feeling about this.'

Angie snorted as she steered the car up the lane towards Lavender Cottage. 'You are *such* a misery!'

Kate realised that she obviously needed more time to convince her sister – and to prevent her from being led up the garden path. She cleared her throat. 'I was wondering if you fancied a girls' night out?'

'What, you and me?'

'Why not? It's ages since we did anything like that, and I'd like to treat you to a drink and a meal as a thank you for transporting me to and from Bodmin. How about The Tinners?'

Angie laughed. 'Such *sophistication*! But hey, why not?'

'I'll be in touch about that. And thanks so much for the lift.' Kate pecked her sister on the cheek, got out of the car, grabbed her case from the back seat and headed towards the cottage. It was good to be home.

Woody held her tight. 'You might not have realised it,' he said, 'but I was with you every inch of the way! I worried about you non-stop. I worried about you walking on your own around Woolwich, I worried about how Father Dominic would react and would he even let you in through the door, and then I worried about you meeting this Rose woman. On top of all that, I worried about you on all those different forms of public transport.' Finally, he released her. 'I know it's late, but I'm going to get you a drink.'

'So long as it's not Scotch!' Kate said with a grin. 'But I'd love a glass of wine.'

'Talking of Scotch,' Woody said, as he uncorked the bottle

of Malbec, 'I wonder if Father Dominic's got through his bottle yet?'

'I wouldn't be surprised,' Kate replied, 'because he was knocking it back with gusto, and he didn't bother much with water either, as far as I could see!'

'All in a good cause,' Woody said, sitting down on the sofa beside her. 'He deserves every damn gulp!'

They clinked glasses. 'Here's to your research coming up with the killer!'

Kate had already told Woody on the phone that it was Wayne who had killed his mother.

'Everything points at him,' she noted, 'and he certainly had the motive. I'd like to find this Wayne before Charlotte nabs him – *if* Charlotte nabs him. But I feel it's important to tell her what I found out. Did you mention to her that I'd gone up to London?'

Woody shook his head. 'I haven't spoken to her since you left.'

'I'm desperate to set eyes on this man,' Kate said, 'but, unlike Damian, he doesn't appear to frequent The Greedy Gull.'

'Of course, he might just be teetotal,' Woody said, smiling. 'But I don't suppose Charlotte will tell me anything about his movements. All the taxis are organised by the police, you see.'

'What do you think we should do?' Kate asked.

'Surely they're using Tom's Taxis, because they're the only ones round here. Tom manages to fit in an hour on his allotment almost every day, says it gives him a break from the driving. I'll go up there tomorrow and wait for him to come so I can get chatting to him.'

Kate grinned. 'Brilliant idea!'

Woody glanced at his watch. 'It's nearly midnight, so finish your drink. You must be utterly exhausted. Let's go to bed.'

'Yes, please,' Kate said, yawning.

THIRTY-TWO

Woody managed to track down Tom the following morning. 'But he wasn't very forthcoming with any information,' he told Kate. 'All he would tell me was that it was Sergeant Davis who normally made the bookings.'

Charlotte Martin was off duty over the weekend, so Woody was able to chat with Pete Davis again, who he knew well from his own days in the force. Kate was at his side with the speaker volume on full.

'This bloody thing goes on and on,' Pete said wearily. 'We thought we'd nailed it when that stupid couple tried to fly back to Spain, but we had nothing on them really, so we had to let them go.'

'So where do they hang out when they want to escape from the delights of Sunshine Park?' Woody asked.

'As far as I can make out, they must get the bus down to the village and then they get a taxi back from your neck of the woods, your local. What's it called again?'

'The Greedy Gull,' Woody replied.

'That's it,' said Pete. 'I should have remembered after that night when the barman was flattened on your road.'

'No clues yet as to who might have killed him?'

'Nope. But Steve Morley was a druggie and obviously needed money to feed his habit – more than the landlord was paying him anyway. We've put two and two together and, as usual, come up with five, because we think he was extorting money from someone.'

'You mean *blackmail*?' Woody asked.

'Most likely. I shouldn't be telling you this of course, being as you're still supposed to be a suspect! Ridiculous you being a bloody suspect, isn't it?' Pete scoffed.

'The only way to get me off that list is to find the real killer,' Woody said. He paused. 'What about the other brothers?'

'Well, the youngest one goes down to The Tinners now and again. On his own. The wife doesn't go out much.'

'That's Jason,' Woody said, 'the one that was supposedly looking after Sid Kinsella, his grandfather?'

'Yeah, that's him.'

'What about the oldest brother?' Woody asked, winking at Kate.

'Same. He gets the bus down during the day and a taxi back at night. He's another one who likes The Tinners; generally gets picked up from there.'

'Alone?'

'No idea,' Pete replied, 'cos obviously we aren't there to check.'

'Final question, Pete. Is there any pattern to this brother's comings and goings? Any particular days or times?'

Kate could hear Pete shuffling papers around.

'Tuesdays, Thursdays and Saturdays, it looks like. I shouldn't really be telling you this, Woody, cos her ladyship would blow a gasket if she knew. Why did you want to know anyway?'

'It's my nosy wife,' Woody said with a sigh. 'She wants to know what he looks like. You *know* what women are like!'

Kate kicked him sharply on the ankle.

'Oh, I do, mate. My missus is just the same! I reckon they're born nosy!'

'You can say that again!' Woody agreed, swiftly moving his left to avoid another kick. 'Anyway, thanks for that, Pete.'

As he switched off his phone, he said to Kate, '*You* wanted to know his schedule and, as you could hear, we've more or less got it. We certainly wouldn't have got all that from Charlotte, that's for sure. So it was worth a few derogatory remarks, bearing in mind Pete is the original male chauvinist!'

'I'll forgive you. Tuesdays, Thursdays and Saturdays, eh? I was planning to treat Angie to a drink and something to eat at The Tinners one night, and suddenly Tuesday, Thursday or Saturday next week seems like a very good idea! It's a bit too late now to arrange it for tonight.'

'No husbands? No partners?'

'Absolutely *not!*' Kate confirmed. 'This is a girlie evening! And, besides, I need to have a serious chat with her, before she gets herself into another fix.'

'And if you do find this Wayne, are you hoping he'll chat you up then?'

Kate snorted. 'It would be interesting if he did because there's quite a few things I'd like to ask him!' She now knew which nights the elusive Wayne Ford might be in The Tinners, but without any idea of what he looked like, how would she know it was him? Did he look like either of his brothers? Both Damian and Jason were dark-haired, well-built and not bad-looking, although there wasn't a strong resemblance between the two.

'I was wondering,' she said to Woody, 'if I should park myself up near the bus stop at Sunshine Park? I mean, it's far enough away from Sunshine so I wouldn't be disobeying Charlotte. I know what Jason looks like, so maybe the two of them go down to the village together? I certainly can't see myself being at The Tinners three nights a week, at closing time, just to see who gets a taxi home!'

'No,' Woody said firmly, 'you are most definitely not going to be around The Tinners at closing time. And you could spend all day watching that bus stop, because sometimes the bus comes, and sometimes it doesn't, which is why most of the villagers don't use it. Does it matter what he looks like?'

'Yes, of course it matters what he looks like! I need to know it's him when he comes into The Tinners.'

'Do you know anything else about him that might help you to pin him down?' Woody asked.

'Apparently, he likes birdwatching, so he'd probably go somewhere with trees. Perhaps the woods behind the church? I could walk Barney up there. The sooner I know what he looks like, the sooner I can keep an eye on him.'

'Why do you want to keep an eye on him? What's he likely to do? If he is the killer, then he's probably killed everyone he considered necessary, and if he sees you watching his every move, you could be next on his list. Talking of lists, have you torn your one up yet?'

'No, and I'm not going to!' Kate snapped. 'He's certainly moved to the top of The List, but I'm not yet ready to exclude everyone else!'

'Oh, very wise!'

'Don't you go patronising me! I'm going to find this man by hook or by crook!'

'Knowing the Fords,' Woody said with a grin, 'I'd settle for a crook!'

The weekend was wet and windy. Woody abandoned any ideas of attending to his beloved allotment and decided instead to paint the kitchen. They'd bought the primrose-coloured paint weeks before but never got round to doing anything about it. It was a big kitchen and it took all day to apply two coats. By Saturday evening, the kitchen looked stunning and both Kate and Woody looked exhausted.

'Let's have fish and chips at The Gull,' Woody suggested as he washed out the paintbrushes.

It was a good idea, although Kate was none too sure about the fish and chips, bearing in mind her ongoing battle with her weight. But anything was better than cooking right now. Not only that, Damian might be there and might even have persuaded his brother to join him. And perhaps Des was still doing salads.

Neither Damian, nor anyone who could possibly be his brother, put in an appearance. And Des had stopped doing salads. 'Summer's over,' he said, 'and it was only the tourists what was wantin' them anyway.'

Kate settled for a lasagne, and Woody asked if they'd heard any more about Steve's killing.

'Nope,' said Des, 'but the police have been in here askin' how much I be payin' him. I told them I was payin' the normal minimum wage.'

Kate was intrigued. 'I wonder why they asked you that?'

'Accordin' to Jacky Bly, a copper who I've known since school, he had wads of money stashed all over the place in his van.'

'He either stole it, or he's been dealing in drugs,' Woody remarked. 'Probably both.'

Des rubbed his nose. 'Looks like it, don't it?'

Sunday passed quietly, but when Kate arrived at the medical centre on Monday morning, Sue and Denise were arguing about something.

Sue rolled her eyes when she saw Kate approach. 'I'm

trying, yet again, to persuade this daft cow not to part with her money. But is she listening? Not on your nelly!'

'I'm fed up of listening to her!' Denise said, red-cheeked with anger. 'Every bloody day, nag, nag, nag! It's *my* money, not *hers*!'

Kate sighed. 'When are you supposed to be paying him?'

'Well,' said Denise, 'the money will be in my current account by Wednesday, so I'll probably do it then.'

'And how does he want the money?' Kate asked. 'I presume you won't be gadding around with a bag full of cash? Will you do it by bank transfer?'

'That's the plan,' Denise replied. She was beginning to calm down. 'I'm seeing him tomorrow night in The Tinners, so we'll finalise the plans then.'

'And then you'll *never* set eyes on him again,' Sue put in.

'Tomorrow night?' Kate asked.

'Yes, what of it?'

'Nothing, nothing,' Kate said hurriedly. 'Just make sure you know what you're doing.'

Sue waylaid her outside their treatment rooms. 'That daft woman is going to lose all her savings,' she said.

'We've got until Wednesday to dream something up,' Kate replied, ideas already forming in her head.

Two gullible women about to be fleeced; she needed to think quickly.

THIRTY-THREE

Kate had made an appointment to see Charlotte at five o'clock, which meant a mad dash to Launceston after she finished work at half-past four. She was keen to get Charlotte's reaction because she felt that the information she'd got in London was of prime importance.

Charlotte looked a little weary at what was probably the end of a long day, but even then she managed to appear groomed and unruffled.

She signalled Kate to sit down and said, 'I gather you've something interesting to tell me?'

Kate took a seat. 'I went up to London,' she said, 'to visit Father Dominic. You remember Father Dominic? He was the priest—'

'Yes, I know who Father Dominic is,' Charlotte interrupted. 'I just wonder why you felt it was necessary to visit him, unless it was for religious reasons of course.' She raised an enquiring eyebrow.

'No, it wasn't for religious reasons, Charlotte. It was concerning the Ford family.'

Charlotte sighed. 'Are you playing sleuth again, Kate?'

Kate ignored the remark. 'When Father Dominic left us, he insinuated that Frank Ford had got himself a fiancée while he was in prison, and that he might have told her who had killed Frank's wife all those years ago.'

'But we've been through all this, haven't we? I mean, Frank spent twenty years in prison for killing his wife. End of.'

'But he *didn't* kill his wife, and I've found out who *did*!'

'And how did you manage to do that?'

Kate was getting the distinct impression that Charlotte was becoming increasingly irritated. Nevertheless, she was determined to impart her information. 'When I met him in London, Father Dominic told me the name of the lady who Frank wanted to marry. Her name is Rose, and she used to visit him in prison.'

'So off you went to visit her? Question her?'

'Yes, I did, because—'

'Because Woody wasn't able to leave Tinworthy and so you thought you'd play detective again?' Charlotte cut in.

'Yes, because my first concern is to prove Woody's innocence. I know you think that the murder of Frank's wife is history, but I think what I found out may be very relevant.'

'In what way?'

Kate was determined to keep her cool. 'Frank told Rose which of his children had killed their mother. He asked her to swear to keep it secret.'

'So she told *you*?'

'I persuaded her to tell me because I had to break the news to her that Frank had been murdered, and how important it was for his killer to be brought to justice.' Kate paused. 'It was Wayne that killed his mother, Pauline Ford. Apparently, he was out of his mind on drugs and Frank didn't want him to spend the best years of his life in prison.'

'Very gallant,' said Charlotte. 'So now you've worked out that Wayne murdered his father and grandfather in case either of them spilled the beans? To stop Frank confessing all to Woody, right?'

'Something like that,' Kate admitted.

'And you believed everything this woman told you?'

'I saw no reason not to,' Kate replied sharply.

'But what proof do you have that everything she told you is true?'

'It's what Frank told her.'

'She could have been lying. Frank could have been lying. Where's the proof?'

'Why would they be lying about such a thing?' Kate was becoming increasingly frustrated. She really had believed that Charlotte would be grateful for this information – that she'd consider it vitally important.

'I'll keep this in mind of course, Kate, but I doubt it has much to do with the current state of play. And I really would ask you not to go hotfooting it up to London, or anywhere else for that matter. You've interfered in police procedures before now, and you should have learned your lesson to leave it to us. Don't think we've completely overlooked the fact that *you* found Frank Ford's body in *your* garden. It did cross my mind that you might have been trying to protect Woody. After all, you knew about the letter. Please don't tempt me to begin following that line of investigation. If we consider something important, then we'll investigate.'

Kate felt quite shaken by what Charlotte had just said. 'But you don't consider *this* to be important?' she asked, trying to regain her composure.

'I told you, I'll keep it in mind. Anyway, is that all?'

'That's all,' Kate said, resigned.

Charlotte stood up. 'Well, I've had a long day.' She smothered a yawn.

'That makes two of us,' Kate said shortly as she got up to go.

. . .

On the way home, Kate felt quite deflated. How dare Charlotte Martin dismiss such relevant information! She'd talk it over with Woody and then do her best to have a look at Wayne and perhaps be able to size him up.

She stopped off at The Old Locker. Apart from a gaggle of six giggling schoolgirls sitting at one table with cans of Coca-Cola, the place was deserted. Angie was sitting at one of the tables reading a fashion magazine and sipping a coffee.

'Did you know that stripes are very *in* this year?' she asked Kate.

Kate shook her head.

'Well, they are apparently. What brings you here?'

'Oh, just the usual sisterly love,' Kate said drily. 'Regarding our night out, how about tomorrow at The Tinners?'

'Tomorrow? Tuesday? Should be OK, because it's not a busy night, but I'd better check with Fergal.' She hesitated. 'Why the hurry?'

'Tomorrow night would suit me.'

After Angie had gone upstairs to find Fergal, Kate, for a brief moment, wondered if it really mattered if it was Tuesday or Thursday, but then rapidly reminded herself that it certainly did. She desperately wanted to meet this Lloyd Bannerman in the hope that she might be able to suss out if he seemed genuine or not, before Denise handed over her money the next day.

When Angie reappeared, she said, 'Yes, OK, I can do tomorrow.'

'Tomorrow it is,' Kate said firmly. 'I'll pick you up at seven.'

'I'm amazed Charlotte didn't appreciate your findings,' Woody said, 'because I would have done so in her shoes. Surely the evidence points to Wayne now?'

'It certainly seems to. Anyway, I'm treating Angie to some supper in The Tinners, so hopefully we'll run into him, given that it'll be Tuesday,' Kate said. 'Not only that, but Denise has this bloke in tow, supposedly a writer, who's after her money, which, she said today, she'll probably hand over on Wednesday. They're going to The Tinners tomorrow night too, so at least I can have a look at *him*.'

'She's always been gullible with men,' Woody said. 'It's a pity she doesn't meet someone decent and get a ring on her finger because that seems to be what she wants, isn't it?'

Kate nodded. 'I do feel sorry for her, but she never seems to learn not to take everyone at their face value.' *Just like my daft sister*, she thought.

'Denise apart,' Woody said, 'I would appreciate you trying to see this Wayne Ford. If you have no luck tomorrow night, you and I could go up to The Tinners on Thursday, and Saturday if he still doesn't show up. I don't want you doing this on your own, Kate, because the man could well be dangerous.'

'I promise to be careful,' Kate said.

THIRTY-FOUR

Kate had a feeling that, somehow or other, she'd just *know* it was Wayne when, or if, he decided to stick to his schedule and visit The Tinners. In any case, she was confident that Denise and her Lloyd Bannerman *would* be there, so it wouldn't be a wasted evening. And, not least, it would be good to have an evening out with Angie because it was a long time since they'd gone out together, without their other halves.

Denise would obviously have to introduce them to her man, and Kate wondered what would be the best way to tackle him. Should she ask something general like 'I hear you've come down here to write a book?' or 'I understand you're starting up your own publishing business?' or should she get straight to the point and ask, 'What assurance can you give Denise that her money's safe?' She'd decide when she met him.

Woody insisted on driving them to The Tinners and back on Tuesday evening. 'You're both going to be drinking,' he said.

There was no need to dress up for The Tinners, so Kate

wore her jeans and a casual sweater, and Angie was similarly attired.

'Are you sure Fergal will cope on his own?' Kate asked as they drove up the hill.

Angie shrugged. 'Shouldn't be busy, but Emma's back in the village and looking for some bar work. Remember Emma? She stood in for us when we went to Marc's wedding? Anyway, she's going to do a couple of hours for us this evening, so that'll help. Clint was in *last* night, and he doesn't usually come in two nights running.'

'Are you still besotted with this guy?' Kate asked.

'Well, he is rather gorgeous, isn't he? I mean, it's not as if I'm *married* to Fergal or anything.'

'So would you desert Fergal if this guy asked you to marry him?'

Angie grinned. 'I'd be tempted!'

As they pulled into the Tinners' car park, Woody said, 'This may not be exactly the Ritz, but they do great steaks.'

'You know what? I don't care – because I'm not going to be cooking it!' Angie said cheerfully.

'Agreed,' said Kate.

The pub was almost full, even at this comparatively early hour, but, as far as Kate could see, there was no sign as yet of Denise and her supposed fancy man. She headed for a vacant table which faced the door so that she could see everyone as they came in.

The Tinners' menu could scarcely be classed as cordon bleu, but, as Woody had said, they did do amazing rump steaks, which is what Kate and Angie both ordered, medium-rare, along with a bottle of Merlot. While they waited, they looked around the crowded bar, both of them spotting acquaintances and giving brief waves.

'There's Polly Lock over there!' Angie exclaimed, pointing at the far end of the bar. 'And who the hell has she got with her? Is *that* her new bloke?'

Polly had previously owned Angie's place when it was The Locker Tearooms. She'd had, according to rumour, an interesting and colourful sex life – even when her husband was still alive. After she'd left The Locker, Polly had moved in with the local undertaker, but that romance, according to Angie, 'had died a death, ha! ha!' Her latest lover was from upcountry somewhere and, apparently, was trying to persuade Polly to move up there with him. But Polly was a Tinworthy girl, and Tinworthy was where she intended to stay.

Kate studied the new man in Polly's life. He was somewhat vertically challenged, reaching only up to around Polly's ear level, and Polly wasn't particularly tall. But what he lacked in height, he certainly compensated for with flamboyance. This included several chains and medallions round his carefully exposed chest, some glittery stud earrings and several jangling chains around his wrist, on either side of what looked like a Rolex.

'My God! He looks like a Christmas tree!' Angie commented. 'But good for her! At least he's more cheerful-looking than the funeral director! Polly never fails to surprise me!'

'Yes, right,' Kate said, keeping her eyes on the doorway.

They'd almost finished their steaks and were refilling their glasses when the door opened and in walked Denise with a tall, dark-haired man. He'd turned around to hold the door open for someone else so Kate couldn't see his face and, as they headed towards the bar, only his back view remained visible. Nevertheless, here was the famous Lloyd Bannerman!

Angie was still studying Polly and her bejewelled boyfriend. 'He's not bad-looking, Kate, and if all that bling is real, then he's probably loaded!'

Kate nodded absently, staring at where Denise and Lloyd were standing at the bar, waiting to be served. There was something even about his back view that was strangely familiar, but she knew there was no way she could have seen him before.

She nudged Angie. 'Denise has just come in with her new bloke, and I'm dying for him to turn round so I can get a decent look at him.'

'Mmm,' Angie said, laying down her knife and fork. 'That was good!' She directed her gaze back to where Kate was pointing, just as Denise turned around. She waved at Kate and Angie, then turned to Lloyd, who was ordering drinks from the bar.

'She'll obviously introduce us in a minute,' Kate said.

'He looks OK from the back,' Angie observed.

At that moment, he turned round, smiling.

Kate almost choked on her drink.

'Come and meet Lloyd!' Denise called out cheerfully.

'God above!' exclaimed Kate.

Angie gasped. '*Clint!*'

There was a horrified split second of silence before Angie got to her feet and headed towards Denise.

'That's my friend Clint!' she shouted. 'What's he doing with you?'

Denise stared back angrily. 'Clint? Who the hell is *Clint?* This is my friend, *Lloyd Bannerman!*'

'Like hell he is!' Angie yelled back. 'You keep your hands off Clint! Have you done this on purpose? Stealing someone else's man?'

'You've already got a man,' Denise snapped, 'so get out of here!'

'Angie...' Kate began, but it was too late because Angie had grabbed Denise by the lapels of her coat. Kate tried to pull her off, without success.

Seeing this fracas taking place, two of the barmen had come round and were busy prising them apart. 'Now, now, ladies!'

While everyone was gawping at the two warring women, Lloyd/Clint was sidling away and trying to sneak towards the door.

Kate rushed after him and caught him by the sleeve. 'This is a *con* man!' she shouted back at the gathering crowd.

He was stronger than she was, and he shrugged her off, but just as he reached the door, a thought suddenly occurred to her.

Kate yelled, '*Wayne!*'

For a brief moment, he stopped, amazement on his face, and then he was gone.

THIRTY-FIVE

The two women were standing apart when Kate got back to the bar. 'For goodness' sake, both of you, take your fury out on that bastard who was trying to con you both and not on each other!'

Angie was still breathing heavily, and Denise was in tears.

Kate put her arm around Denise. 'We're all going to have a drink,' she said, 'and thank our lucky stars that neither of you two idiots have parted with any money yet!'

'But he was so lovely...' Denise wept.

'I know. Angie thought so too.'

Angie had recovered her composure and nodded in agreement. 'I'm sorry I had a go at you, Denise.'

'What I shall never understand,' said Kate, looking from Denise to Angie, 'is why you two didn't lay into *him*, instead of each other!'

As they sat down together, one of the barmen appeared with another bottle of wine. 'Here we are, ladies! I'm not sure what that was all about, but this should help to calm things down. On the house!'

They thanked him profusely and, as they filled up their glasses, Angie said, 'So who was he? Clint or Lloyd?'

'Just a con man,' Denise said sadly.

'Yes, he is a con man, and I rather think his name is Wayne Ford,' Kate added.

By the time they'd got through most of the wine, Angie and Denise were friends again. Best buddies, in fact.

'You both need to report this to the police first thing in the morning,' Kate said. 'But what I don't understand is why neither of you ever thought to check him out? I mean, Denise, didn't you ever think to see where he was supposed to be staying? Where he was supposedly writing his book?'

Denise said nothing.

'And, Angie,' Kate continued, 'I asked you this before, but didn't it enter your head to check where this so-called Clint was supposed to be filming, or where he said the film crew were staying?'

'Well it wasn't as if I was having a *romance* with him!' Angie snapped.

'Maybe not, but you were all set to hand over ten thousand pounds, weren't you?'

'And do *you* know who he really is?' Denise asked.

'I'm ninety-nine per cent sure his name is Wayne Ford,' Kate replied.

'Any relation of that bloke who was found dead in your garden?' Denise asked. 'Wasn't his name Ford?'

'Indeed it was,' Kate replied.

'You're sure?' Woody asked when, an hour later, he and Kate were sitting by the wood burner. 'I mean, you've had a few drinks, haven't you?'

'Yes, perhaps I have, but nevertheless everything points to Wayne. For one thing, I realised he looks a little like his sister.

He looked nothing like his brothers, which is why I never suspected when I saw him at The Locker as Clint. And I knew first of all it was one of the nights he was supposed to be a regular at The Tinners. Secondly, he was known to be good-looking and "fond of the ladies", as someone put it. Thirdly, since neither Clint nor Lloyd actually existed, who else could he be? He must have been very bored up in that caravan, and this was his way of amusing himself and extracting money from gullible women.'

'Holy moly! You need to tell all this to Charlotte in the morning because he's got to be taken in for questioning, if nothing else,' Woody said. 'And these two dozy birds need to report how nearly they were conned '

'Now we know what sort of *birdwatching* Wayne was up to,' Kate said. 'I just hope he doesn't do a runner during the night.'

'He's unlikely to get very far without his car,' Woody remarked.

'I shouldn't think anyone with his morals would think twice about helping himself to someone else's car,' said Kate.

Kate telephoned Charlotte at half-past nine the following morning, by which time both Angie and Denise had reported their experiences.

'Yes, Kate, I am aware of what's going on, and I will bring in Wayne Ford for questioning, and ask both Denise and your sister to identify him as their respective companions.'

For once, Charlotte appeared to believe Kate's certainty that the con man might in fact be Wayne Ford. While she had him in custody, surely Charlotte would question him about his motives for the murders? Or would she?

. . .

On Wednesday evening, around five o'clock, Kate popped into The Old Locker on her way back from walking Barney along the beach. She found a somewhat subdued Angie behind the bar.

'There goes our function room!' Angie said gloomily.

'Well, you had no intention of having any function room until the so-called Clint came up with an idea to relieve you of your money,' Kate remarked.

'Don't rub it in,' Angie groaned.

'If you're so keen on this function-room idea, why don't you and Fergal go ahead with it? You did say that you still had some money left.'

'You could well be right,' Angie said, 'but I doubt I have that much.'

'Have you been to the police station yet?'

'Yes, I had to go up there at two o'clock.'

'And?'

'Charlotte Martin asked me to identify the man I knew as Clint. I had to look at him through a window. Don't think he could see me.'

'And did you identify him?' Kate asked.

Angie sighed. 'Yes, it was Clint.'

'Who is, presumably, Wayne Ford?'

'She wouldn't tell me,' Angie said.

'What about Denise?'

'Yes, her appointment was for two thirty, so I waited outside for her.'

'And was her Lloyd Bannerman one and the same?'

'Yes.'

'And did Charlotte tell *her* it was Wayne Ford?'

'No, she wouldn't tell Denise either.'

'I'll get Woody to find out.' Kate put her hand over Angie's. 'I'm sorry, Angie, really I am. I was taken in too. I thought he was very fanciable.'

'Yes, I know.' Angie grinned. 'No fools like old fools, eh?'

'Don't torture yourself. What did Fergal have to say?'

'Oh, all very predictable. He said that if you hadn't taken me to The Tinners last night I would be ten thousand pounds poorer. I have to admit he was never happy about the deal, so perhaps I should listen to him more in future.'

'Perhaps you should,' Kate agreed.

One of the things that irritated Kate about Charlotte Martin was the fact that she'd tell Woody stuff that she wouldn't disclose to a woman. Why wouldn't she tell Angie and Denise that the guy who was about to fleece them was Wayne Ford? And why had she not acknowledged Kate's findings with a little more credulity? Did she not like her own sex? Because when Woody phoned her that evening, she told him, without persuasion, that she was keeping Wayne Ford in custody for twenty-four hours for duping two women with the intention of accessing their bank accounts, and for the possible motive for killing his father and grandfather.

'Kate, don't judge her too harshly,' Woody said. 'She probably tells me stuff because I used to do her job and she's had to pick my brains on several occasions, as you know. Anyway, neither Angie nor Denise are known for keeping their mouths shut, so don't go telling them anything for the present.'

'I won't,' Kate said, 'but I just wish she'd shown more interest in what I had to tell her. That's the reason I take matters into my own hands because she either appears not to believe me or else she gives me a lecture on interfering with police procedures. It's a no-win situation for me.'

'I do understand how you feel, Kate,' Woody replied earnestly, 'and I do think your findings about Wayne are very relevant. But those Fords are a dangerous lot, so when I tell you to leave it to the police, it's because I don't want you coming to grief. How many times have I told you that?'

'Yes, but she's supposed to be trying to solve this case and I was only trying to give her Wayne's possible motive for killing his father and grandfather.'

'I'm sure she'll have taken everything you said into account,' Woody said.

'Let's hope so,' Kate replied with a rueful smile.

THIRTY-SIX

On Thursday, with Wayne presumably still in custody, Kate struggled to decide what to do next with the information she'd gleaned. Perhaps now was the time to visit the other Fords, if only to get their reactions. That would, of course, be tricky, since she wasn't allowed to visit Sunshine Park.

But there was nothing to stop her from visiting Sharon Mason.

With Woody at his allotment in the afternoon, and Barney having been walked in the morning, Kate set out to visit the enterprising Masons. Sharon might be out, but that was a chance she'd have to take.

So it was with some relief that she spotted the black BMW parked outside Sharon's house. Kate rang the bell.

'Oh,' said Sharon, when she opened the door, 'it's *you*. This is a surprise! What can I do for you?'

'I wonder if I might have a word?' Kate asked.

'About what?'

'It's not something I think we can discuss on the doorstep,' Kate said firmly, 'so could I come in for a moment please?'

'Well, OK then.' Sharon stood aside to let her enter, and

Kate found herself again in the vast kitchen, although less mini-
malistic than before, due to a sullen-looking teenage boy
slumped on the pristine white leather sofa by the window. He
was surrounded by empty cups and plates, and didn't even look
up but stayed glued to his phone.

'That's Liam,' said Sharon, 'who should be in school, but he
wasn't feeling too well this morning.' She sighed. 'Kids don't
half make the place untidy, don't they?' She turned to the boy.
'Why don't you go to your bedroom, Liam?'

Liam scowled at her before going back to his phone.

'You'd better come into the snug,' Sharon said to Kate,
leading the way into a big room with leather sofas built round
three walls and a giant TV screen on the fourth. If this was the
snug, Kate wondered what size their sitting room might be.

'Take a seat.'

Kate obeyed, sitting on a seat opposite the TV screen, while
Sharon faced her from the left.

'OK, what's this all about?' Sharon asked.

Kate cleared her throat. 'Well, I went up to London as a
result of a visit we had from a Father Dominic.'

'I've never heard of him,' Sharon said.

'Father Dominic was the priest who oversaw your father's
conversion to Catholicism. He became very close to your father,
who confessed that he hadn't killed your mother but that it was
one of his children. The priest himself had no idea which one of
you it might have been,' Kate said.

'Are you accusing me of killing my mother or something?'
Sharon asked, looking astounded.

'No, I'm not,' Kate replied, 'but Father Dominic said that
the person who might know was the woman your father was
planning to marry. And I've spoken to her.'

Sharon's eyes widened. '*Woman he was planning to marry?*
What rot! Dad had no intention of marrying anyone!'

'I'm afraid he did,' Kate said, 'because he'd become very

friendly with a lady who visited him in prison, and he was going to ask her to marry him, according to the priest.'

'And you believed this Father What's-it?'

'Yes, I did, and I tracked down the lady concerned.'

'How come he never mentioned this big romance to us? And how come he didn't bring her down here to meet the family when we were all together?'

'I don't know. Perhaps that was the reason he wanted to come to see you all.'

'And you say you spoke to this woman? What did she have to say?'

'She said that your father had told her who it was that killed your mother.'

'Oh yeah?' Sharon was plainly sceptical.

'Yes, she said that your father told her it was Wayne.'

'*Wayne*? Why would Wayne have wanted to kill our mum?'

'He was high on drugs at the time, and your mother had refused to let his equally druggie girlfriend move in with him.'

Sharon looked bewildered. 'I remember Wayne being high as a kite,' she said, 'but I can't believe for a moment that he killed Mum, but, then again, I never did believe that Dad could have done it either.' She hesitated. 'Did this woman tell you why Dad confessed to killing Mum, if he didn't do it?'

'Your dad didn't want Wayne to – and here I quote - "spend the best years of his life in prison". So he took the blame because he reckoned Wayne wasn't in his right mind at the time.'

Kate could see that Sharon was absorbing this information.

'Well we've only got this woman's word for all that, haven't we? Who is she anyway? What's her name?'

'I can't tell you that,' Kate said. 'She only told me because it might help to solve the mystery of who killed your father, and I don't think she was particularly keen to meet any of the family.'

'Not a bad judge then!' Sharon remarked. 'But you'll appreciate that it's hard to believe what some anonymous woman told you? No name? No proof?'

'But do *you* think it's possible that Wayne might have killed your mother?'

Sharon shrugged. 'I don't know.'

'I also wanted tell you that Wayne, under various guises, has been chatting up Tinworthy women in an attempt to extract money from them,' Kate added.

Sharon snorted. 'I *do* believe that cos he's been doing it for years. Sometimes he wins, sometimes he loses, but that's Wayne for you.'

'We think that your father, with his new religious zeal, was perhaps planning to tell my husband what had really happened back then. And your grandfather, apparently, had found out the truth too and was inclined to come out with the occasional coherent comment.'

Sharon sat silently for a minute. Then she took a deep breath. 'I've already told you what I think of my brothers. But I find it hard to believe some woman, whose name I don't know, unless I have proof. Your policewoman is going to have to *prove* that our Wayne is a killer! Anyway, that's what she's paid for, so let her get on with it!'

'I just wanted to know if you thought it was at all possible,' Kate said, standing up. 'I thought you should know.'

'Mainly because you want to prove your hubby's innocence more like! Still, I don't blame you; I'd probably do the same. Shall I make coffee?'

'No thanks, Sharon, I'll be on my way,' Kate said.

Driving home, Kate wondered how much of an impression her information had made on Sharon Mason. She'd already known that Sharon didn't think much of her brothers but plainly wasn't totally convinced about Wayne killing their mother. And who could blame her?

Kate didn't feel it safe to reveal Rose's name or whereabouts to any of the Fords, particularly as Rose had said that she'd never met any of Frank's family and had no wish to do so. Kate wondered if she'd get a similar reaction from both Damian and Jason. If she was going to contact them, she'd need to do it while Wayne was still in custody.

Wayne! Had he known all along who *she* was when she'd met him, as Clint, in The Old Locker? Had he known Angie was her sister? Would she *ever* know? What Kate *did* know was that Wayne knew now who she was, when she'd correctly identified him for that split second in The Tinners. She could certainly be in danger if and when he was released.

On the way up the lane, Kate stopped at The Greedy Gull.

Des, who was polishing glasses in preparation for the evening trade, looked surprised. 'Don't often see you in here on your own.'

'Not stopping, Des. Just wondered if Damian Ford still drinks in here regularly?'

Des nodded. 'Reckon he comes in here Wednesday and Friday lunchtimes, if I remember rightly, and sometimes at night. Nice enough bloke – likes a chat, he does. Don't bring the missus in very often though. Shall I tell him you want to see him?'

'No, no,' Kate said hastily. 'Not important. I'll look in tomorrow to see if he's here.'

Des looked at her quizzically but didn't comment.

'Thanks, Des,' Kate called out as she hurried towards the door. Now she had to decide if she should go into the pub tomorrow lunchtime, or should she try to speak to Damian Ford while he waited for his taxi? Suppose the taxi came early and he didn't have time to listen to her?

She'd go inside, and hope for the best.

THIRTY-SEVEN

Kate wasn't sure if Woody was going to be around the following day, but, as luck would have it, he needed a new headlight bulb and some other bits and pieces for his precious Mercedes, which necessitated a trip to the local garage who'd got the parts in from St Austell.

'I'll have to wait while they work on it,' he said, 'but while I'm up there, I'll grab a sandwich at The Tinners.'

And I shall have a drink in The Gull, Kate thought but didn't say.

At around one o'clock, Kate decided it might be a good time to have a quick look in The Gull to see if Damian was there. He was, and he was alone. Avoiding Des's eye, she walked round to where Damian was standing at the bar, nursing a pint of bitter.

'Oh hello,' he said. 'What brings you here?'

'I was hoping to see you,' Kate replied.

'Well I'm very flattered. Can I buy you a drink?'

'Thank you,' she said, 'I'd like a lime and soda. I really wanted to talk to you about something.'

'Sounds ominous,' he said with a grin before turning round to Des and ordering her drink. 'You want to grab a table?'

Kate nodded and made her way to a vacant table beside the window.

When he joined her and set her drink down, Damian said, 'How's your husband?'

'He's well, thanks,' Kate replied. Then, out of politeness, she asked, 'How's Jackie?'

Damian shrugged. 'Fed up to the back teeth with being imprisoned in that bloody caravan. She's gone to get her hair done today and I'm picking her up in the taxi on the way back. So, what was it you wanted to talk about?'

Kate told him about the priest's visit, what he'd said and her trip to London.

Damian guffawed. 'Dad planning to marry again? You're joking! Silly old fool!'

'He'd told his lady friend that he'd gone to prison for a crime he didn't commit to spare his son years in jail.'

Damian stared at her over the rim of his glass. '*What*? Are you serious? *Which* son?'

'Wayne.'

He let out a long whistle. 'You expect me to believe that? Did you know that Wayne's in the nick at the moment for chatting up women and trying to get at their money?'

'Yes, I had heard.'

Damian shook his head slowly. 'He's always done drugs, has Wayne, and he's always liked women, and conning people, but I can't believe he killed Mum.'

Kate then told him, as gently as she could, the story about Wayne, his girlfriend and his mother. 'He was so high on drugs that your father reckoned he wasn't in his right mind.'

Damian looked shaken. He put down his glass. 'I believe the bit about Wayne being out of his mind on drugs,' he said, 'but I find the rest hard to credit. Who is this woman anyway?'

'I can't tell you her name, but I can assure you she exists, and I believe what she told me,' Kate said.

'I've only got your word for all this,' Damian commented, looking suspicious.

'I'm afraid so. I don't think the lady in question would want to be identified because she wasn't keen to meet the family.'

Damian snorted. 'Who could blame her? So, you're telling me that Wayne killed our mum, and Dad took the can for it?'

'Yes,' Kate confirmed.

'And now you're going to tell me that Wayne killed Dad and Grandpa as well?'

'That hasn't been proved,' Kate said, 'but it does seem likely.'

Damian sat silently gazing out of the window for a few minutes. Then he said, 'Me and Jackie tried to get away.'

'So I heard.'

'We had enough of that bloody van, stuck out in the middle of nowhere. If we gotta stay here any longer, then I'm going to ask that woman detective if we can move in to the Atlantic Hotel.'

'I'm sure she'd agree,' Kate said. But, of course, you never quite knew with Charlotte.

'I tried to get in there when they dragged us back from the airport and took our sodding car and our passports away, but it was all *booked up*! Who the hell comes down here for their holidays at this time of year?'

'Lots of people do,' Kate informed him. 'It's still warmer here than most places in the UK.'

'Not as warm as Spain,' Damian said wistfully.

'Probably not.'

'Fancy another drink? Something stronger? Because I bloody well need one!'

'No thank you. I only wanted to let you know what I'd found out, and I'm sorry that I can't give you names. I did tell your sister, but I'm not at all sure she believed me. I'm not allowed to visit Sunshine Park, so I haven't been able to contact Jason.'

'He's difficult to get hold of, but I'll tell him what you've told me, and then it's up to him to get in touch with you if he wants the details. But if what you told me is true, then I'll kill that bloody brother of mine with my bare hands! When I think how heartbroken we were! Our dear mum, killed by our dad! Do you really believe what this woman told you could be true?'

'She had no reason to lie to me, Damian. And she obviously believed what your father had told her. In my experience, when people become so committed to religion in later life, they feel a great need to confess the truth.'

'I wonder if he planned to confess to us?'

'We'll never know.'

Kate made her way to the door.

'What have you been up to?' Woody asked when he got back a short while later.

'I haven't been up to anything,' Kate said defensively.

'You haven't been up to Sunshine Park, have you?'

'Of course not! You know I've been forbidden to go there.'

Woody frowned. 'You have a guilty look about you.'

Kate thought quickly. She hadn't been able to decide whether to tell him about her meetings with the Ford siblings, but he'd probably find out and then she'd be in real trouble. 'I saw Damian Ford waiting for his taxi outside The Gull,' she said. Outside, inside, it wasn't too much of a fib.

He was looking at her sceptically. 'And what did he have to say? Or, more importantly, what did *you* have to say?'

Kate decided to be truthful. She was a bad liar, and Woody knew it. 'I told him about Father Dominic and what he'd told us, about going up to London and about meeting Frank's lady friend. But I didn't tell them who she was or what her name was.'

'*Them*? What do you mean, *them*? Who else have you been talking to?'

'Well,' Kate said, 'I did have a little chat with Sharon Mason.'

'Did she come here?' Woody asked.

'Um, no. I decided to pay her a visit.' Seeing Woody's face, she added quickly, 'I thought they should know that Wayne killed their mother and that their father went to jail for him.'

Woody sighed loudly. 'I'm not at all sure you should have done that, Kate.'

'Why not?'

'There's no proof against Wayne, and he could sue you for defamation of character and, knowing him, he's probably been told by one of his siblings what you've been up to.'

Kate felt a little shaken, not having considered this. 'I don't think either of them were entirely convinced anyway, because I refused to name Frank's friend. Let's face it, if Charlotte doesn't deem the information important enough, then perhaps his siblings can quiz Wayne.'

'You're in very dangerous territory here, *yet again*. If Wayne is released from custody and he hears about what you've been telling his brother and sister, and he most likely will, then he's going to be gunning for you, particularly if he's *not* guilty of killing his father and grandfather.'

Kate bit her lip. 'But he *must* be!'

'It might look that way, but there's no absolute proof.'

'But they should know about Wayne killing their mother,' Kate said.

'I'm not sure they should. If Frank didn't see fit to tell them when he was alive, then that's how he would have wanted it to be.'

'But, Woody, Frank was *murdered*! And surely by one of his

family, because who else down here would have had any reason to kill him?'

'Well, there was Steve, and I'm not sure where he fitted into all this. There has to be a connection, and I think that's the line Charlotte's working on.'

'Oh my God!' Kate exclaimed. 'Have I done the wrong thing, Woody?'

'Not necessarily, but I'd keep a low profile if I were you.'

'I'm going to.'

It wasn't that Kate had forgotten about Steve, but she had calculated that he must have been yet another of the killer's victims. The chances were he knew them in London, knew that Wayne was, or had been, a drug dealer, and he needed somewhere he could get a fix. She remembered how he'd tried to warn her off Damian and the Fords in general. Was that because of drugs and Wayne being a dealer? Were the two connected? There didn't seem to be any other reason why Steve too had met such a brutal death. And what about the money stashed in Steve's van?

Kate could feel a headache coming on as her thoughts whirled round and round.

THIRTY-EIGHT

On Saturday afternoon, Woody said, 'If I go up to my allotment for a couple of hours, will you either come with me or promise to stay at home? If you're good, I might even take you out to dinner tonight.'

'I'll be good,' Kate promised, 'and I have a stack of ironing to do.'

'No dog-walking or visiting?'

'No dog-walking or visiting,' Kate confirmed.

'See you later then,' Woody said, kissing her on the cheek as he headed out towards his car.

Kate looked without enthusiasm at the pile of ironing and sighed. These shirts, sheets and duvet covers weren't going to smooth themselves out. She switched the iron on and was about to tackle a pillowcase when her phone rang. She hoped it wouldn't be a long conversation or she'd lose what little urge she had to begin this chore.

'Is that Kate?'

Kate couldn't quite place the voice. 'Yes?'

'It's Meghan here, Meghan Ford. Jason's wife. You remember me?'

'Yes, of course I do!' Kate replied, switching off the iron.

'I'm in the area and wondered if I might have a word?' Meghan asked. 'I've got some important information which I think you'll find most interesting.'

Kate was dumbfounded for a minute. 'Really?'

'Yes, but I need to talk to you alone. Are you on your own?'

'Yes, I am. My husband's just gone up to his allotment.'

'Good! Get the kettle on then! I'll be with you in under ten minutes.' Then she hung up.

Wow, Kate thought, *information being brought to* me! *What can Meghan Ford be about to tell me? Sod the ironing!*

She went into the kitchen and filled up the kettle. Woody would never believe that she'd been able to glean important information without having to step outside the door!

Her heart pounding in anticipation, Kate awaited her guest.

Meghan Ford had plainly not been far away because she arrived on the doorstep about five minutes later.

'Well, this is a surprise!' Kate exclaimed as she stood aside to let Meghan enter.

'Let's have that cup of tea, because I'm dying of thirst!' Meghan said, plonking herself on the sofa in the sitting room. 'Then I'll tell you all I know.'

'Good idea.'

Having established that Meghan only took milk in her tea, Kate carried the two mugs into the sitting room and placed them on the coffee table. She'd only taken a sip when her mobile, which she'd left in the kitchen, rang. 'Excuse me for a minute,' she said to Meghan.

'Sorry, wrong number,' said the caller before she'd had time to speak. How strange!

Kate felt somewhat mystified as she returned to her guest. She sat down opposite Meghan.

'This is so intriguing!' she said as she sipped her tea. 'I can't imagine what you're going to tell me.'

'Well,' said Meghan, 'it all stems from the fact that you've met some woman who's told you that it was Wayne who killed his mother and Frank took the blame.'

'That's right,' Kate said. 'I was trying to work out how to tell Jason and yourself because I'm not allowed to go to Sunshine Park.' She drank some more of her tea.

'Not to worry, because Damian told us everything.'

Kate was beginning to be aware that she was feeling decidedly woozy. She drained her mug of tea and tried to concentrate on Megan's face, which had become somewhat blurred. She noticed Megan's four eyes and two noses, and thought that to be strange...

Kate was in some form of transport which was being driven by Frank Ford. Sitting beside her was none other than Sid Kinsella.

'Sid!' Kate exclaimed. 'I thought you were dead!'

'Not me!' he said cheerfully, patting her hand.

'And I thought Frank was dead too!'

'No, no, dear, Frank's fine. Did you know that he didn't kill my little girl?'

'Yes, I did know that,' Kate replied, 'and I know who did!'

'Oh, Frank and I know who it was. You don't need to tell us that!'

Both men laughed heartily.

'We'll be in heaven in just a minute,' Frank said from the front seat.

'We will?' Kate looked out of the window to see some fluffy pink clouds scurrying by. She was on her way to heaven! Then she had a thought. 'But I didn't say goodbye to Woody! I can't leave Woody!'

'Oh yes you can!' said Sid.

'Oh yes you can!' chorused Frank, and they both dissolved into raucous laughter, just before they hit a big black cloud which had formed in front of them.

Kate felt herself emerge from darkness. Her head ached, her eyes had difficulty focusing and her mouth was so very dry. Water – she needed water.

Slowly, she began to focus, but where on earth *was* she? She tried to look around and, as the mist cleared a little, she found she was lying on a beige sofa in a small beige room. There was a beige chair as well, and a big TV screen (which wasn't beige). Everyone had such big TV screens! She could hear a voice somewhere nearby.

Kate tried to sit up, but her legs felt too wobbly to stand. She collapsed back onto the sofa and managed to see out of the window. There were so many windows everywhere! Why would anyone want big windows round three sides of a room?

She focused on what she could see outside: rows of big, white boxes. No, not boxes, *caravans*! Kate realised with a jolt that she was in a caravan in Sunshine Park. But whose caravan was this? Not Jason's – the layout was different. And who had been talking?

Slowly, Kate's memory was returning. She'd been drinking tea with Meghan Ford in Lavender Cottage. Meghan had something to tell her. What was that? And how had she come to be in this caravan? It took a few minutes for it to dawn on her what had probably happened. She'd obviously been drugged, but why?

Someone was coming. Kate slumped back across the sofa and feigned sleep. She needed the person, whoever it was, to think that she was still unconscious.

As the person neared, Kate realised, through half-shut eyelids, that it was Meghan.

'Still out for the count?' Meghan asked pleasantly.

Kate groaned in reply.

Meghan must have felt confident enough to move into the kitchen area and pick up her mobile.

'Hi, darling! Well I put a good dose in her tea, so she's probably going to be comatose for another ten minutes or so.' Meghan sounded very pleased with herself.

Kate became alert. Who in hell was she talking to? She then heard Meghan ask, 'Are you *certain* you've moved everything of yours from this shithole, Wayne? Good! No, I'm quite sure no one saw us carrying her in.'

Everything was now coming into focus and making sense. Meghan was obviously talking to Wayne, and this was Wayne's caravan. But where was Wayne? Elusive as ever?

There was a pause while Meghan listened. Then she said, 'Oh don't worry about *Jason*! Damian and Jackie persuaded him to join them for a drink at The Tinners. Damian said he had something else very interesting to tell Jason; something he'd got from *Kate Palmer*.' She shrieked with laughter at this. 'Apparently there's a quiz or something on at the pub, so they'll be there for a while.'

Another pause while Meghan appeared to listen intently.

'So we've to pick up the passports from Basingstoke, did you say? Yeah, OK. I'll try to get used to your new name, *Mr Davidson*!' Another shriek of laughter. 'And what time is the Costa Rica flight?' She listened again, the phone clamped against her ear, her eyes on Kate. 'OK, darling. Well I think we'd better leave soon – the sooner, the better, so get yourself back here. Oh, Wayne, I couldn't *bear* it if it all caught up with you now!' Meghan lowered her voice. 'Hey, darling, I think I saw her eyelids flicker. She's coming round.'

Kate's thoughts were in turmoil. Should she continue to feign sleep to see what happened next? They had obviously decided to leave her here and she had to get out somehow. She opened her eyes.

'Huh!' said Meghan. 'The sleeping beauty has awakened.'

Kate forced herself to sit up. She tried to speak, but her mouth was so dry that her teeth had stuck to her lips.

'Could I have a glass of water?' she managed to ask.

'No, you can't.'

Kate licked her tongue over her teeth. 'You aren't going to get away with this,' she said and then thought, What *a cliché*! Gleaned, no doubt, from the countless crime programmes she'd watched on TV!

'Oh, I think we will,' Meghan said with a smile, 'and you aren't going to be telling anyone anything. Got it?'

'Why are you doing this, Meghan?'

'Why? I'll tell you why. Because I love Wayne and I'm not having him go to jail now for a crime he committed twenty years ago, that's why.'

'But he kills everyone who gets in his way!' Kate exclaimed. 'His father! His grandfather! How can you love a man like that?'

Megan snorted.

'*He* didn't kill his father and grandfather,' Meghan said, adding with a cackle of laughter, '*I* did!'

THIRTY-NINE

'*You* did?' Kate stared at her in horror and disbelief.

'Needs must, you know. Frank was about to tell your bloody husband, and we couldn't be having that!'

Kate swallowed. 'I can't believe what I'm hearing! And Sid?'

'Sid had started remembering some stuff, silly old sod. I was sick of supposedly looking after him anyway, and I should have done it sooner, save me from chasing around after him. Why are you looking at me like that?'

Kate was still in shock. 'You killed those two men? And what about Steve? Where did he fit into all this?'

'Steve! He was a greedy bastard! I've known him for years. We used to go out together, before I met Jason. I persuaded him to come down here, knowing we'd be coming later. He still loved me and I knew he'd do anything for me. I told him I'd leave Jason for him, and he believed me. It wasn't a total lie because I was planning to leave Jason, but not for *him*. Anyway, I thought he might be useful, and he helped me to lug Frank's body into your garden, and also he helped me finish off old Sid.'

'Why would he do that?' Kate asked through parched lips.

'Because firstly he thought he'd win me back and, when that

didn't work, he thought he'd blackmail me, that's why. I had to raid Sid's bank account to pay him, cos we've got power of attorney, see? But the bastard wanted more and more, so I had to get rid of him.'

'So you decided to kill Steve too?'

'Bloody right! Only problem was that the damn police got to his tacky caravan before I did, and I wanted that money back. Understandable, don't you think?'

Kate was rendered speechless for a moment. Finally, she said, 'And Jason, your husband, had no idea that all this was going on? That's unbelievable!'

'Oh, don't you go worrying about Jason,' Meghan said cheerfully. 'He's already got Sid's garage, which is what he wanted. And now he'll be free to get himself a boyfriend, which is also what he wanted. Our marriage was a sham anyway.'

'Surely he knew about you and Wayne?' Kate asked.

'We never asked each other questions,' Megan replied. 'We've always led separate lives. One of us had to be there to look after Sid, but the other could do what they liked.'

Kate was having difficulty absorbing so much horrendous information. Why was Meghan telling her this? She was obviously confident that Kate Palmer wasn't going to be telling anyone. She realised, with horror, that of course Meghan was planning to kill her, and she looked around in the hope of seeing a means of escape, an open window or something. But she could see nothing, only the doorway.

And then, suddenly, *someone* was standing there, watching her. Wayne was a big man and she didn't fancy her chances there. In fact, she didn't fancy her chances with either of this evil pair.

She began to feel a wave of fear flowing through her body. Kate thought of Woody then. He would never believe that she hadn't come up here of her own free will! If she died, he would always think that she'd broken her promise to him to stay at home. How many times had he said to her 'You're in dangerous territory'? He'd never uttered a truer word.

If I'm lucky, Kate thought, *they might just lock me in here until they make their getaway to Costa Rica*. For an instant, she thought of tropical vegetation, white, palm-fringed beaches, monkeys in the trees. She'd seen a film about Costa Rica once and it had looked beautiful.

Meghan picked up a large holdall which had been placed behind where Wayne was standing, near the door.

'So, farewell, Kate,' she said with a pleasant smile, 'it's been nice knowing you.' They both laughed and went out of the door, locking it behind them.

Kate reckoned it could be worse. After all, Damian, Jackie and Jason should be back from the pub before too long. She could shout and hammer on the walls. At least she could get herself a drink of water.

She got up shakily, steadied herself and walked slowly towards the sink in the kitchen area. There was a selection of glasses in every shape and size in the cupboard. She chose a tumbler and held it under the tap, then turned the tap on.

Nothing. Nothing happened.

Kate tried both taps. Still nothing.

Perhaps there was some in the shower room so Kate made her way there.

Nothing. They had turned the water off.

As she came out into the passageway, Kate realised with mounting horror that flames were snaking their way towards her from the bedroom. Wayne and Meghan had locked her in a burning caravan without water.

Kate tried to keep calm. She didn't have her mobile of course, because Megan had seen to that. There was no phone in here, unless it was in the bedroom where the fire was now blazing. She'd need a CO_2 extinguisher to cope with burning furniture and mattresses, and there should be one mounted on the wall somewhere. She found the fitting on the wall, but no extinguisher. They'd thought of everything.

Already she could smell toxic fumes.

How long would it take to spread to the living area? The flames were now devouring the bedroom door, and getting ever closer.

Kate tried in vain to open the windows in the living area, but they were all locked. She looked round in desperation, to see if there was anything heavy with which she could batter the door or windows. Her eyes alighted on the TV set. Could she pick the thing up and clobber the glass with it?

There were plenty of windows to choose from, and she tried to lift the TV up to the level of the window nearest to it. No matter how hard she tried, she couldn't position the heavy TV high enough to crack a window. Then she looked at the chair. It was heavy, but not as heavy as the TV, and it did have wooden legs. If she could manoeuvre the chair in such a way as to get a leg at window level, she might, just *might*, be able to crack it. It looked like being her only hope.

With all her strength, she hoisted it up into position and, as fast as she could, ran towards the front window. It battered the glass but didn't break it. She'd have to gather her strength and try again.

Kate took a deep breath in readiness and coughed. With horror, she realised that the black smoke was now enveloping the kitchen area and heading towards her. She'd have only one more attempt to get out of here before it was too late.

Her eyes watering and her lungs choking, Kate's attempt to break the window met without success again.

She remembered then that the smoke would rise and that the cleanest air would be at floor level. The flames were now devouring the kitchen cupboards, including the one that acted as a room divider.

Kate lay down, knowing she was going to die but determined to breathe for as long as she could. Shortly before she passed out, she heard a wailing noise somewhere.

Then she knew no more.

FORTY

'She's coming round,' someone said away in the distance.

She tried to speak, but there was some sort of mask over her face. What was going on? Where was she? Was she dead? Or in some sort of transit out of the world? Wherever it was, she was warm and comfortable, and she hoped they'd leave her alone.

'Kate!' A man's voice. She knew that voice.

'Kate, darling...' That voice again.

Perhaps if she opened one eye, she might see where she was, what was going on.

She opened one eye; there seemed to be an awful lot of white around.

'Oh, Kate,' said the voice again.

That's me, she thought, *and I do know that voice!*

She tried to move her lips to form some words, but they weren't working properly.

'You're in hospital, Kate, and you're going to be fine.'

She tried to ask if she was dead or not, but the mask got in the way. She opened the other eye, and then she knew for sure who the voice belonged to. That slight American accent. Woody.

· · ·

A few minutes later, Kate became more aware. 'Costa Rica,' she said.

'She'll still be hallucinating a little,' one of the nurses reassured Woody.

'No, Kate, you're in *Plymouth*, not Costa Rica!' Woody said.

Kate struggled to sit up, pulling off the mask. She was gently pushed back down and the mask replaced with some little tubes up her nose.

'Is that better?' a nurse asked.

'Mmm.' Kate was fully awake now. 'Why am I in Plymouth?'

'Because you're at Derriford Hospital,' said Woody, holding her hand. 'You needed specialist treatment for smoke inhalation.'

Kate's thoughts were in a whirl. Smoke inhalation? Then, slowly, her memory began to return.

'How did I...?' she began.

'We'll explain later,' Woody said, 'but just get your strength back first.

'Costa Rica,' Kate repeated.

'No, Kate, you're in Plymouth!'

'Costa Rica,' Kate said clearly, 'is where they're going.'

'*Who* are going to Costa Rica?'

'Wayne and Meghan of course. Mr and Mrs *Davidson*!'

'*What*?'

'Via Basingstoke.'

'*Basingstoke*? That's nowhere near Costa Rica!'

'For their passports,' Kate said, now fully conscious. 'Passports in Basingstoke, then on to Costa Rica.'

'Excuse me for one minute,' Woody said, getting up rapidly from his seat. He headed towards the door.

'Where's he gone?' Kate asked crossly.

'Probably to talk to the policeman outside the door,' the nurse said soothingly.

Woody, accompanied by a uniformed police officer, came into the room. The policeman had his phone clamped to his ear.

'Kate,' Woody said, 'can you tell the officer here as much as you can remember?'

'I've told you,' Kate said, beginning to feel weary again. 'Meghan and Wayne are going to Costa Rica. Megan killed Frank and Sid, and then killed Steve too, because he was blackmailing her. They're getting new names.'

The policeman repeated all this into his phone.

'They're now Mr and Mrs Davidson,' Kate added, 'and they're getting their passports in Basingstoke.'

She continued answering all the officer's questions, which he then repeated into his phone, presumably to Charlotte.

'Don't you worry,' he said, after he'd got all his information and was heading out of the door, 'we're going to get them.'

Woody was sitting down again next to Kate.

'Woody, I didn't break my promise to you! I *did* stay at home!'

'I know you did, Kate. I realised you had a visitor when I saw the empty cups on the coffee table!'

'But,' Kate asked, 'how on earth did you know where I was?'

Woody smiled. 'I'd just got back from the allotment when Des phoned from The Gull.'

'*Des*?'

'Yes. He'd been outside clearing up glasses or something when he saw a white Range Rover drive up the lane to Lavender Cottage. He knew that the police had been looking for a white four-by-four after Steve was killed, so he waited inside by the window to see if it came back again. Half an hour later it did.'

'So what did he do?'

'Des managed to get most of the registration number, and

then he phoned the police in case they were still looking for the vehicle. The police, followed by myself, went straight up to Sunshine, hoping it would be parked there. It wasn't. All we saw was a caravan ablaze.'

'And me in it,' Kate said.

'Yes, you in it. I must say the fire brigade were fantastic; they were there in a flash, if you'll excuse the pun! It was touch-and-go, Kate, because you'd inhaled a lot of smoke.'

'I remembered to keep low,' Kate said with a smile.

'Wise move. Anyway, the police will be on their way to Heathrow, now we know what we're likely to be looking for.'

'Good old Des!' Kate said, amazed. 'He saved my life.'

'We'll buy him a drink,' Woody said with a wink, 'or three.'

'We were quite convinced that Wayne was the killer,' Kate said, 'but it was Meghan and Steve who did all the dirty work. I suppose Wayne *must* have known what was going on?'

Woody shrugged. 'We'll never know for sure, I suppose. Apart from anything else, he wouldn't want to go to jail now for a crime committed so long ago. Perhaps Meghan was his means of escape, or perhaps he really did love her. Who knows?'

FORTY-ONE

The day after her release from hospital, Kate took a stroll with Barney down to the beach, to gulp in some beautiful sea air, and called in at The Old Locker on her way back.

'I wonder why Woody puts up with you,' Angie said, placing a cappuccino on the bar in front of Kate, who was sitting on her usual bar stool. 'You just keep on looking for trouble.'

'I was *not* looking for trouble,' Kate protested. 'I was at home, about to start ironing.' She thought for a moment. 'That's a point: I noticed that the ironing's been done. Good old Woody!'

'*I* did it,' snapped Angie, 'because I'm a bloody saint!'

'Oh, Angie, thanks so much!' Kate was almost moved to tears. 'That was such a kind thing to do!'

'Well, Woody had gone to the hospital to see if you were dead or alive, and I went up to make sure Barney was OK, and that's when I saw the pile of ironing.'

'You really are *so* kind!'

'No I'm not. I'm a dutiful sister.'

'For whatever reason, thank you!'

Angie poured herself a gin. 'Next time you take off on one of your adventures, could you do the ironing first?'

Kate laughed. 'Thing is, I didn't take off on any adventure, Angie. The woman came to my door with what she called "important information", and I made her a cup of tea. I only left the room for a minute to answer the phone, which was a wrong number, but was plainly Wayne, giving her time to doctor my drink. And if it hadn't been for good old Des phoning the police, when he saw the white Range Rover going up and down, I wouldn't be here now.'

'So isn't it time now to stop all this detective malarkey?' Angie asked, pouring a shot of brandy into Kate's coffee. 'I know cats are supposed to have nine lives' – here she glanced at Maximus, who was sitting in his usual place on the bar top – 'but they've got nothing on you!'

'Yes, it's time to stop, so keep your fingers crossed that there are no more crimes around here.' Kate shuddered. 'I shall *never* go anywhere near Sunshine Park again!'

'Not even to see the burned-out shell of a caravan?'

'Definitely not to see that!' Kate replied firmly. 'At least Damian and Jackie have finally got back to Malaga, and I believe Jason's gone back to London, where, according to Meghan, he's probably looking for a boyfriend.'

Angie shrugged. 'Each to his own. And what about Bonnie and Clyde, or whatever they call themselves these days? Davidsons was it?'

'Caught at Heathrow, and now in police custody, thank God!'

'I'm going to have nightmares for the rest of my life about water supplies being turned off,' Kate said to Woody later in the evening.

'What a hellish woman she is!' Woody said. 'She'd already killed three people and was damned determined to get you.'

'I only hope Charlotte now realises she almost had *four* killings on her hands. If she'd listened to me in the first place, at least I could have been spared my ordeal. How come she never found the white Range Rover? Surely it must have been around somewhere?'

'Yes. They'd very cleverly hidden it underneath an enormous old tarpaulin in the ancient ramshackle barn up there. For years, a rusting tractor was hidden there, and my guess is that the police reckoned it was still there. They probably only glanced inside the door, if they even bothered to do that.'

'My admiration for Charlotte has taken a bit of a bashing,' Kate remarked ruefully.

'I think Charlotte is ready to move on,' Woody said. 'Like everyone else, she thought policing down here was going to be a doddle. She did admit she was sorry not to have acted immediately on what you told her but that she was merely following police procedures because she had no proof.'

Kate snorted. 'Well, she's got plenty of proof now! And I shall *never* take a glass of water for granted again! I feel thirsty just thinking about it!'

'Well, my darling, how about I go straight to the tap in the kitchen and get you a glass of the stuff?' Woody suggested. 'But, do you know, it might taste even nicer with a drop of Scotch in it?'

'You're a very persuasive man,' Kate said, laughing. 'But if you don't mind, I'd rather have a gin and tonic!'

'*Women!*' Woody sighed as he made his way into the kitchen.

Kate looked around. How fortunate she was to live in this lovely cottage, with this wonderful man, in glorious Cornwall! And how lucky she was to still be alive after yet *another* close shave. She resolved, there and then, to cut out all this Miss

Marple stuff in future and take up a new hobby. Watercolour painting? Pilates? Baking perhaps? No, not baking, because she had to consider her figure. Badminton? Crafts maybe?

She'd think of something.

A LETTER FROM DEE

Dear Reader,

I very much hope you've enjoyed *A Body at Lavender Cottage*, which is the sixth in the Kate Palmer crime series. If you'd like to catch up with the other Kate Palmers, or any of my women's fiction novels, just sign up with the link below. Your email address will never be shared and you can unsubscribe at any time.

www.bookouture.com/dee-macdonald

If you did enjoy the book, I'd be very grateful if you would write a review. I love to know what my readers think, and it also helps new readers to discover my books for the first time.

You can get in touch with me at any time via my Facebook page, or through Twitter.

With many thanks,

Dee

 facebook.com/AuthorDeeMacDonald
twitter.com/DMacDonaldAuth

ACKNOWLEDGEMENTS

Thank you, first and foremost, to my lovely, patient, understanding editor at Bookouture, Natasha Harding, because her guidance and enthusiasm are invaluable.

And thank you to Amanda Preston, my agent, and everyone at the LBA, who introduced me to Bookouture in the first place and continues to look after my interests.

I'm grateful, as always, to my friend and mentor, Rosemary Brown, who is so much cleverer than I am, and takes the time to sort out my errors and clichés! I have to say that the odd glass of wine helps too!

I must not forget my husband, Stan Noakes, for putting up with my writing sessions and providing the necessary refreshments, and my son, Dan, and his family, who take a keen interest in my sales and reviews – and generally get me out of trouble with my (lack of) technological expertise!

Thank you, Bookouture, who are the friendliest and loveliest publisher on earth! There's a large team who've helped to produce this book, including Lizzie Brien, Ruth Tross, Alba Proko, Peta Nightingale, Alex Holmes and the brilliant marketing team. And particular thanks to Kim Nash and Noelle Holten for all the promotion work they do on our behalf.

Finally, thank you to you, the reader, and to all the book groups who kindly choose to read my books and take the trouble to contact me. I am most grateful to you all.

Printed in Great Britain
by Amazon